Dear Reader:

*I'm delighted to pre*_____*he first books in the HarperMonogram imprint. This is a new imprint dedicated to publishing quality women's fiction and we believe it has all the makings of a surefire hit. From contemporary fiction to historical tales, to page-turning suspense thrillers, our goal at HarperMonogram is to publish romantic stories that will have you coming back for more.*

Each month HarperMonogram will feature some of your favorite bestselling authors and introduce you to the most talented new writers around. We hope you enjoy this Monogram and all the HarperMonograms to come.

We'd love to know what you think. If you have any comments or suggestions please write to me at the address below:

HarperMonogram
10 East 53rd Street
New York, NY 10022

Karen Solem
Editor-in-chief

TOO CLOSE FOR COMFORT

She wasn't sure when they had stopped walking and started standing very close, face to face.

"Should I let you go first?" Sir Daffyd asked. He leaned closer, his breath brushing across her cheek.

Softly and seductively, he continued, "Or should I drag you off with me? To where, Lady Jehane? Some deep, moss-covered bank in the woods?"

Abruptly, before she could answer, he stepped back, his expression distant and unreadable. "My apologies," he said stiffly. "A small joke. I didn't mean to frighten you."

The hot, melting sensation running through her blood had nothing to do with fear. "You don't frighten me," Jane said.

Which wasn't true. He did frighten her. Not with his size, or the threat of violence in the proud way he carried himself. He frightened her because she was attracted to him.

❖   ❖   ❖

Harper
Monogram

Wings
of the
Storm

Susan Sizemore

HarperPaperbacks
A Division of HarperCollinsPublishers

This is a work of fiction. The characters, incidents, and dialogues are products of the author's imagination and are not to be construed as real. Any resemblance to actual events or persons, living or dead, is entirely coincidental.

HarperPaperbacks   *A Division of* HarperCollins*Publishers*
10 East 53rd Street, New York, N.Y. 10022

Copyright © 1992 by Susan Sizemore
All rights reserved. No part of this book may be used or reproduced in any manner whatsoever without written permission of the publisher, except in the case of brief quotations embodied in critical articles and reviews. For information address HarperCollins*Publishers,*
10 East 53rd Street, New York, N.Y. 10022.

Cover illustration by John Ennis

First printing: November 1992

Printed in the United States of America

HarperPaperbacks, HarperMonogram, and colophon are trademarks of HarperCollins*Publishers*

❖ 10 9 8 7 6 5 4 3 2 1

For the Dream Team—Cary, Jane, Lois, Marguerite, Nellie, Nora, and Sharon

1

"Step into my time machine," said the drunken boy. He wasn't joking.

David Wolfe had Jane cornered in the back of his private lab, and it was obvious he wasn't going to let her out of the door. There was a tall blue booth behind her. He kept trying to herd her into it.

He was smiling stupidly, an expression ill-suited to his unfinished-looking face. Normally, he wore a furious scowl. It went well with his fashionably shaved head and the gold hoop earring in his right ear.

"It'll be fun," he told her, taking a step closer. "You want to go. I know you do. You have to. It'll only be for five years."

"No, I don't." She tried to be reasonable. "Dr. Wolfe, you're not yourself."

"You know too much. You said you saw five years into the future. Can't allow you to know about the future. You want to know about the past."

Jane Florian wished she hadn't stayed late in her lab at the Feynman Institute's Time Search Project.

She'd remained long after the rest of the Time Search Staff left, partly because she didn't want to drive home in a bad spring thunderstorm, partly because she found her work more interesting than what she had to drive home to.

She'd even declined an invitation to party with the particle physicists down by the accelerator ring. It seemed a new quark had just gotten discovered and it had been declared an occasion for champagne.

She wished she'd gone. If she had, she wouldn't have been by the screen when the lightning caused the power surge and the impossible happened. She'd ended up seeing into the future instead of the past. The time monitor was only supposed to scan backward, not forward.

The whole thing had lasted for no more than five seconds. In those five seconds she'd seen previews of five years' worth of upcoming events—wars, celebrity weddings, earthquakes. Wolfe had come in just as the screen faded to black. He hadn't seemed his usual serious self, but she'd been too upset to notice at first. She'd told the young physicist what happened.

He hadn't wanted to know what she'd seen. He'd said it was best if no one knew. He wasn't really interested in listening to her at all. It had become obvious to her that he'd been partying down in the quark lab. A rare occurrence for the reclusive young genius.

"This is the perfect opportunity. You've got to come to my lab," he'd said, smirking. "I've got something better than quarks."

In his lab he'd shown her the blue booth and told her what it was. Apparently the little twerp had actually gone and invented a time machine. He wanted to use it on her.

If anyone could do it, Jane supposed, it was David Wolfe. Actually, he wasn't little or exactly a boy. He was only twenty, but he was well over six feet tall. This egotistical twenty-year-old was in charge of Time Search, the Feynman Institute's most prestigious research program.

He backed her another step toward the machine. He was not small, and he was not giving her any chance to duck past him and out of the room. "You have to go," he said. "You'll destroy the future." Another step. She backed up. "I know the perfect place in the twelfth century. In 1168, to be precise," he went on. "At that big convent in the south of France. Font . . ."

"Fontrevault? It's not in the—"

"Right. You'll be safe and out of the wa—"

"I don't want to be a nun!"

"Can you think of anywhere safer in the Middle Ages?"

"Nothing was safe. Nowhere was safe. Not from fighting or disease or famine. This is murder."

"You'll be fine. I'll see you in five years."

She started to protest, but as she took another backward step she tripped over something. She fell into the booth. The walls were made of blue glass. Before she could get up, Wolfe quickly tossed the bags she'd tripped over in on top of her. He hurried to a control console on the side of the room.

The glass room disappeared. She teetered forward; the world rushed up to slam in her face. She fell through the blue tiled floor. The blueness rippled and changed; it was like water, then like the sky, then like being dragged through an undertow in an ocean of blue paint. As she fell out of the paint she saw the round stone tower rushing up to meet her. She slid, screaming, but insubstantial as smoke, through the rotting boards of the roof to land—

Jane sat up with a spine-wrenching jolt, her eyes wide with terror. She saw a stone wall in front of her. When she reached out tentatively her hands encountered hard stone beneath her.

She blinked. Stone? Closing her eyes, she waited for her ragged breathing to return to normal. She tried to think. Stone. Cold. "Where am I?" She opened her eyes.

What she saw was far from promising. She was in a circular stone room with no door, just a narrow arched opening letting in watery light and a damp breeze. There was windblown bracken lodged in the crevices, and a fuzzy patch of moss was growing up the wall opposite the doorway, splotching the gray, pitted surface a dark green. A rotting timber staircase circled up to a second story.

The damp cold penetrated her skin. She was shivering as she got slowly to her feet. She noticed the short skirt and knit top she'd been wearing were now little more than tattered rags. She'd been left uninjured by the long, impossible fall, but her clothing was so badly torn and singed she thought it might fall off if she moved. She hugged herself to try to stop the shivering, and the right sleeve of her sweater slid from her shoulder to dangle like a knit bracelet from her wrist.

Jane wondered what she was going to do. Then she noticed a trio of large canvas bags. She remembered tripping over them. She remembered them landing on top of her before she was engulfed in suffocating blue. She quickly went to investigate whatever it was David Wolfe had sent into the past with her.

The first thing she found was a bundle of clothing wrapped in a green wool cloak. There were three long, simply cut dresses. She recognized the style of the clothing, and knew how it was supposed to be worn. Her clothes were falling off, and she was cold.

She quickly stripped off her modern clothing and dressed in the triple layers of linen, silk, and wool. She found a belt, shoes, and head veils. She put them all on. Medieval clothing was one of her hobbies; she'd made and worn many costumes when she'd been involved with a medievalist club for years. This was not a costume she'd made herself, though the rich colors suited her tawny complexion perfectly.

So where was she? Had Wolfe's crazy experiment with the time machine really worked? No. She must be dreaming.

But the tight knot of fear in her stomach and the all-too-vivid memories told her this was no dream.

Dr. Wolfe had been planning this little trip all along, she thought, remembering the speculative look he had given her when he'd asked her to recommend a reading list a few weeks ago. She had thought the boy genius was getting interested in the fun part of the Time Search Project. He had been planning a little excursion instead. Planning on sending the resident historian where no one had gone before.

She shook her head. The egomaniac had actually expected her to volunteer. The accident had just been a convenient excuse.

Jane dashed her tears away and tried to shake off the memory of David Wolfe's face and glittering gold-green eyes. He didn't care. He had a mission to use his time machine. She'd ended up doing exactly what he planned.

But where was she? she wondered, making herself accept the present, whenever this present was. Did it work? Was she near Fontrevault Abbey? Or was this Oz? Or a ruined silo just up the road from Feynman? Her head ached and she was hungry and chilly despite the heavy clothes.

She dragged the canvas bags into the patch of sunlight coming through the doorway. Sitting down, she pulled the nearest bag to her, untying the leather string holding it closed. Out tumbled several more dresses, yards and yards of brightly colored silk fabric, and many skeins of embroidery thread. She reveled in color for a few minutes, realizing Wolfe had sent it along as trade goods. How nice, she thought sourly, refolding and stuffing the material away in the bag. It looked like the man had raided a fabric store in search of items he thought a medieval lady might find handy.

"I'd rather have five years' worth of M and M's," Jane complained, and went on to the two smaller bags. In them she found other rare items such as semiprecious stones and Chinese lacquer boxes filled with heady incense, foodstuffs, spices, and dried fruit. Expensive delicacies, she acknowledged as she ate a few apricots. She'd have preferred some camping equipment and a large supply of toilet paper, though.

"A few good paperbacks," she added aloud. "An old cassette player, batteries, tapes. A flashlight. Aspirin. An Uzi. Yeah"—she rubbed her hands together—"something in a semiautomatic with a large supply of ammo would do nicely."

At the bottom of the last bag she found a change of clothes. There was also a silver-hilted dagger in a brown leather sheath and a pouch containing small squares of gold and silver bars tucked inside one of a pair of cloth shoes.

She repacked everything, then stood and fastened the dagger and pouch to her belt. Time to inspect the premises, she told herself, knowing she couldn't hide in the stone tower forever. She took a deep breath, squared her broad shoulders, and stepped through the doorway. Before her stretched an overgrown clearing; beyond that were dark woods. A narrow but steep-banked stream snaked past the tower and into the trees. She could barely make out the rutted line of an unused path. The ground underfoot was damp and muddy, but there were traces of snow still in the withered undergrowth. What time of year was it? she wondered. It was spring at home. Late winter, perhaps? She sniffed the air. It smelled of moss and rainwater and, faintly, of pig.

For someone who'd spent her life in downstate Illinois, this earthy aroma was almost reassuring. It meant there was a farm nearby. People. Civilization. But was that necessarily a good thing? Jane's full lips pressed firmly together as she balled her hands into fists.

She concentrated on being angry rather than afraid. Angry at fate, at herself for not finding a way out of the situation, at David Wolfe. She concentrated on coping because panic never helped anybody survive. Damn Wolfe, anyway!

Stop thinking about him, she commanded herself—the shaved-head little geek! Six foot one was not little. Fine. He wasn't little. He was still a scrawny geek, and she was still stuck in the twelfth century.

"What a wonderful opportunity for a historian," she mocked, her rich contralto voice dripping venom.

She turned her attention to the ruins in the middle of the clearing. The round tower was only two stories high, with narrow windows cut in the thick stone of the second story. The defensive tower of a manor house, she guessed. Jane crossed her arms beneath her cloak and walked around the clearing, trying carefully to avoid ice-glazed puddles, afraid of what would happen if the flimsy leather shoes she wore got soaked. It didn't take her long to find evidence of tumbledown outbuildings. The wattle-and-daub structures would have been flimsy to begin with; a few seasons left to the weather and they'd molder back into the earth. The place looked to have been abandoned for quite a while.

Of course, the question wasn't so much what the ruins were, but where and when. She was *supposed* to have arrived in France, near the abbey of Fontrevault, in Anjou. Jane rubbed her upper arms briskly, not so much from cold as from nerves.

"Well, it isn't Kansas," she said to a crow perched on a fallen branch. "And I bet it isn't even France." The crow gave a scoffing cry and flew away.

Jane watched black wings beating the air until the bird disappeared into the trees. As she turned to follow its flight, she heard something crashing through the undergrowth, followed by a loud snuffling noise. Her gaze shifted from the sky to the ground, coming to rest on a humped-backed creature with short, brindled fur and a great tusked head with small, evil eyes. She jumped, gasping with alarm as the cloven-hoofed animal barreled forward, followed by a half dozen large beasts just like it. She ran, mindless of puddles now, until she was inside the vague shelter of the tower.

She peeped out the doorway, watching as the snorting and squealing animals fanned out across the clearing, blunt noses pushing hungrily at the wet bracken. Their stench reached her and she began to laugh, the sound fueled by the adrenaline that was still coursing through her.

"Pigs," she said, wiping her hand across her veiled brow. "Just pigs." She stepped back to the center of the doorway—just as the swineherd came into view. He was a boy of no more than ten, muddy and dressed in ragged homespun, butter-yellow hair hanging in braids. He leaped nimbly across the narrow stream. Jane started to retreat into the shadows, but the lad had seen her. He hurried forward, a pair of his pigs following like puppies on his heels. He called to her. Jane didn't recognize the language.

He stopped in front of her, questioning her in a guttural chatter. She listened carefully but couldn't make out a word of it. It sounded sort of like German, sort of like Dutch, and seemed as though it should be familiar. Jane read Latin, and two types of medieval French, the everyday langue d'oïl and the langue d'oc, language of the troubadours. She had a feeling what she was hearing was English, of a sort. Not the recognizable language of Chaucer's time, but an earlier dialect. Perhaps she had landed in the right time after all. But if this was English, she certainly wasn't in the right place.

When the boy stopped talking, she shrugged, and

replied in Norman French. "Hello. Those are very nice pigs. Could you tell me where I am?" She spoke slowly because she was more used to reading langue d'oïl than speaking it.

The boy blinked pale fringed lashes at her as she spoke. His eyes were very blue, the expression in them changing from curiosity to cautious neutrality. She supposed he was a Saxon. He probably didn't know a word of his country's conquerors' language.

And what did he make of her in her bright colors, with her brown eyes and creamy brown complexion and her slender height? She was five foot seven, tall for a male in this time, ridiculously tall for a woman.

The boy might not speak her language, but he reacted, though not as Jane expected. He wheeled around and, shouting loudly and waving his arms, he gathered up his herd and drove them back into the woods. He gave Jane only one furtive look before leaving the clearing. She wiggled her fingers in an attempt at a friendly wave. Perhaps the lad took this gesture as some sort of evil sign, because her waving only made him move faster.

Forgetting the short veil, Jane scratched her head. The gesture dislodged the square of linen. A breeze caught the light cloth, blowing it back into the tower room. Jane followed after, grumbling, and tripped over the canvas bags. Once she righted herself she retrieved the veil and fastened it securely over her recently permed brown curls. Then she took a seat on the tower stairs, stared out the doorway, and wondered what would happen next.

2

Not overly long after the swineherd's retreat, Jane heard the clop of a horse's hooves approaching the clearing. She reacted by scrambling up the steps to the second floor of the tower. The floorboards beneath her feet were rotting, covered in decaying leaves. Three tall but very narrow windows were cut in the deep stone. They let in some light, but more came from the hole near the center of the low ceiling. She stepped cautiously across the creaking floorboards to peek through one of the arrow-slit openings and had a clear view of the rider as he came into sight.

His horse was very large, powerful muscles rippling beneath its shiny black coat. The high-stepping animal moved with almost delicate grace across the uneven ground. Jane's knowledge of horseflesh was minimal, but even she could recognize a warhorse when she saw one. That, she told herself, was a Rolls-Royce on the hoof. On the horse's back rode a man swathed in a heavy black cape. Jane could make out spurred boots and a sheathed sword riding on his left hip. A knight, she realized.

"The perfect accessory, found on better warhorses everywhere," she muttered sarcastically.

When the horse halted before the tower door the rider threw back his hood, revealing a great deal of long dark hair. He looked up toward the window, and she saw a starkly handsome face. Jane caught her breath and corrected herself. His attractiveness wasn't so much stark as it was minimalist, as though a brilliant artist had sketched an ideal of masculine beauty in simple, bold lines. He was also young, she realized, eighteen, maybe nineteen. When he jumped lightly down from the horse she saw that he was taller than she'd expected a man of his time to be. He was long and slender; his body looked to be wiry and strong, but not quite finished. The young man's coloring was all dark and light, pale skin contrasting with blue-black hair and brows.

Even as she stared at this remarkably handsome young man, she was asking herself what she was going to do. What would a Norman lady do? Go out and face the armed foe or cower in terror? She was personally rather in favor of cowering, but there wasn't anywhere in this bare tower to hide. She backed away from the window.

Besides, she added in thought, lifting her head proudly, she wasn't very good at cowering. If Wolfe hadn't been drunk— Forget about it. That was in the past—future.

"I can see tenses are going to be a real problem from now on," she muttered. Men in armor might be more of an immediate danger, she reminded herself, getting a firm hold on her nerves. She was apparently going to have to live in this world, so she might as well get on with it. If she didn't get on with it she might as well curl up and die right there and then.

She adjusted her headgear, flicked some dried mud off her green cape, and forced herself to walk down the stairs, her long skirts trailing gracefully behind her.

The knight was standing inside the doorway by the time she reached the bottom of the circular staircase. When she paused on the second step, Jane found herself meeting a pair of intense black eyes. From the distance of the tower window she'd thought the young man's features ascetic, but the expression she saw in his dark-fringed eyes hinted at passion far from any religious calling. And his mouth was amazing, almost too wide for the narrowing face, the lips almost too thin, yet wondrously expressive. As he gazed up the stairs at her, he was managing to convey interest, a hint of worldly sophistication that said he appreciated what he was seeing, and a bit of reassurance, all with only a hint of a smile. Jane found herself smiling, rather shyly, back.

He put his hands on his narrow hips and said, "I see Arnulf was wrong."

Jane's smile turned into a grin, not at the man's words, but because she had no trouble understanding them. He spoke langue d'oïl. Staying put on the stairs, she questioned, "Arnulf?"

The young knight's smile widened. "My swineherd," he explained. "He came running to the reeve, and the reeve came running to me. It seems the lad claimed he saw a giantess, or a man dressed as a fine lady." His eyes sparkled as he surveyed her critically, his smile never wavering. "I see no giant, though I may not be a fair judge, being so long-shanked myself. Nor do I see a man garbed as a woman. I've seen such oddness at Christmas revels; I don't think your soft curves are padding."

Jane felt herself blush, and for the first time in her life she found the warm sensation rather pleasant. "No, my lord," she answered. "I'm quite all me. I'm afraid I can't help being tall, or my deep voice."

"A pleasant voice," he assured her easily. "But I do wonder why a beautiful lady is hiding in this old ruin."

"I'm not hiding," Jane declared, trying to think of an explanation of why she was here. "I'm lost."

"Lost? A lady as lovely as you should be lost in a bower of roses."

"And you're a flatterer," Jane told him with a chuckle. And she was glad of it. Far better that her first encounter in this world be with this charming young man than with some hulk with a sword in his hand. His sword and spurs and the horse outside told her he was a warrior, but she also felt instantly at ease with him. Maybe it was the smile.

"I should hope so," he responded to her. "I've been well trained in the flattering of ladies. Though of late I've had little practice. "He stepped forward, gesturing toward the stairs."Perhaps we could sit awhile and talk of the world beyond this lonely tower."

He seated himself next to her feet, gazing up at her expectantly, rather like a friendly, black-eyed hunting hound. Jane hesitated for only a moment before easing down next to him. "I am Sir Stephan DuVrai," he introduced himself. "Lord of Passfair Castle. And of this crumbling ruin as well," he added, waving his hand as though apologizing for the building's deficiencies. "Though this wood is more often used as a pig pasture than for housing guests."

Jane looked at her toes, encased in stiffening damp leather. Tucking her hands into her sleeves, she confessed, "My lord, I have no idea where I am. My name . . ." She hadn't thought about what she would say when confronted by the natives; Wolfe certainly hadn't thought about it.

She couldn't very well explain that she'd been minding her own business monitoring a Time Search screen on a rainy night in 2002 when she'd accidentally gotten a glimpse of the future. Or that her crazy boss had used the accident as an excuse to toss her into his experimental time machine.

But she did have an explanation ready, she realized suddenly. She'd spent years playacting a role in the Medievalist Society. She had a persona she slipped into when the club did living history demos.

"I am Jehane FitzRose," she told DuVrai. She bowed her head sadly, just the way she did when explaining to curious high school kids. "A widow. My husband and father died in the Holy Land. That's where I'm from," she added. "I was born in the kingdom of Jerusalem." She could only hope she'd landed in the right period for her story to sound authentic.

"Jerusalem." The young knight sounded impressed. "That would explain your accent. I confess, some of your words are a bit hard to understand."

It's my midwestern twang, she thought. Looking up at Stephan demurely, she went on, "My father was a native of this land. He left his father's lands to go on

Crusade, a younger son seeking his fortune," she explained.

Stephan nodded his understanding.

Jane warmed to the subject. "He did well and settled in Palestine. I was his only child, so he married me to a knight he thought of as a son. I was very happy with Geoffrey." She sighed and gave a fatalistic shrug. "But the Saracens . . ."

"They killed your family? Overran your land?"

"Something like that," Jane agreed. "I was alone in the world." Outside she could hear the horse pawing the ground restlessly.

Stephan cocked his head to listen to the animal for a moment, then said, "Go on, Lady Jehane."

"I couldn't stay in Palestine."

"Far too dangerous for a woman alone," he agreed. "Far too dangerous for any but the bravest Christians since the late king's Crusade failed. I've heard many horror stories about that war from my father."

Jane's fingers began to itch for her pocket word processor. She'd thought picking up random data from the time monitor had been fun. Now, here she was talking to a living history book—a book with a very nice cover—and she didn't dare ask him specific questions. In fact, she was the one being questioned, and she had to be very cautious in her answers.

"The late king," she went on tentatively. "Richard?" Stephan nodded. Late? Like in d-e-a-d? Richard the Lion Heart was *dead*. Her head spun with confusion. That was wrong. No, she was wrong. In the wrong time. She was supposed to show up at Fontrevault in 1168, long *before* the Lion Heart was king. Where had Wolfe plunked her down?

What was she going to do? Where would she go?

"Where am I?" she heard herself say, her voice a frightened rasp. Sir Stephan put a reassuring hand on her shoulder.

She tried to take up the thread of Jehane's story before she broke into sobs, trying to shape her club persona to fit conjectured circumstance. "I . . . and my maid and two men-at-arms left the Holy Land. We brought all we had with us. I was widowed, but not impoverished. We made the journey in slow stages. There was illness; my maid died, then one of the soldiers. I was ill on the Channel crossing. I don't know what port—"

"Dover?" Stephan suggested. "Reculver? It's the nearest to Passfair."

Jane gave a confused shake of her head. "I know nothing of England, and I was feverish. I don't remember much of the journey. My last retainer— he'd been with my father all his life—he was bringing me to my grandfather's estate. Apparently it was destroyed, or had changed hands. Perhaps he didn't even remember where it was. He was quite old. We grew lost. I don't know how I got here or where he went. When I woke up this morning I felt better." She looked gratefully at Sir Stephan. "Then you came."

She didn't recognize the other town he'd mentioned, but she knew Dover was in the south of England. It had been the main Channel port before the tunnel opened a few years ago. She was also realizing how dangerous it was for her to be running around loose in this time. She knew too little. And too much. Knowing the period as she did would certainly help her survive, or at least cope. But she was a danger to the future, or could be if she said even a few wrong words to the wrong person. She knew the politics and the power struggles of the Normans better than they did. It was as dangerous for her to be able to reveal what was going to happen five years from this date as it was for her to reveal what was going to happen five years ahead in her own time. In all her studies she'd never come across any mention of a Sir Stephan DuVrai. Perhaps an encounter with him wouldn't matter. But what if she met someone famous? Wolfe had been right in one thing: she was going to have to hide herself away. She needed to be somewhere she could live in silence and obscurity. Somewhere the world would be safe from Dr. Jane Florian.

"A convent," she said sharply.

Stephan almost jumped at her tone. "What?"

"A convent, an abbey, a priory, a—" She caught herself and took a deep breath, forcing herself to calm down, to remember she was now Jehane FitzRose. She took her hands out of her sleeves and folded them on her lap, trying for an imitation of serenity. "I should like to take holy vows," she told the young knight. "I wish only to escape this world."

"Oh." He looked a bit unhappy at the thought. "If you must. I've no great love for the Church myself, but . . ." His wide mouth flattened in a sudden frown, the heavy brows lowering. "No, you can't. Foolish of me of all people to forget."

Jane stared. "No? Why not?" she asked suspiciously.

"The damned king's being excommunicated again. By the archbishop of Canterbury this time. You've chosen a holy calling at an unholy time," he explained.

Jane threw her hands in the air, annoyed with Wolfe's bad timing. "Don't tell me—John's king of England and the country's under interdict. No masses, no burials in consecrated ground, no marriages, no sacraments at all."

"That is the usual procedure," he agreed dryly. "And our king's turning the clergy out of their holdings as well, at least all the ones near Canterbury. There's nowhere for you to be a nun just now, at least not nearby. I hope you don't want it too badly," he added with a boyishly charming smile.

"It would be best for me." She sighed and got up to pace across the cold stone floor of the tower. "What am I supposed to do now?"

Stephan rose, leaning casually against the wall as he watched her marching worriedly back and forth. "You needn't agitate yourself," he said after a while.

She turned on him. As she opened her mouth to yell, she managed to remember that medieval ladies were supposed to be demure and gentle. A tantrum would not do, even though she might enjoy it. So she stood there gaping at the young man instead.

Stephan strode forward. Tucking a forefinger under her chin, he closed her mouth for her. "You'll stay at Passfair for now," he informed her.

She eyed him suspiciously. His tone was that of a man used to having his way. She was alone and lost and too aware she really couldn't survive on her own. He had offered her nothing but kindness so far, and she was trespassing on his land. He also had a sword. She didn't relish the thought of a confrontation with an armed man. She didn't like being meek and mild, but there wasn't much choice at the moment.

"I—" she began.

"There are wolves in the forest," he added before she could fumble on. His dark eyes were sparkling with mischief as he informed her, "And brigands, of course. And I've an annoying neighbor who's been terrorizing travelers of late. It's best you come home with me." Stephan placed his right hand over his heart. "Your virtue's safe, Lady Jehane," he said as he ran his eyes appreciatively over her once more. "For now, at least."

Jane dropped her gaze demurely—before she did something stupid like respond to his flirting. No one had flirted with her for a while. He was just a boy, and he probably had fleas or something worse, she reminded herself. The last thing she needed was to get involved with someone in the twelfth or thirteenth or whatever century this was. "I'm grateful, Sir Stephan," she said after some hesitation.

"Good." He looked past her, out the doorway. The horse was snuffling and pawing the ground. "He thinks he runs my life, you know."

Sounds like my car, Jane thought. *I will never again buy one that talks at me. No,* she realized, *I won't.*

She had a sudden sensation that was rather like having her brain hit with a brick wall. The tower and Sir Stephan spun briefly out of focus.

She heard him ask, "Are you all right? The fever?"

She grasped his arm to remain upright as the dizziness passed. She blinked owlishly. "Fever? Oh, yes, the fever."

"We best go."

"Right," she agreed. She went to the bags and hefted the two smaller ones with a grunt. Their contents made her a rich woman in this time, and she wasn't about to forget them. They weighed about twenty pounds each. When she turned around, Stephan was holding the larger canvas bag and looking at her in surprise.

"I could have sent a servant back for these," he said, half-chiding. He added, "You're strong for a woman."

For a lady, he meant. Jane blushed. "Without servants, one learns," she pointed out rather primly. He nodded. She followed him outside.

Within a few minutes he had the bags lashed to the skittish animal's high saddle peak. He mounted, then helped her up, settling her behind him.

Jane wrapped her arms tightly around the young knight's very narrow waist, her wide skirts spread out around her and her short linen veil stirred by the breeze. It probably looked terribly romantic, she thought, even if it wasn't all that comfortable. Things could be much worse, she supposed. She had been invited to a castle, with a handsome knight as her champion. Maybe the Middle Ages wouldn't be so bad after all.

3

"What a dump," Jane said under her breath as she viewed the great hall of Passfair Castle.

Sir Stephan had led her into the hall through a door cut in a movable wooden screen placed several feet back from the outer door. She paused, squinting in the murky light. She made out a large room with a low, soot-covered ceiling. Very little light seeped in from the two narrow windows in the wall above the high table at the other end of the room. A smoky fire in a round central hearth was responsible for the soot, if for very little illumination or warmth. The floor was covered in a thick layer of withered and stinking rushes. The rushes were covered in a layer of rough-coated dogs. Well, dotted was perhaps a better word, Jane thought, but there were at least a dozen of them. She sniffed distastefully. Not exactly housebroken, either.

Stephan noticed her staring at the dogs. "Deerhounds," he said. "The estate borders on the royal forest of Blean. I'm not allowed to hunt the king's deer, but I have the privilege of housing and providing for a pack of our lord John's hounds. Not," he added with a sarcastic twitch of his lips, "that those curs would recognize a deer if it wandered into the hall and offered to slit its own throat."

Jane breathed a sigh of relief. "Then the King doesn't come here to hunt?"

"Not in living memory. He prefers other sport."

She followed Stephan to the central fire. She stepped carefully, the rushes not so much rustling as squashing underfoot. She heard the skittering and squeaking of mice in the foul matting.

As they reached the glowing hearth and held their hands out to warm, one of the hounds rose on long, slender legs. It stretched, then trotted up to Stephan, butting its head insistently against his hand. He reached down automatically to pet the long white head.

"This," he said, scratching the dog's short, floppy ears, "is Melisande, the true chatelaine of Passfair." As he spoke a pair of puppies caught up to Melisande and began happily weaving in and out between her legs. "She's something of a wanton," he added.

"You haven't been home much lately, have you?" Jane guessed as she and Stephan made their way through the dog pack to the long wooden table on the dais. Melisande followed at Stephan's heel, her puppies clamoring after. The little ones had some trouble with the dais step, so Stephan absentmindedly helped them up with the toe of his boot.

Jane hid a smile as she seated herself at a hard but beautifully carved chair behind the table. Stephan's gallantry was unconscious and quite boyishly charming. In fact, he was looking more boyish to her with each passing moment, especially as his mobile mouth took on an almost petulant pout. She resisted an urge to pat him affectionately on the head.

"Well?" she questioned instead.

He pulled another unwieldy chair up beside hers. When he sat down, Melisande took the opportunity to rest her elegant head in his lap. He played with her ears while he answered.

"It's a long tale." His lips lifted in a mocking half smile. "A long winter, actually. I was away for most of it, in my liege's service. A fever struck Passfair and my village of Hwit between here and the river. The priest died first, I'm told. No loss since he wouldn't shrive the dying anyway."

Stephan threw off his cape, letting it drape across the back of his chair. He wore a black tunic, embroidered at the neck in a gray-and-white geometric pattern. Jane followed his example, shedding her own cape.

"Over the course of the winter," he continued, "my steward died, and his wife, and the bailiff. By the time I got home only the Saxon reeve was left in the village. There's been no one but the cook and a crippled old guard sergeant to keep the place running at all." He gestured around the hall with one elegantly long-fingered hand. "My late lady mother would kill me if she knew I'd let her hall come to this."

He smiled warmly at Jane. "The problem is," he went on earnestly, "Passfair needs a lady. Running a household's no job for a man. I've been trying, but I hardly know the buttery from the brew house. The reeve's keeping the demesne farm running all right.

Peasants don't need a nobleman trying to teach them farming. But the hall . . ." He trailed off, mobile mouth downcast, but Jane thought she detected a gleam of speculation in his dark eyes.

She ignored it, recalling the ride across the estate from the tower. There'd been men and oxen working in two of the three fields she'd seen, a little girl minding a gaggle of geese, and a few other people going slowly about their business while studiously ignoring their passing lord, but she'd gotten the feeling the place was almost deserted. There seemed to be a lack of purpose or interest about the inhabitants. From the look of the castle interior, Sir Stephan's home was falling rapidly into decay.

It was a small keep, square in shape and only two stories high. The main building's walls were thick gray stone with a flat, crenellated roof, surrounded by a ditch and a double wall. The outer wall was of heavy wooden staves, wickedly pointed at the top. Inside the walls the bailey held the keep and quite a few thatched-roofed wattle-and-daub buildings. She'd identified a sturdily built stable and noticed servants lingering around a wooden kitchen structure connected to the castle by a covered walkway.

Stephan grimaced at her lack of response to his silent plea and yelled for some ale. Almost instantly the old servant who had brought her bags in came shuffling over with a pair of wooden tankards, making his way to the dais through a traffic jam of suddenly awake and restive dogs. Those mutts had to go, Jane thought as she watched his weaving progress.

As the servant stepped up to Stephan she just barely caught herself from crossing her legs to get more comfortable. The chair was hard and her muscles ached, but she knew she'd have to be careful to be as still as possible until she could pick up local body language. Better to be thought stiff than improper. She did drum her fingers on the chair arm and nudge a pup chewing on her hem.

"No wife?" she questioned cautiously.

"Wife?" he said as he took the tankards from the old man. He passed one to Jane, who sniffed distastefully at the brown liquid. She knew the barley-based beverage was safer to drink than water and supposed she'd better get used to it. As she took a cautious swallow Stephan repeated, "Wife? Not yet."

Jane balanced the tankard on the wide arm of her chair. "No?" Stephan was looking melancholy, and she didn't think she liked it. "What's wrong with being married?" she asked.

"Nothing." He lifted his square chin proudly. "I am betrothed to Lady Sibelle LeGauche of Sturry," he announced, sounding more as though he were trying to impress himself than her. Then he added unhappily, "There really isn't any better choice."

"Local heiress?" Jane guessed. He nodded and sat moodily staring at his boots while Melisande licked his hand. Jane watched him for a minute before asking, "All right, what's wrong with her?"

He looked at her through his thick black lashes. "I've never met the girl," he admitted. "But I have my suspicions. She'll not make a good chatelaine, I know that already," he declared forcefully. Giving Jane the full potency of his most beguiling smile, he cajoled, "You'll help me, won't you?"

Jane really wished she could scratch her head. It

wasn't just that all the hours under a veil made her scalp itch. She always scratched her head when she was totally confused. She knew her expression must be reflecting her unease at his odd request. She didn't think this was an offer of marriage. Rich heiresses weren't exactly thick on the ground, and young knights had a certain yuppielike hankering after upward mobility. Jane had a treasure in her bags, but it would mean nothing to Sir Stephan. He was part of a class structure that valued land above all else. He wouldn't be marrying this Sibelle person if she weren't bringing him at least one estate as a dowry.

"Please, dear nut-brown Jehane."

"How can I help?" she asked. She knew it wasn't a wise question, but he'd offered her shelter—and he looked so appealing.

He ran his right hand around his long jaw and chin. "It's Sibelle. She's fifteen. Ripe for marriage, yes, but from what I've heard . . . she was raised in Davington Priory. To pray," he added sardonically. "No one seemed to think she had it in her to be prioress despite her family's wealth. The nuns were turned out of the priory about the same time Baron LeGauche's two sons died. He was left with the girl as an heiress. He had need of a husband for the girl, someone to protect her lands. He chose me. He preferred a near neighbor to other alliances he could make. He's ailing, and in difficult times it's best to stay close to home. The choice was between me and Hugh of Lilydrake, Hugh's wife being recently dead. The lucky woman," Stephan added. "The baron's a feeling enough father not to want his girl wed to the likes of Hugh. And I'm better connected," Stephan added with a shameless grin.

Not to mention he was about the cutest thing in the country, Jane added silently, rubbing her own chin to hide a smile. Not that she supposed that counted in the marital transaction. "So you're betrothed to a nun. What's that got to do with me, Sir Stephan? I wish to become a nun, remember?"

"I need a woman to run my household," he told her, waving his hand around the deserted and dirty hall. "How can I bring a bride into this muck? Especially a bride with no sense to manage it?"

"But—"

"I'd like to appoint you my chatelaine," he told her before she could go on. "I knew you'd suit as soon as you told me of your life and travels. You're a strong woman, Lady Jehane."

She found herself scratching her head despite the veil. "But I know nothing about running an estate. I'm from a different land, a different ti—climate. I'm a stranger."

He didn't seem to care. "You'll manage," he said smugly.

"What do you mean, I'll *manage*?" Why was she suddenly running into men who insisted on throwing her into impossible situations?

"You've survived the Saracens and the journey to England," Stephan pointed out reasonably. "Running a manor's only a matter of giving the right orders and keeping accounts. I don't suppose you can read?"

Jane bristled, snapping out, "Four languages," before thinking about it.

Stephan's heavy black brows lifted at this statement. "Reading's a useful skill. I've no Latin myself,

but I can manage French well enough for love poems.
You have the skills I need, and I'm offering you a
place until the interdict's over." He nodded his stubbornly set square jaw. "It's settled, then."

Jane didn't see it that way, but her protest wasn't
heard since the dogs suddenly started yapping again.
Several of them bounded up to the screen doorway,
one of them knocking a stack of peat into the
already smoking fire as it lunged forward. The
smoke drifted inexorably toward the dais. Jane
quickly tucked the end of her veil over her mouth
and nose so she wouldn't start coughing from smoke
inhalation.

Melisande had stiffened. It was clear she had
seen something. She came and stood protectively
next to Stephan's chair. The knight had to push her
aside to rise to his feet. Jane looked eagerly toward
the entrance, straining through the hearth smoke
for a better view of what all the excitement was
about.

She was rather disappointed when a horde didn't
come rushing into the great hall. Instead, a grizzled
old guard came limping in, his ring-sewn leather
jerkin jingling as he made his jerky way toward the
dais. Jane sat back with a sigh that was mostly one of
relief. Apparently the peasants were not revolting.
Maybe the hounds were just bored. She bent over to
disconnect the tangled puppy from her hem once
more.

"My lord," the guard said as he came up to
Stephan. "Sir Daffyd—"

"Is perfectly capable of announcing himself."

"—ap Bleddyn," the guard finished lamely.

The voice that had interrupted the guard was deep,

rich, and amused. The sound of it made Jane think of heavy cream and dark chocolate even before she looked up to see the tall blond man who'd followed the guard into the room. The dogs had quieted their barking, but their attention was centered warily on the broad-shouldered newcomer.

Jane didn't blame them a bit. He radiated danger far more than the fire radiated heat. There was something about the man's swaggering walk and the proud thrust of his jaw that spoke volumes about his arrogant self-importance. He had an aquiline, if slightly crooked, nose that seemed tailor-made for looking down. The shoulder-length gold hair that framed his face resembled a lion's mane. He was dressed in full chain mail with a belted black surcoat pulled on over the heavy armor.

Coming to a halt in front of Stephan, he rested one spurred boot on the dais and leaned forward, the fingers of his left hand curled loosely around the pommel of his sword. Jane couldn't help but notice how large and competent that hand looked. He squinted through the murk at Sir Stephan.

"I've some news about your bride," he said in his deep, richly accented voice. He peered around Stephan at where Jane sat. "If you want to hear it," he added.

His deep voice held only the faintest hint of insinuation, but it was enough to make her go hot with outraged embarrassment. Stephan's back muscles tensed as he moved so that he was between her and Sir Daffyd.

"The lady is the widow of Sir Geoffrey FitzRose," Stephan informed the knight coolly. "A kinswoman from the kingdom of Jerusalem. My chatelaine," he added, throwing a look over his shoulder for Jane. She gave an unconscious shrug in reply.

Sir Daffyd nodded curtly. "Lady," he rumbled. "Welcome. About the girl?" he went on.

The man was big and impressive and wore an air of danger like an invisible cloak around his shoulders. Jane was glad of the shadows and smoke that obscured the room, glad Stephan stood between her chair and the warrior at the foot of the dais. There was an air of disdainful pride about him she found threatening. He scared her without having done anything more than walk in the room and casually glance her way. She didn't suppose the combination of fear and fascination she was experiencing made any sense. But it reminded her that she was in a time when brute strength counted for a great deal, where men with swords took what they wanted. In 2002 the idea of needing a man to protect her was ludicrous. But this was 1200 something, and she knew she was fortunate to have a chivalrous warrior to champion her.

Cheeks still flushed, she looked away from Sir Daffyd's face and caught sight of the insignia decorating his black surcoat. On the right shoulder of the black wool garment was embroidered a gold lion; a red dragon decorated the left. Jane interpreted the symbols to mean the knight was a Welshman in the service of the English king. She recalled that Daffyd was a Welsh name.

The old servant appeared with another wooden tankard of ale. Daffyd took it and drained it before tossing it back. He wiped the back of his hand across his mouth, then spoke to Stephan again. "I stopped at Sturry on my way from Canterbury. The baron's dying. He's not likely to last long and wants the girl settled. He asked me to escort the child's party to you." He made a sour face. "But my orders are to garrison my men in Reculver."

"Still hunting Sikes and Pwyll and their men?" Stephan asked.

The Welshman nodded.

Stephan turned to Jane to explain, "The brigands I was telling you about. Sir Daffyd's been sent by our lord John to—"

"Ride over the local barons and threaten the archbishop in my spare time," Daffyd interrupted. "But hunting the outlaws has more sport in it." Stephan laughed and Daffyd joined him. "You better fetch the girl yourself," he went on. "Before your neighbor snatches the heiress for himself."

"Hugh of Lilydrake isn't getting his hands on my marriage prize," Stephan said. "I'll leave for Sturry in the morning." He gestured around the hall. "Accept my hospitality for the night, Sir Daffyd."

The Welshman straightened and backed two steps away from the dais. One of the dogs came up and sniffed at him. Impatiently he pushed the animal's head away. "Another time," he answered. "I just wanted to bring the baron's request to you." He gave a vague nod in Jane's direction. "Lady."

The single word sounded more like a sneering dismissal than a mere farewell. Jane wondered if she was expected to make some gracious answer when she'd much rather say something rude. She held her temper and racked her brain for mild words. Fortunately she was saved from trying out the Medievalist Society's idea of courtliness when Sir Daffyd spun around and marched out as swiftly as he'd entered.

She discovered after he'd disappeared through the screen that her knuckles had gone numb from gripping the arms of her chair. She didn't know why he made her so nervous, but she was very glad he hadn't stayed for dinner. She forced herself to relax, made herself think about something other than the abrupt appearance of the lion-maned Welshman. She had to swallow hard to relieve her dry throat.

"Hugh of Lilydrake?" she asked as Stephan took his chair again.

He ran a hand through his silky black hair. His eyes snapped with anger as he answered. "The fool's going to try to kidnap Sibelle. He knows I'd storm his keep to get her back."

She removed the veil from across her mouth and coughed lightly when she took a breath. "How romantic," she said.

He gave her a sardonic look. It was the sort of expression his eyebrows were made for. "Isn't it?" A delighted smile suddenly squared his wide mouth. "Sibelle will think I'm wonderful, won't she?

"I'm sure," Jane agreed. Her estimation of Stephan's age dropped to about seventeen. Then she shook her head in confusion. "But the country's under interdict. What good will it do you or this Hugh to have Sibelle if you can't get married?"

He laughed loudly, the sound filling the hall. "It's having the heiress that counts," he told her. "Whoever holds the girl when her father dies will get her lands."

"Right. Important point. How could I have forgotten?" It was the land they wanted, not the girl. She'd tumbled into the time that had seen the birth of the romantic ideal, but when love had nothing to do with marriage. Marriage was a business transaction; romance was a ritual you conducted with somebody else's wife. She tucked her hands in her sleeves and added primly, "I'm glad I'm soon to be away from such worldly matters."

"Of course you are, Jehane," he agreed with a humorous glint in his dark eyes. "You'll make a fine nun. In the meantime you'll make Passfair a good chatelaine."

She sighed. "Yes, I suppose I'll have to try." It was a living, she thought. She supposed technically Sir Stephan was her liege lord, and she owed him service. Besides, where else could she go? What else could she do?

Her eyes stung from the smoke. Or maybe they stung from an effort not to cry as the hopelessness of her situation tried to overwhelm her.

No, she told herself firmly. *You can cry all you want if you ever have a moment alone. Things aren't all that bad. You could have ended up with Sir Daffyd. Survive,* she told herself. *Survive so you can strangle David Wolfe if you ever see him again.*

The idea of somehow getting revenge on David Wolfe had a bracing effect. She smiled and sank down on the high-backed chair. Almost every vertebra creaked with exhaustion. All she really wanted was to go to sleep. Waking to find out this was all a dream would be nice, too. She didn't think that was going to happen. So forget being tired, she ordered her weary limbs.

She stretched out her legs, levered herself to her feet, and looked around the dismal mess of Passfair's great hall. Hands on hips, she surveyed its dogs and smoke and stinking rushes. Lord knew what the rest of the place was like. It wasn't going to be easy.

She glanced at the eagerly smiling Sir Stephan. "When do I start?"

4

"*Now,*" *the boy said, and went off,* shouting for his guard sergeant as he left the hall. There was an exuberant bounce to Stephan's step. Several of the dogs followed at his heels.

"Teenagers," Jane muttered after him, an affectionate glow permeating her exasperation. Off to rescue fair maidens and terrorize the neighborhood. Odd, she thought, she'd known the kid a few hours and already she was feeling maternal. And a good thing that was, too, considering the kid's looks. The script read virtuous widow, she reminded herself sternly. And he was engaged—in looting and pillaging, probably. No, he was a nice boy. She chuckled.

She folded her arms and stared once more into the morass of damp and dirty rushes. She wasn't crossing that again without immunization. She returned to her chair, where she pulled her cloak back around her shoulders and tried to organize her thoughts.

She didn't have long to consider her situation in private. Servants soon shuffled in and began rearranging the hall. She watched them carefully in the dim light, fighting the impulse to toss back reassuring smiles at the few furtive looks thrown her way. She remained carefully still and neutral as she tried to assess how to play the role Sir Stephan had thrust on her.

The dogs were shooed aside long enough for a pair of trestle tables to be set up for the household and Stephan's men-at-arms. Wooden trenchers clattered onto the tables. Stephan, his sergeant, and his men came into the hall soon after the tables were ready, bringing with them the heavy aroma of horse manure. Supper was served soon after. The food was late-winter fare, fish in a sauce of dried herbs, cheese curds, boiled dried beans and a bread made of a mixture of roughly ground grains. The ale was plentiful, and a sour wine was served to Stephan and Jane in tarnished silver goblets. He gave her a pleased look when she fingered the dirty silver dish.

She kept her acknowledging chortle to herself. Okay, she conceded silently, maybe she could make a good housekeeper for the kid. She ate sparingly, drank not at all, and tried not to suggest sending out for pizza.

During the meal Stephan introduced his household to their new chatelaine. She got a few openly curious and surly looks after the announcement and glared them down with as much Norman arrogance as she could fake. It helped that she had a long nose to look down. She'd had a boyfriend once who'd described it as "elegant" and "aristocratic." She'd kept him for a long time.

Most of the people below the salt concentrated on wolfing down their evening meals, probably not car-ing who gave the orders as long as they got fed. The dogs wandered around begging and snatching food shamelessly, most people just shoving the big deer-hounds out of the way without paying them any mind. Melisande sat regally by Stephan's chair. Jane was happy to slip the hound and her pups much of her own dinner.

It was well after sunset when the few dishes and trestle tables were taken away. The room emptied, but for a few servants who settled by the banked central hearth to sleep. The dogs found places with the humans, all the bodies melding into a warm heap.

Stephan rose from his chair and took Jane's hand to help her up. "The hour of coverfire," he told her, voice soft as though not to disturb the sleepers. "Time to be abed. There's a sleeping space behind the tower storeroom. Bertram will show you."

The old servant approached, a sputtering oil lamp in one gnarled hand. "I've left your bags and bedding for you there, Lady Jehane," he told her as he led the way up the tower stairs.

She followed his bent figure, suppressing the urge to grasp him by the elbow and help him along. She wondered how old he was. Forty, maybe? The thought was not a pleasant one, and she quickly put it aside.

He led her to a curtained alcove at the back of a big, dusty room on the first of the tower's two floors. She got the impression of many barrels and chests occupying the room's shadowed depths.

He handed her the lamps and the heavy iron key he'd used to unlock the storeroom's thick wooden door. "Rest well, Lady Jehane," he said, and was gone, his footsteps echoing faintly back out of the dark.

It took a few minutes of banging into wooden barrels and bins and stirring up dust in the feeble light before she finally found the notch in the wall containing a narrow bed frame. After setting the lamp down on a leather-bound chest next to the bed, she turned too quickly and tripped over one of her bags. Landing on the straw mattress, she stayed put. Her skirts snuffed out the wick as she fell, saving her from having to blow out the light.

"Lucky I didn't catch my dress on fire," she murmured.

She knelt in the center of the bed to wriggle out of her layers of clothes. As she recalled, nightgowns were unknown in this period, but she didn't want to have to sleep in the same clothes she would have to wear again tomorrow. And the next day, and the next. Maybe she would adopt a few laundry innovations as chatelaine of Passfair.

She rolled around, settling the fur covering comfortably, and almost immediately discarded any plan for change. She didn't dare alter a thing. Not one single, uncomfortable thing. She had a responsibility not to influence this alien culture. She could change the future. And stuck back here she'd have no way of knowing whether a ripple effect from one tiny alteration would prove good or ill for her own time. She sighed unhappily. She'd just have to live by this place and time's rules. Observe and not participate and get herself to a nunnery ASAP.

She just hoped she didn't forget, screw up, or get fed up with life in a time warp.

The straw-stuffed mattress wasn't much different from the thin cotton futon she slept on at home. The mattress did rustle dryly when she moved, and there were things in it that nibbled on her. But it was neither the straw nor the bugs, nor even her spinning thoughts, that kept her awake. It was the silence. It was the dead still quiet of the night inside these stone walls that convinced her she was no longer at home. Alone in the silent darkness she faced the realization that she wasn't really in some weird overauthentic theme park produced by David Wolfe.

Even in her quiet neighborhood in an Illinois town there was white noise that went unnoticed except in its absence. Here in the south of England, probably sometime around 1209, there wasn't a dishwasher or airplane or car engine or stereo or lawn mower or air conditioner—not a mechanical *whoosh* or roar or thrum or blare or rattle or hum to be heard anywhere on the planet. She didn't like the dark silence; it pressed in on her ears and her mind.

In the silence she couldn't stop thinking about what had brought her to this alien place. She was an alien here, no matter what Wolfe thought. He thought she lived for history. Maybe she did; her job had become her life in the last year. She gradually lost track of friends and family and the real world to concentrate on historical research. She practically lived at the institute. She'd drifted away from the Medievalist Society, hardly ever called her mother anymore. There were no men in her life. She had thought she was satisfied with what she was doing.

She suddenly knew she'd gotten so caught up in the project that she hadn't made time for anything else in her life. She thought her historical research was enough. She'd been enjoying herself.

Enjoying herself and forgetting reality, she castigated herself. Now reality didn't exist for her. Not the reality she wanted and didn't even realize she wanted until she'd lost her chance for it. It wasn't as if she hadn't planned to get on with real life someday. She'd hoped to find someone to love. It was just that she hadn't found anyone who'd met what her standards were. Maybe someone who looked like Daffyd ap Bleddyn but acted like a gentleman.

She tried not to feel sorry for herself despite the strangeness and discomfort of her surroundings. She tried not to be frightened. She tried not to be homesick. She tried not to listen to the silence, but the silence wouldn't go away, though she tried to populate it with memories of familiar sounds. It kept her awake for many hours until exhaustion finally forced sleep on her. Even then she had nightmares.

In her dreams the broad-shouldered form of Sir Daffyd, grown to giant size, stood over her, sword drawn while she worked frantically at a piece of embroidery. She kept trying to form red dragons with her needle, but the design kept turning into a lion. He kept threatening and badgering her to get it right until she got fed up and began shouting back. He grabbed her shoulders. She kicked him, and he laughed, telling her he liked a fiery wench. She told him he sounded damn silly, which was when he kissed her and the dream changed from nightmare to something else.

First his lips brushed across hers, then the kiss deepened, became demanding, filled her with a glowing heat. In the dream he was suddenly holding her as no man of her time ever had: fiercely possessive, wanting her, knowing how to make her want him. His hands cupped her breasts. He pinned her between himself and the cool stones of a wall, his hips grinding against hers. His need was obvious, hard against her thigh. His kiss became more passionately insistent.

Jane wound her arms around his neck, wholly consumed by the desire he aroused so demandingly in her. She responded eagerly to his touch. She offered herself to the sure touch of his hands and lips. In the dream she matched his passion with her own, molded her flesh to his, drank in the masculine, erotic scent and hardness and—

She woke up shivering, very aware of the fur covering rubbing sensuously against her bare skin. "Well," she complained to the ceiling, "I never thought I liked them butch." Her mother would say that it was about time she had a thing for a man in uniform. Which she didn't, of course. She tried to make a joke of the unsettling erotic experience. Forget the dangerous good looks and the narrow-hipped swagger; the dream was probably caused by moldy rye in last night's bread.

She chuckled, her usual good humor restored as she threw off the blanket and flopped onto her back. And yelped as the chill air caught her by surprise. Yep, still in the thirteenth century, she decided as she leapt up and began to pull on layer after layer of clothing. Her tower cubbyhole possessed one tiny slit window, enough to let in light to dress by. She remembered the fire in the hall. It pulled her like a magnet through the storeroom and down to the hall.

"You're late rising," Bertram told her with the slightest hint of disapproval as she arrived by the blazing hearthfire. With Bertram was the grizzled guard sergeant, Raoul DeCorte, and a bearded man she hadn't seen before. She knew she hadn't seen him because she would have remembered the silly baby-cap of a hat he was wearing. It was made of faded blue wool, tied snugly under his yellow-bearded chin.

"There's porridge and bread saved for you," Bertram added.

What she needed was a cup of coffee, she thought, ignoring the food to warm her hands by the hearth. The stench of the hall had hit her anew as she came down the stairs. She'd woken up hungry, but her stomach was now informing her she'd better not dare try to put anything in it in this noxious atmosphere. She swallowed and shook her head at the servant. Her skin itched, and she wanted to brush her teeth.

The men made room for her, all of them looking at her worriedly. She threw a sour glance over her shoulder at the pale-lit windows. In an age that lived by fire and rushlight, every second of daylight was important. Only someone who was very ill would spend time sleeping past the break of day. Oops.

She tucked her warmed fingers into her wide sleeves and told them, "A touch of lingering fever, I think."

The men looked at each other anxiously, and she recalled what Sir Stephan had told her about a fever devastating his holding. "I doubt it's catching," she hastened to reassure them.

Caffeine withdrawal wasn't, she grumbled to herself. For their benefit she explained, "A woman's illness." The tension relaxed immediately into knowing and sympathetic nods.

"My wife's had such," the man in the silly hat said. He spoke slowly, with a thick Germanic accent. "She's learned much about herbs from brewing her own remedies. She might be of help, Lady Jehane."

"Switha's a useful woman," DeCorte interjected. "This is Cerdic," he went on. "Reeve of Hwit and Passfair villages. Sir Stephan said you would want to speak with us this morning."

Bertram handed her a heavy brass key ring. "I've been keeping these," he told her as she fingered the keys one by one. "The cook and I can help you with an inventory of the keep. Cerdic has knowledge of the villages. Sir Stephan said—"

"And where is Sir Stephan?" she interrupted.

Raoul DeCorte gave a gap-toothed grin. "Rode for Sturry at daybreak. Took most of the men with him, my lady."

"A savings of the late-winter stores," Bertram contributed. He gave the others a jealous look as he added, "The inventory, my lady?"

"Your orders, Lady Jehane?" DeCorte requested, elbowing Bertram aside.

"Will you have need of me, my lady?" Cerdic asked with a respectful nod of his baby-cap. She wondered if he was going to tug his forelock in an excess of loyal zeal.

And just what threats did Sir Stephan use to gain such enthusiastic cooperation from his household? Or maybe these three mature gentlemen were just tired of chaos. Or maybe the masses *liked* being downtrodden. She backed a few steps from the fire, nearly tripping over one of the deerhounds in the process. It growled. So did she.

She was the boss, was she? The men were eyeing her pensively as she considered how to proceed. She was more familiar with user-friendly software and self-service everything than with any kind of labor relations. Shorting a tip for the occasional

surly waitress was about all she knew of disciplin-
ing the peasants. Fortunately this bunch seemed
eager to be led.

"Woman's got to do what a woman's got to do,"
she said under her breath in English. She squared her
shoulders, looked the trio in the eye one by one, then
announced to Bertram, "I want those hounds kenneled, the floor cleaned, and fresh rushes down by
tonight."

"Rushes, my lady?" Bertram asked, his wrinkles
rippling with puzzlement. "At this time of year?"

"Our lady is from a warmer land," DeCorte interjected gallantly while she swore to herself.

She gave the guard sergeant a grateful look. She
also remembered something her mother had told her
she'd learned in the army. When in doubt, delegate.

Mom the colonel would probably be enjoying this
adventure. It was just the sort of thing she'd fanta-
sized about doing ever since she'd gotten involved in
the study of medieval military history. She'd become
so fascinated with the whole period, she'd helped
found the Medievalist Society so she could play dress-
up and mock battles. And Jane had grown up sharing
eagerly in Mom the colonel's off-duty pastime. She'd
never thought it would land her here.

"You'll find something," she assured Bertram with
a steely-eyed confidence that dared him to contradict
her. He just looked at her in dumbfounded confusion.

"We've straw enough in the stables." DeCorte
came to the rescue.

Jane began to understand the respect for sergeants
her mother had brought from her tank commanding
days. "Suitable," she agreed. The stench of the hall
was beginning to make her eyes water. Her stomach

was still threatening revolt. She had to get out before she threw up.

"Fetch my cloak," she ordered the servant. "DeCorte and I will inspect the outbuildings while the hall is cleaned."

5

Nearly a week later, Jane was having trouble deciding which of several aching spots to rub when she spotted Bertram approaching from the direction of the kitchen. She squinted at him painfully. She only had sight in one eye at the moment; the other was swollen closed. His hobbling steps were slow, but he looked determined. No doubt he'd found another task needing his chatelaine's urgent attention. To think she'd been worried about figuring out how to do the job. She'd scarcely had time to breathe in the five days since Stephan had left the holding.

Bertram and the others were having a wonderful time finding things for her to give orders about. It seemed the inhabitants at Passfair had assumed their amiable young lord didn't mind living in squalor; young knights were supposed to have war and wenching rather than the state of the storerooms on their minds. His putting a proper chatelaine in charge was the same as giving notice to the peasants that times were changing.

And they wanted the place to look nice for their new young mistress, as well. There was an eagerness about the serving women working on new linens in the bower, a cheerful willingness in the way two other women were beating the dust from the tapestry they'd carefully taken down and into the courtyard to air out. Knowing the lord of the manor was bringing home a bride made everything about the castle seem more purposeful and alive. Especially old Bertram. Old Bertram, who turned out to be fifty-two and quite spry.

Jane sighed with tired fondness at his approach, then contemplated her injuries while waiting for his arrival. Her eye hurt worse than her hip, so she settled on cradling her swollen cheek with her palm. She rested the other hand on the cool stone of the freshly swept step where she was sitting. A puppy came up and licked it.

The sky overhead was a brilliant blue, there was a hint of warmth in the air, and she was getting some satisfaction out of watching people scurrying around the courtyard doing her bidding. There was steamy smoke rising from the wash house. Rich, yeasty smells were drifting her way from both the brew house and the wide mouths of the ovens next to the kitchen. Of course, none of this made up for the physical discomfort of sitting around nursing a black eye and bruised bottom.

Last night's fall down the tower steps was the dog's fault, of course. Melisande was simply too much the willful pet to put up with being kenneled with the common riffraff. Not a day had passed before she'd bitten the boy put in charge of the deer-hounds, escaped from the enclosure, and marched boldly into the hall, her puppies bounding happily after. Jane didn't have the heart to throw any of them out again. Melisande was Stephan's particular favorite, after all. So she'd named the puppies Nikki and Vince, and somehow the three canines all ended up in her bed. This did not help the bug problem, but she welcomed the company.

Last night, while she'd been climbing the pitted old stone steps with a puppy in each arm, Melisande had affectionately butted the back of Jane's knees with her head. Hard. Jane was knocked off balance, tripped over her voluminous skirts, and ended up tumbling head over heels all the way back down to the hall.

Nikki and Vince were unhurt. She was lucky to sustain only some heavy bruising and the black eye. She hated to think what might have happened if she'd really been hurt. A broken bone in this era could be fatal. She didn't want to think about it. She rose carefully and greeted Bertram instead.

The old man's first words were, "The hall needs more servants, my lady."

Jane tugged at the veil of her wimple. The gesture was becoming the substitute for her old habit of playing with her hair when she was puzzled. As far as she was concerned, the place was crawling with servants. What sort of project did Bertram have in mind? Rebuilding the hall completely by the time Stephan and his lady arrived?

"Oh?" she asked, hoping her tone conveyed dignity along with healthy skepticism. Bertram was very concerned for her dignity and sense of status. He was very much in favor of her having both. She tried to live up to his standards.

"You have no women of your own to attend you."

"They died on the journey," she recounted hastily.

"Of course, my lady. But you really should not go unattended," he persisted. "It is not—"

"Proper," she finished for him. She felt a great deal of fondness for Bertram. She wondered what he would have been if he had lived in her time. The CEO of a major corporation, perhaps.

She tucked her hands in the voluminous sleeves of her gown and gave a judicious nod. "Quite right, good Bertram." She looked at him speculatively out of the eye not swollen shut. "You know where I might find a decent woman or two to serve me?"

He gave a decisive nod. "There are three young village widows you might choose from. They lost their men in the winter's fever. Cerdic can bring them for your inspection."

Mention of the village and its reeve reminded Jane that she hadn't yet inspected the houses or tithe barn, or any of the demesne beyond the fortress's wooden outer walls. She said, "Yes. I must talk to Cerdic." She picked up her cloak from where she'd left it on the top step. "Where would the reeve be this time of day?"

Bertram wasn't sure, but he gave her directions to the reeve's house. "Shall I come with you, Lady Jehane?"

"No need." She patted the old man's arm. "I need you here to manage while I'm gone." He lifted his head at her words, his bent shoulders straightening a bit.

She walked off, happy her slight praise brought him some pleasure. She walked slowly toward the gate, her sore hip reminding her it wasn't happy at all with this walking nonsense. She told it exercise was the best thing for the stiffness. At the gate one of the stable lads hurried past her, no doubt sent by Bertram to warn the reeve of her impending visit. She supposed his forethought saved her the additional exercise of searching out Cerdic. She didn't try to hurry her steps but carefully made her way down the rutted track leading to the group of low, thatched huts clustered at the foot of the hill. It had rained last night, and her hem had an extra border of mud by the time she reached Passfair village.

She found the house without trouble; it was the largest daub-and-wattle hut in the village, after all. Cerdic was there, hurriedly back from whatever task he'd been overseeing. He greeted her with a respectful bob of his head. He'd taken off his hat, revealing a wealth of gray-tinged red-gold curls.

The Saxon reeve knew every inch of Stephan's two villages, fields and orchards and pastures and mill and barns and houses. Jane walked him over the well-trodden ground, asking questions as they went. The sunny day brought a hint of warmth in the air; several of the small fields were greening with early wheat and barley crops. She found out it was late February and that the river running beneath the mill wheel was the Stour. He told her eighteen people had died during the winter fever and that there were twenty-one families in Hwit, which was on the river, and eleven families in Passfair.

They walked to the edge of the wood where Jane first arrived. Now that she saw it on foot rather than on horseback, the place seemed somehow more formidable, dark and mysterious. Bare branches seemed to reach out for her, or beckon her onward to explore ancient secrets.

All right, all right, she told herself. There was nothing dark and wild about the place. It was where they pastured the pigs and gathered firewood and—

"There are outlaws in the woods," Cerdic told her, breaking in on her mental catalog.

Jane jumped. "What?" she squeaked nervously. She remembered now that Stephan had warned her.

"A band of outlaws."

"Not like Robin Hood, I bet." The words slipped out before she could catch them.

The reeve blinked his china blue eyes at her in momentary confusion. "Robin Hood's band was in the north. In Lincolnshire, I'm told. Or Sherwood. This forest is the Blean. Sikes's band of brigands is smaller but not so kindly. Though the Robin Hood band was in my father's time. There's nothing left of them but the tales. Sikes's leaves bodies and burned houses right now." He scratched his beard thoughtfully while Jane tried to keep her head from spinning right out of its wimple.

She almost had to bite down on her tongue to keep from demanding every word of Cerdic's father's tales. She was *not* a historian, she told herself firmly. She was chatelaine of Passfair. She was not going to take notes or write monographs. Robin Hood was not real. And even if he was, who was she going to impress with her well-researched, documented knowledge?

As she stood on the edge of the wood trying to forget Dr. Jane Florian's passion for the past, a slight figure stepped from behind an oak's wide trunk, onto the narrow track leading out of the wood. It was an elfin-featured woman with gray-streaked black braids. She was wearing a brown dress and a faded green shawl. She carried a reed basket on one arm.

Cerdic raised a hand in greeting. His affable face lit with pleasure. "My wife, Switha," he explained. "She can help you choose a woman to serve you at the hall."

Switha arrived beside them and looked up at Jane with sooty-lidded blue eyes. Jane remembered being told Cerdic's wife was the village midwife and wise-woman.

"I've heard you have a woman's illness," she said. Like Cerdic, she spoke to Jane in Norman French, but her accent was not as thick. "And about the fall," she went on, reaching up to touch the swollen and discolored skin around Jane's eye. "I've herbs for both problems, my lady. You'll be well soon," she said reassuringly.

"May I return to the fields, my lady?" Cerdic requested, backing a pace from the two women on the edge of the woods.

Jane's gaze was caught by Switha's. The woman was studying her critically, her head cocked to one side. It was almost as if Switha's intent scrutiny was more for the ills inside her head than for the injuries to her body. Jane barely had enough attention left over to nod dismissal at the reeve. She was too caught up in Switha's stare.

She didn't know how long she and the little woman stood staring eye to eye, but when she managed to blink her good eye and look around, it seemed as if the sun had moved nearer to the horizon.

"What time is it?" she asked, her voice barely a whisper.

"The wrong time for you, I think," Switha answered

equally softly. The woman shook her head sadly, her braids swinging gently on her breasts.

A natural empath, the reasonable part of Jane's mind supplied as she gave her head a hard shake herself. Back home Switha'd be wearing crystals and reading tarot cards and conducting seminars. Village wisewomen were supposed to be wise women. It was in the job description. Jane laughed nervously. The sound seemed too loud, spreading out to fill the silent landscape on the edge of the wood.

"You said something about herbs?" she questioned, her voice still too loud in her own ears. "Actually," she went on, "apparently what I really need is an attendant. I was told you—"

"I'll send Berthild to you," Switha interjected. She fiddled with a clump of moss in her basket, breaking it up into tiny pieces. Its earthy smell tickled the back of Jane's nose.

Switha went on, "Berthild's gentle and biddable." Her far-seeing blue eyes took on a glint of amusement as she admitted, "Also my sister. One of the castle guards taught her some of your language while her husband journeyed to London town last year. She'll be happy to serve in the castle now her man's gone."

"I see," Jane said. "Thank you."

She was prepared to take her leave then, but Switha tugged on her sleeve and pointed into the forest. "As for your other problem, I think I know the way to the cure for it. Come with me." She marched off the way she'd come, down the faint trail among the ancient trees. She didn't bother to see if Jane would follow.

Intrigued, Jane trailed slowly behind, glad her long walk with Cerdic had helped ease the stiffness from her sore leg. Her skirts and veil immediately began catching on the thick undergrowth. This side of the wood was darker, the trees bunched together more closely, than the area around the old tower. Switha moved with fleet assurance, leaving the trail to pick a path between the trees.

Jane moved with more care. The layers of leaf mold under her feet were springy. The aromas of impending spring, damp earth, wood rot, and moss filled the air. In sheltered spots she saw the beginnings of ferns and fungi, and maybe violets. The wind was still, but the birds overhead were raucously noisy. The place was dark, but it soon lost its air of mystery for Jane. She began to enjoy the walk despite the trouble with her voluminous layers of clothing.

She had no way of guessing how far they'd strayed from their starting point when the unmistakable sound of hooves hitting the earth echoed off to the left.

A horse! Her first thought was of outlaws, her first instinct to climb a tree and hide.

Ahead of her, Switha stopped. She tilted her head to listen for a moment before turning to look at Jane. She seemed rather pleased with herself.

Jane whispered a nervous "What?"

"Sir Daffyd's been quartering this part of the woods with his men all day. But I doubt he'll find any outlaws here today."

Jane relaxed, glad to know the unseen rider was a soldier, not a criminal. She got the impression the peasant woman wasn't exactly in favor of the man-hunt. She supposed the arrogant Sir Daffyd was unpopular with the locals. He was a king's man after all.

"I think the lad should find what he seeks," Switha said, apparently reading Jane's thoughts. "Then he'll go away and leave us alone." She pointed to where a clearing appeared through a gap in the trees. She set off once more, and Jane followed.

The horseman was waiting on the other side of the small clearing. His gold head was bared to the sun, his sword drawn and resting on the high saddle front. Sir Daffyd glared down his aquiline nose at them from the back of a deep-chested gray warhorse. He sat still as a statue, cape thrown back, muscular body poised in the center of a sunbeam. The sight of Daffyd ap Bleddyn against a backdrop of mistletoe-draped oak and clear blue sky was riveting. He seemed to Jane the living personification of ancient war.

Switha continued toward the knight. Jane hesitated at the edge of the clearing, half tempted to run from this theoretical protector of the people. He looked anything but benign. Stephan armored, with sword in hand, looked a bit like a child playing dress-up in his father's clothes. Sir Daffyd looked as though he meant business.

But she was also half tempted to move forward. The dangerous figure of the horseman was oddly compelling. Jane found herself waiting, one foot in the wood, one in the clearing, biting her lip while indecision and the half-recalled memory of a dream froze her in place.

Sir Daffyd solved her dilemma by spurring the big gray forward. He stopped briefly to speak to Switha, curt words in the Saxon woman's own language. From the look of pained concentration on the woman's face, Jane assumed the man spoke

Saxon with a particularly garbled accent. The woman eventually bobbed her head in understanding, pointing at Jane.

Sir Daffyd moved the horse closer. When she could feel its warm breath on her shoulder, he jumped out of the saddle to stand before her. Loom. He was shorter than Stephan, but not by much. He was a looming sort of guy. His sword disappeared into its sheath with a dangerous snick. She noticed his eyes were hazel, highlighted with green. They looked her up and down with chilling contempt.

"What?" he demanded. "Did your husband beat you?"

"What?" Jane asked in her turn.

He pointed to her cheek.

She had almost forgotten her bruised and swollen face. She touched the swollen eye while reminding the knight sternly, "I'm a widow. I fell down some stairs." He didn't look as though he believed her. Not that how she'd injured herself was any business of his. "It was one of those stupid dogs," she started to explain.

"And what are you doing out here alone?" he demanded. He rested his hands on his narrow hips.

She didn't suppose it would do any good to point out to Sir Daffyd that he had a definite attitude problem. She was seething inwardly, but she tried for a conciliatory smile. All the gesture did was pull at the aching muscles of her cheek.

"I'm with Switha," she said reasonably.

He looked around the clearing, then raised a heavy, pale eyebrow at her. "Oh?"

She peered over his shoulder. The Saxon woman

had disappeared from the clearing. So much for finding the cure for her problem.

"I sent her home," he explained shortly. "I doubt there's anyone in the region who'd dare to harm the goodwife, so she's safe enough. But you." He pointed an accusing finger at her.

"Me?" she heard herself squeak. She cleared her throat. "I'm chatelaine of this holding," she went on defensively. "Who would dare . . ."

"Any outlaw who can catch you alone," he cut in. "You've guards at the castle," he pointed out. "Bring some with you when you venture out."

It was good advice, though his contemptuous tone was anything but endearing. She gave him a curt, imperious nod, thinking with annoyance that she wasn't used to living life with a bodyguard in tow. She was not a rock star. Although *he* certainly looked like one with all that gorgeous naturally blond hair and the gold hoop earring in his right ear.

He took her arm and said, "Come along, lady. I haven't got all day." It was a large hand. She could feel its warmth, and a heavy layer of callusing, through her three layers of sleeves. The calluses were from wielding a sword, she supposed.

"What! Where?"

While she protested, he dragged her forward a few steps, until they were next to the horse's warm gray flank, then placed his hands around her waist. The next thing she knew she was perched precariously on the rump of his horse. He swung easily up in the saddle before her. She watched his fluid movements with a certain amount of admiration. She managed to keep her sputtering indignation in check only by reminding herself just which one of them carried the sword—

and muscles enough to treat her as though she were no heavier than a feather.

"Where are you taking me?" she asked with deceptive meekness as he guided the animal forward.

"To Passfair," was the succinct answer. He gave a swift glance over his shoulder and instructed, "Try not to fall off."

The high rear of the saddle didn't seem like a particularly good object to cling to, and this horse was nowhere in the black destrier's league. It had a far rougher gait. Her sore hip made her position even more uncomfortable. She found herself flinging her arms around Sir Daffyd's waist.

It didn't feel at all like Sir Stephan's. There was more of it, for one thing. Stephan was all lanky skin and bones. This man was made up of hard muscle and sinew. Wide shoulders arrowed down to the waist she was holding. Even though she could feel the chain mail beneath cape and surcoat, she could tell most of what she was holding and leaning against was him. His gold hair was soft against her cheek, the thickness and texture very different from Stephan's black silk. He smelled different, too. Less of wood smoke and stable and more of . . .

"Lavender?"

She felt the chuckle ripple down his back. They were so close that the movement almost tickled her. "Switha recommends it for fleas. You should try some, my lady," he suggested.

She wasn't sure if he was being helpful or implying she was flea-ridden. She probably was. She'd didn't know if lavender would keep bugs away, but it certainly smelled good. She breathed deeply but didn't bother to reply, and they rode on in silence.

Daffyd stopped twice to speak to soldiers they encountered as they neared the fields, then moved on. He seemed to forget her presence behind him. She held on tight and endured the bumpy ride.

As they reached the track leading up the hill from the village, she recalled her dream of several nights before. She remembered how, in the nightmare turned into erotic fantasy, it had been Daffyd ap Bleddyn who'd kissed and caressed her. She realized the subconscious pleasure she'd been getting from pressing so close to him. Her grip slackened so much that she almost fell into the mud as the horse began plodding toward the outer bailey.

She was going into a convent, she reminded herself sternly. And Sir Daffyd was a brutish man with a big sword. He gave orders. He probably beat his own wife. She wasn't interested. She repeated the simple phrases several times with her eyes firmly closed so she couldn't look at the man riding the horse.

She kept her eyes closed until they reached the bustling activity of the inner bailey. Then she slid to the ground without any help from Sir Daffyd. Looking around the courtyard rather than at the Welshman, she couldn't help but notice there was rather more activity than she'd expected. There were certainly more guards than she remembered.

It was Sir Daffyd who explained from his vantage point atop the gray horse. "It seems Sir Stephan's returned."

6

Sir Stephan approached from the stable, his purposeful long strides lacking their usual zest. He was tired, Jane decided as a group of laughing guards parted to let their young lord pass.

He turned on them, snapping, "Why are you men standing around idle?" They dispersed quickly, their abrupt silence testimony to their shock at the lad's unaccustomed reproof. He continued on toward Jane and Sir Daffyd.

Tired and cranky, she amended as she made out the weary slump of his narrow shoulders. His black eyes, however, were full of angry fire. She hoped it wouldn't get turned on her. Perhaps his mission had gone badly and the heiress was now in Hugh of Lilydrake's hands. She was full of sympathy for the young man by the time he arrived at her side. She bobbed him a quick curtsy and got her shoulders grabbed by him on her way back up.

He held her, giving her bruised face and black eye a critical once-over before turning an angry glare up to Daffyd. "Did you . . . ?"

"I thought you did."

"It was the dog."

Stephan's hold loosened at her explanation. "What?"

"I fell down the tower stairs after tripping over Melisande."

"Oh."

Something about his tense manner told her he was spoiling for some reason on which to vent his temper. He would gladly have taken on Daffyd in order to defend her honor. Stephan was chivalrous, and she was a lady under his protection. And it would have made a wonderful excuse to pick a fight.

Never mind if a few days ago she'd gotten the impression he liked Sir Daffyd.

Daffyd asked, "Is your lady bride well? Safe within your walls?" He leaned a forearm on the high saddle horn, voice lowering suggestively. "Is she pretty?"

"She's here," was as much answer as Stephan seemed willing to give. Jane was shocked by the look of sour disdain twisting Stephan's pale features. "As for well . . ." He gave a mocking laugh.

"Worse than you expected?" Daffyd questioned sardonically. "Not to your taste? No beauty?" He backed his horse and turned it toward the gate. "If it's a choice between a fortune and a pretty face," he went on, tossing the last words over his shoulder as he reached the gate, "I'll take the pretty face every time."

"I bet," Jane mumbled under her breath.

Stephan made a rude gesture at Sir Daffyd's departing back before facing Jane squarely. Alone with her, his expression changed from arrogant annoyance to boyish petulance. He ran a soothing thumb, very gently, under her sore eye. "Poor lamb." He sighed. "Sweet Jehane . . ."

"Did you come to the Lady Sibelle's rescue before Hugh could carry her off?" she interjected, hoping to raise his spirits by dwelling on his heroic exploits. He straightened his shoulders and gave his wide grin. Some teasing devil in her prompted her to add, "Does Sibelle think you're wonderful?"

His face fell back into depressed lines. "Yes," he said unhappily.

How bad could the girl be? Jane wondered. She was only fifteen. Even in this time fifteen had to be kind of unfinished. She touched his cheek sympathetically. "Tell me."

He brightened. "About the fight?"

About Sibelle, you . . . "So there was a fight," she coaxed agreeably.

He linked his arm in hers, leading her toward the castle door. The servants gave them a wide berth, but Melisande and her kids came bounding up as they neared the steps. This closeness with Stephan felt good after the uncomfortable proximity of the ride with Sir Daffyd. Stephan was safe.

He told her, "There's truth to the rumor Hugh harbors Sikes and his men."

She hunted through her memory for the reference. "The outlaw leader?"

"Aye. At least Hugh must have let them know there was gold in it for them, even if he didn't actually send the brigands to set the ambush. Oh, he put on quite a show." He gave a delighted laugh. "We were attacked at a narrow turning of the road, and I was burdened down with the girl and her women and her baggage."

He waved a long-fingered hand toward a row of three two-wheeled wooden carts and a box-shaped closed carriage, drawn up in a ragged line near the entrance steps. Jehane assumed the carriage, which was a springless monstrosity, had conveyed the baron's daughter from her home to Passfair. Riding pillion behind Stephan would have been more comfortable, certainly more fun. Of course, a girl raised in a convent wouldn't have any experience of riding and might be shocked by the intimacy the position required. She turned her attention back to Stephan as he went on.

"We were set on by the outlaws first. They didn't fight very hard. They ran off, expecting me to give chase into the forest while Hugh and his men came up from behind to snatch the girl." He snorted derisively.

"It didn't work," Jane concluded.

"My liege would whip any first-year squire who fell into such a ruse."

"And who is your liege?" she asked.

He hesitated dramatically before saying, "You would have heard of him, even in Jerusalem. Guillaume le Marechal." He preened, giving her a proud, expectant look.

She didn't disappoint him. "*The* Guillaume le Marechal! The man who trained King Richard? The perfect knight? The crusader? The man who was with King Henry when he died?" William the Marshal himself. The man whose contemporary biography she had done the newest and most definitive translation of. Her jaw dropped.

She forced herself to calm down and say, "Real-

ly?" though the word came out high-pitched and none
too steady.

He nodded and went back to his tale. "I've had
better training than to be tricked by the likes of
Lilydrake. He's a dull-witted, greedy fool with
more ambition than sense. There was a small fight
with very little blood. Hugh showed us his backside fast enough. I brought the lass home. She's
mine," he added as they entered the hall. "I suppose I really must keep her. But she'll have no joy
of it," he declared miserably. His long, handsome
face took on a determinedly stubborn expression,
the wide, mobile lips pressed together in a thin
line.

"Now, Sir Stephan," Jane coaxed gently. "That's
not a chivalrous way to treat a lady."

His black eyes sparked with defiance. "She'll come
to no harm," he promised. "But she must understand
our arrangement from the first. It's a pity one can't
expect more from marriage than just an arrangement," he added wistfully.

The poor boy was trapped by his own culture, she
thought. It bothered her to see the charming young
man unhappy. She reached up to pat his cheek sympathetically as they walked through the screen into the
freshly cleaned main hall. The scent of dried herbs was
stirred up as they trod across the layer of fresh straw.
She noted the cleaned tapestry had been rehung on the
back wall during her afternoon in the woods.

The room was empty but for three women clustered around the warmly glowing central hearth. All
three were plump and frumpy-looking. All three
turned disapproving faces on Stephan and Jane as
they approached.

As they neared the fire Jane saw the one in the middle was young, her heavily padded form swathed in layers of saffron wool, deeply bordered in red-and-gold embroidery. The color went horribly with her pink complexion; the decoration was overdone. The wide purple belt around what passed for a waist cut her too round form in half. Her head and several chins were blanketed in gray-and-black barbette and veils. The inappropriate combination of finery and heavy veiling gave the impression the girl was half nun and half— What? Heiress to a barony?

Jane didn't need any introduction to know she was being stared at with pure loathing by the Lady Sibelle LeGauche. Quickly she took a decorous step away from Stephan. She wondered disloyally if the lad had planned their cozy entrance to inform his betrothed he wasn't completely hers.

Well, he's not mine, Jane wanted to shout. Actually she wanted to kick the young strategist on his tiny behind.

Stephan grabbed her hand and led her to the girl. "Lady Sibelle," he announced. "Lady Jehane FitzRose, my chatelaine." He put a lot of emphasis on the last two words. It seemed he wanted to make it perfectly clear who was in charge here.

The girl refused to look at her. She merely gave a cold, wobbly nod in Jane's direction. Her women, on the other hand, glared in open hatred. Jane responded with an edged smile and a rattling of the official keys dangling from her belt. It made her feel like the warden, but imperious behavior seemed to be expected from her. The women sniffed disdainfully in unison but judiciously went back to warming their hands around the fire. While everyone stood in uncomfortable silence for a few minutes, Bertram led in the servants, who efficiently went about setting up the hall for the evening meal.

Sibelle had eyes only for Stephan as he grudgingly offered his arm to lead her to the high table. The girl wiped her hand furtively on her skirt before placing two fingers on the edge of Stephan's black sleeve. Keeping as far away from him as she could without letting go, she tripped her way up the dais step.

Jane winced as she watched Sibelle lurch to her chair. It really would help if she watched where she was going, she thought. And what fashion guerrilla had put together that outfit? She shook her head and caught sight of Bertram watching the young couple from the pantry door. She and the old man exchanged one pained, understanding look. His assessment was easily read. Things were not going to be easy around here for a while. Jane agreed. Bertram waved the scullery servants forward to serve the first course. Jane squared her shoulders and went to take a place at the main table.

She ended up seated on Sibelle's left. The girl turned out to be left-handed. Jane's bruised face hurt when she chewed, and she still hadn't worked up much appetite for the local cuisine. She made a meal by dipping coarse bread in greasy goose broth flavored with old onions and played a mental game of considering the origins of Sibelle's name to keep her mind off the taste of her dinner.

Perhaps they were a left-handed family; therefore they were of the left—*le gauche*. Or the first baron was born on the wrong side of the blanket and was rather proud of the fact. It could be, she considered as she watched Sibelle first spill soup on her bosom, then knock the salt cellar across the table, that she was called LeGauche because she came from a long line of klutzes. The poor kid was quivering from terror. Too bad there was so much of her to shake.

As the meal proceeded in ever more strained silence, Jane began to be annoyed with Stephan. He was drinking sour wine and petting Melisande. The girl beside him might as well not exist. Sibelle did nothing but chew and throw furtive, adoring glances his way. Jane oversaw the servants with her good eye and tapped a foot under the table in annoyance until Nikki and Vince decided this was the signal for them to start chewing on her toes.

The conversation from the tables below the salt was far quieter than usual. The members of the household were eating their meal with most of their attention focused on the strained movements of their betters. The tension in the air could be sliced with a dagger. Jane especially didn't like the disdainful looks the household women were aiming at Sibelle more and more openly as the evening went on.

It wouldn't hurt Stephan to say something to the kid, she fumed as he accepted another cup of wine from Bertram. Okay, she decided finally. If he wouldn't do it, she would.

She cleared her throat, opening her mouth to speak. Her mind went blank. "Uh . . ." She hadn't talked to a fifteen-year-old in a long time. She had never talked to a fifteen-year-old ex-nun heiress to a barony who'd already labeled her as an enemy. She supposed they didn't really have conversational ground in common, since it wouldn't be politic to discuss Stephan's acting like jerk. Still, something had to be done.

She opened her mouth and tried again. "I'll show you around Passfair tomorrow, my lady," she offered politely.

Sibelle didn't answer. Sibelle didn't look at her. Sibelle did stiffen with disapproval and lift her chins haughtily. Stephan did not rush in to fill the conversational gap. Wherever had the charming boy who'd brought her home gotten to?

Jane resigned herself to silence and studied the profile Lady Sibelle turned to her. The girl would never succeed in looking down her nose, Jane decided, since she hardly had one at all. It was kind of a cute little button, actually. Not like her own long beak. Sibelle's skin was really not too bad, just blotched from crying. Or maybe the pink cheeks were from a bit of windburn. There seemed to be a cleft down there somewhere on her original chin. Weren't nuns supposed to be ascetic and sacrificing? Where was it Stephan said Sibelle had been? Davington Priory? Maybe she should apply there herself after the interdict was lifted. It couldn't be too hard of a life if the graduates turned out like Her Ladyship here.

Jane went back to slowly finishing her bread and broth while the dinner dragged to its conclusion. She was grateful to rise from her deep wooden chair when the last of the dishes were finally cleared away. She wanted nothing more than to escape to her cubbyhole behind the storeroom. Only she couldn't just run up the stairs and hide. As chatelaine she had duties yet to perform.

As the servants settled down by the fire, Stephan grabbed his cloak and waded in among them, taking the choicest spot for himself, in the fresh straw laid down near the hearth. He didn't even bother with wishing his betrothed the most cursory of goodnights.

Jane decided to put his churlish behavior down to the influence of too much wine. Much to her surprise, Melisande and the pups stayed at her side rather than settle down with Stephan. She fervently wished him an enormous hangover and steeled herself to deal with the girl. She turned to find the two dragons had come up from the servants' table to flank their mistress once more.

Their presence made communicating with the now crying Sibelle a bit easier. "The bower's this way," she said, and pointed the servants toward the tower stairs. The first floor of the tower held the storage room. The second held two connected rooms: the bower, where the household women were meant to spend their days with weaving and needlework, and the castle's only bedchamber.

She led the dragons up the stairs, and they led the wailing Sibelle. It wasn't long before they reached the upper pair of rooms set aside for the lord and his lady. Since the lord was snoring peacefully on the floor downstairs, Sibelle was installed alone in the large, curtained bed. She was sitting in the center of it, snuffling disconsolately, when Jane made her hurried exit back down to her own quarters.

Poor kid, she thought, not for the first and probably not for the last time. She tried to put the sad image of the lonely Sibelle out of her mind as she threw herself onto her own straw mattress.

Melisande and the puppies gathered around her. "Right," she said, rubbing the deerhound's ears. "Us womenfolk have to stay together, don't we?"

She fell asleep soon after winning the nightly argument with the dogs over who got the most bed space. Sometime in the middle of the night, Melisande woke her briefly with a low growl. The bed creaked as the dog got up to investigate some minor noise. She came back soon enough. Jane went immediately back to sleep.

She dreamed once again of Sir Daffyd. In her dream they lay down together in a sun-warmed field of lavender, crushing a bed of tiny purple flowers to cushion their ardent embrace.

His mouth claimed hers, making her giddy with desire. Without a word she told him he reminded her of chocolate. He asked her what chocolate was. His mouth covered hers. Does it taste like this?

She undid his sword belt and told him how no man of her own time was like him.

The thought woke her. Sitting up, she scrubbed her palms over her face. The dogs were warm lumps around her feet, the fur blanket was soft and warm, yet she was cold. Cold with dread? She shook her still somewhat sleep-fogged head. Why did she dream about the man? she wondered. She'd met him twice, but her subconscious seemed to have latched on to him as an object of desire.

All right, she conceded, he was gorgeous. Perhaps she had a weird subconscious. Or maybe it was her conscious mind that had always been weird. She'd always looked to the past, hadn't she? She'd made the past her hobby and her profession. Maybe she'd been secretly longing for a knight in shining armor. Knights didn't wear shining armor in 1209, she reminded herself, and chivalry had been invented by women while the menfolk were out pillaging and crusading. Knights wore rusting chain mail and chased down peasants who had to steal to survive.

But Daffyd wore chain mail better than anyone she'd ever seen, she told herself. He'd been worried about her safety this afternoon. That was almost chivalrous. This afternoon . . . She settled back on the bed and closed her eyes. She could see him clearly, gold hair flaming in the shaft of sunlight, the hard, handsome lines of his face. She remembered the feel of his hands on her waist, of her hands on his, the softness of his hair, the scent of lavender and leather.

He was very real, she warned herself. He was not any idealized, sanitized, twenty-first-century version of a medieval man. He was himself, and being attracted to him would be very dangerous indeed. He was a landless knight, and she was masquerading as a rich widow. He might be interested in a rich widow for her dowry. She didn't let herself encourage his attention in any way. He might get ideas. She had to remember marriage was a business arrangement. It was an arrangement with only one side benefiting: the man. She was not from this time, she couldn't be an obedient chattel. She didn't dare let herself be attracted to any man from this time. A convent was safe, a marriage to a man from this time was not.

"Not that he'd necessarily be interested in marriage," she mumbled as she rolled over and tried to get back to sleep. "That would be even worse. Can't ruin my reputation if I want a convent to accept me. Can't think about Daffyd ap Bleddyn anymore."

She fell asleep, and immediately back into the dream.

7

"*No! Not on the floor!*"

Jane cracked the squatting dog hard on the backside. "Outside!"

Melisande yelped and skittered away. She whimpered impatiently by the alcove curtain while Jane hurriedly finished struggling into her shift and underdress. Jane slipped her feet into shoes and fastened a veil over her uncombed brown curls.

The first light of dawn was creeping in through her narrow window, and Melisande had been trying once again to use the far corner of the storeroom. "Another morning at Passfair has begun," Jane said around a yawn.

The barest hint of dream memory teased at the back of her conscious mind, but she ignored it purposefully. She knew there was no use dwelling on erotic nonsense. She vowed not to think of the Welshman at all. Or chocolate. She had more than enough to fill her attention with a full day's worth of duties before her. She had promised Bertram she'd finally inspect the main storerooms in the deep cellar today.

Actually, Jane reflected, grabbing Melisande by the scruff of the neck, the housebreaking wasn't going too bad considering she was a grown dog. The puppies jumped down from the bed to follow after them. Their training was going very well. The deerhounds really were intelligent animals. Probably because they weren't too distant relatives of their smarter wolf cousins.

"In my time," she told them, "your species has descended to little more than mindless toys."

She threw open the curtain blocking her alcove from the rest of the storeroom and pulled the dog with her through the opening, only to trip over the lump lying across the doorway. She fell flat on her face with a startled shout. She hit her nose on the hard stone this time. She came up clutching her painfully throbbing nose to find a young red-haired woman staring at her in horrified surprise.

"My lady, I'm so sorry!"

"Who are you? What are you doing here?" Jane noticed Melisande sitting calmly on her haunches, watching the two of them with a happy doggy expression. "And why didn't you at least bark?" she demanded irritably of the hound. She looked at her fingers. They were sticky with blood from the tip of her nose. It felt like a pavement burn. Nothing broken; just another bruise.

"I could use some aspirin," she muttered in English.

The woman had backed toward the alcove, staring at Jane in wide-eyed expectation. She was a tiny thing, with carrot-red hair and freckle-dotted milk-white skin. Very pretty, really. "My lady?" she questioned, stepping forward eagerly when Jane spoke.

Jane climbed to her feet, glad she hadn't hit her already bruised hip when she fell. She noticed the soreness in her backside was much improved this morning. She looked down at the little woman and repeated, "Who are you?"

"Berthild," the redhead answered promptly. "Switha sent me to serve you."

Berthild? Right, she recalled. Switha's sister. The one with the soldier boyfriend. "What were you doing on my floor? You are what I fell over, aren't you?"

"I was sleeping by your door, my lady," was the swift explanation. "It is my duty."

Jane looked down at the bare wood. Duty? That sort of duty could lead to arthritis and who knew what else in the drafty air. "I see."

It seemed she now had a personal servant to be responsible for. The thought left her kind of unnerved. It was one thing to supervise the large group of people needed to keep Passfair running. It was definitely a challenge—an enjoyable challenge. But she had an uncomfortable feeling about having a peasant girl to call her own. Berthild here didn't have any rights. She was totally dependent on her mistress's goodwill. Jane knew it would be pleasant to have someone to take care of all her little needs. She didn't like the responsibility that went with it.

"Owning people is icky," she mumbled behind her hand as she touched her nose again. The bleeding had stopped, at least. The entertainment over, Melisande rose and rushed out the open storeroom door with her pups. The dogs' hasty exit reminded Jane of her original purpose. She was also reminded that the key to the room was missing. If she could lock the door,

she wouldn't have ended up with a sore nose to go
with the black eye.

Oh, well, Berthild was there. She undoubtedly
expected to be put to work. Jane smiled at her. "First
you can clean up the mess in the alcove. And I need
some laundry done. The yellow underdress is silk.
The washing instructions for the material has got to
be cold-water wa— Never mind, the river is cold.
And I've been thinking maybe I could get one of the
smaller tubs from the wash house moved up here so I
could take a bath. Maybe you could see to that?"

Berthild gave a quick curtsy. "Yes, my lady."

"And if you must sleep by the door, tell Bertram I
said you need a pallet and some blankets."

The servant's freckled face lit with delight. "Yes,
my lady."

Jane hurried down to the hall, where the usual
morning activity was well under way. Breakfast porridge was being served. Neither Sibelle nor her
women were anywhere to be seen. Jane didn't know if
this was good or bad. The kid probably had to be really upset to miss a meal. On the other hand, missing a
few meals certainly wouldn't hurt her.

She didn't see Stephan anywhere in the hall, either.
She took the time to shovel in a few bites of porridge
with a wooden spoon before going to look for him.
She finished quickly, then rinsed her mouth with a
cup of new ale. She grimaced at the raw taste, but at
least it helped wash the sleep out of her mouth. She'd
wiped her teeth on a square of linen when she first
woke up, but the combination of cloth and ale was no
substitute for a tube of toothpaste. She sent a prayer
of thanks for the dentist who'd talked her mother into
having her teeth coated with sealant when she was a

teenager. Whatever fate might bring to her here, at least she didn't have to worry about the mouth problems that were such a plague to the natives.

She forgot about her teeth as Bertram approached her, looking as if he were ready to shoo her into the cellar. Instead, the first thing he said was, "The cook needs to speak with you about the fish pond."

"Fish pond?"

"He's insisting on Lenten fare whether we have mass or no."

Jane hurried to cross herself. Sometimes she forgot she was supposed to be seeking life in a religious order. "Quite right," she approved. "What else?"

"Alfred says you promised him men to help rebuild the dovecote. Cerdic says he has too few men to help with the planting as it is, and won't send any more."

"Hmm. I thought Wat and Oswy were going to help him."

"They're working on the stable roof this morning," he explained.

She understood Alfred's impatience to get the work done. Hawks had been getting at the pigeons, and they were an important source of meat for the castle table. "I had better talk to Cerdic." Anything to stay out of the cellar a while longer. "Where's Sir Stephan?" She wanted to say a few words to her liege lord as well.

"In the stable."

Where else? "I'll be back soon."

Bertram cleared his throat and gave her a chilly once-over. The gesture reminded her that she was only partially dressed. She hurried upstairs. Berthild had left on the tasks she'd set for her. Jane pulled out one of her three canvas bags. First she gobbled down a handful of dried fruit, then she brought out her second overdress. This one was black, decorated in blue and gray. She pulled it on and wrapped her belt around a waist that was a touch narrower than it had been a week before. She added the lightweight cloak Bertram had rummaged from Stephan's late mother's clothes chest for her. Then she headed for Passfair village.

It was midmorning before she settled matters to the satisfaction of both the reeve and the pigeon keeper. She entered the courtyard with a keen feeling of satisfaction at a job well done. A warm sun was casting butter-cream light across the landscape. She'd noticed the beginning of buds on the trees in the apple orchard on her way back up the hill. The birds were trilling overhead, and her face wasn't hurting quite so badly as the day before.

Now she wanted to talk to Stephan. She was hoping she might be able diplomatically to suggest he try to get to know the girl he was going to marry. She wanted to point out to him that domestic harmony between them would be good for the whole Passfair household. With gentle words ready to trip from her tongue, she went to the stable.

Raoul DeCorte was waiting for her at the stable door. "My lady," he said, looking at her nervously. "I have a message for you."

The boys working on the stable roof began hammering loudly with heavy wooden mallets. She drew him aside so she could hear without either of them having to shout. As they walked together toward the hall she said, "Yes?" There was a knot in her stomach telling her she already knew what the guard sergeant was going to say.

"Sir Stephan said to tell you he felt compelled to renew his vows of service to his liege. His conscience bade him to journey to Striguil. Or wherever Lord Guillaume might be holding winter court."

Her brows knit in a thunderous frown. "He slunk off while I was gone, you mean?"

"Just so, my lady," Raoul agreed with a devilish smile. "You're one to cut to the heart of a matter. The lad's fled the maiden."

"Leaving me to take care of her." She made the unladylike gesture of banging her fist into her palm. *Wait until I get my hands on you, Stephan DuVrai!*

Guillaume le Marechal was one of the richest landholders in England. He could be at any of his vast estates, which covered the length and breadth of the country. Stephan could spend weeks dawdling his way from one holding to the next.

That rat! she growled to herself. Running off just because he didn't want to face the girl he was going to marry. To DeCorte she posed a more practical concern. "How many men did he take?"

"Ten, my lady. He left enough to hold the castle in case of trouble."

"Will there be? Trouble, I mean? Will Hugh of Lilydrake try to snatch Sibelle again?"

The sergeant shook his head. "That game's won. Lilydrake will think her bedded and already with child by the time he hears the lad's gone. And Sir Stephan said he trusts Daffyd ap Bleddyn to keep the countryside safe."

The devil with Daffyd ap Bleddyn! Daffyd ap Bleddyn keeping the countryside safe wasn't going to help her keep peace inside the walls of Passfair, she fumed. "Does Lady Sibelle know he's gone?"

He drew himself up to his full height. She was still a good six inches taller. "I don't concern myself with matters in the ladies' bower," he informed her. Then he quickly took himself off to the armory.

"Right," she railed at his retreating back. "Another coward leaving me to do all the work!"

She sighed. It was both an angry and a frustrated sound. She suddenly felt as if the weight of the world were being dumped on her. The morning had gone so well. She'd almost been starting to enjoy this forced exile. Now she had to face Sibelle with the news—and cope with the girl through all the days until Sir Stephan chose to put in another appearance at his castle.

"Face it, girl," she chided herself. "You are very much alone, and it's never going to get any better."

The bright, sunny day was suddenly cold and dark for her. She sighed again and went into the castle. Bertram was waiting just inside the screen to let her know Lady Sibelle hadn't ventured out of the bedchamber. Her women had informed him she didn't intend to. "About the cellar, my lady?"

His news sent Jane marching up the tower stairs.

Her knock on the stout bower door was eventually answered. It was the shorter and rounder of the two dragons who opened the door, but she only cracked it a few inches.

She looked as if she'd tasted something nasty when she caught sight of Jane. "What do *you* want?" she demanded haughtily.

Jane considered pushing her way in. Instead she offered a patient smile and said, "I have to talk to your mistress."

"She won't speak to *you*." The door began to close.

Jane already had a foot stuck in the opening. She added a hand pushing against the outside of the door for good measure. "I have news about Sir Stephan."

"Then give it to me," the woman snapped.

"You're not his betrothed. Let me in." Jane didn't know why she was being so insistent about a confrontation she didn't want in the first place. Sense of duty or something, she guessed. She thought about the girl having cried herself to sleep the night before. Maybe what she was feeling was a little compassion for Sibelle's untenable situation.

"Who is it?" she heard a young female voice asking from inside the room.

So the kid could talk, Jane thought as the servant turned her head to answer. "*That* woman, my lamb."

"I don't want to talk to *her*!" came the shrill reply.

"Perhaps you'd best, my dove," she heard the other attendant coax soothingly.

"No! She's an ugly giant, and I won't have her near me!"

"Forget this nonsense," Jane fumed. She gave an irritated shove on the door. The woman trying to hold it against her was knocked aside. Jane strode in angrily.

Sibelle jumped up from a bench as Jane approached her, and pointed a pudgy forefinger dramatically at the door. "Cast her out!" she ordered her women.

Jane gave them a challenging look. The women backed to the far side of the room. Jane stalked forward and planted herself squarely in front of Lady Sibelle. "My lady," she said in crisply enunciated tones. "I am the chatelaine of this castle. It is my duty to care for you. I wish to make your life here as pleasant as possible. Now, if you ju—"

"Where's Sir Stephan?" the girl interrupted. "Why doesn't he come to me? I want you to go away." She crossed her arms over her full breasts and added imperiously, "Now."

"We have to talk first," Jane continued doggedly.

"I'm to be his lady," Sibelle told her. "I don't have to talk to his leman." Jane gasped at being called Stephan's mistress. "I don't want you here," Sibelle continued. "Go away. Marguerite, make her go away."

"Lady Jehane," ventured the more reasonable of the two attendants. "Perhaps you should go. Perhaps Sir Stephan will come and speak with our la—"

"He's not here," Jane cut in. She kept a steady gaze on Sibelle as she explained, "I'm not his mistress."

"You are!" the girl declared. "He beat you so you wouldn't complain about his marrying me. Soon he's going to throw you to his guards and then I'll—"

"It was the dog," Jane explained once more, through clenched teeth this time. "The dog tripped me and I fell down the stairs. No one beat me. Sit down," she ordered the girl, her tone so full of authority that it would have made her military mother proud.

The girl sat. And began sniffling.

Jane had to concede the girl had quite an active imagination. "Sir Stephan wouldn't beat anyone," she defended him loyally. "He's a chivalrous young knight."

Her words calmed Sibelle a bit. The girl gave a romantic sigh. "He's the handsomest man I've ever seen."

Jane doubted that Sibelle had seen that many, but a

few days ago she might have agreed with the girl. Now, for some reason, she found herself mentally comparing Stephan's slender good looks with the lionlike masculinity of Sir Daffyd. "One of the handsomest," she agreed.

"He shall be mine."

"Of course, my lady," she soothed. "I am not his mistress. I have never been his mistress. I will never be his mistress. I'm a widowed kinswoman from the Holy Land." Suddenly all three of the other women were looking at her in bug-eyed awe. They crossed themselves in unison.

She went on. "As soon as the Church returns to England, I will enter a convent and spend the rest of my life in prayer." There, she added silently, was that a good enough explanation? "I swear by Saint—uh—Bernard."

"Bernard?"

"Hasn't he been canonized yet?" Damn. "We heard so in Jerusalem. Saint George, then. And the Holy Sepulcher," she threw in for good measure. "Where my dear husband and I often prayed before the paynim overran the Holy City."

Sibelle's fair skin blushed hot pink. "Oh," she said. She looked at her servants. "You said she was hi—"

"They were wrong." Jane gave the older women a dirty look. "And we don't encourage gossiping here at Passfair," she added warningly. So there.

"But where is Sir Stephan?" Sibelle asked, drawing Jane's attention back to the subject she'd come to discuss.

"Sir Stephan's been called away."

Fresh tears began to trickle down Sibelle's cheeks.

"Oh." Her lower lip quivered miserably. "When will he return?"

"I don't know. He has to serve his liege for a time."

"He's very brave."

"Yes."

With a romantic sigh, Sibelle folded her hands in her lap. "Then I will wait for him."

Jane was relieved at how well the girl was taking it. Of course, she was probably used to waiting. It was what women did while the menfolk were off bashing each other's heads in.

She wanted to say something reassuring about how things would be better when Stephan returned. She was probably wrong, but she felt the urge to give the girl some comfort.

As she opened her mouth to tell some placating lie, one of the stable lads rushed into the bower shouting, "Lady Jehane, come quickly! It's Oswy! He's fallen from the roof!"

The smell of dung hung about the boy like a cloud. His face was pale under a thick layer of dirt. Jane stared at him, speechless for the moment.

"Come to the stable, my lady. Now. Please!" he urged. He ran back out the door.

"What's happened?" she asked, following quickly to catch up as he raced down the two flights of stairs. Her heart was pounding with fear as they rushed across the hall. She'd seen the look of horror in the boy's face. "How bad?"

It wasn't a high roof. How bad could it it—

"His back's all twisted."

A broken spine.

"Oh, my God." She grabbed the boy by the shoulder. "Go for Switha. Send her to me at the . . ." She thought swiftly, quickly latching on to a place both clean and quiet. "At the chapel."

The boy hurried off toward the village. Jane lifted her skirts and sprinted toward the stable.

8

This was her fault, Jane thought as she leaned tiredly against the cool stones of the chapel wall. She didn't know how much time had passed since she'd reached the stable. There she'd found the small, silent crowd gathered around the lad lying in a pitiful, twisted heap in the mixed mud and straw of the paddock. She knelt beside the boy, wishing she knew something about first aid, as the lad who'd been working with Oswy on the roof babbled out an explanation. She didn't hear a word he said. Someone, it must have been she, gave the stablemen and guards surrounding the boy orders. She remembered her hands moving, her muscles straining, as she helped the men ease Oswy onto the wide board the cook brought from the kitchen. She remembered holding Oswy's cold hand as the board was carried gently into the chapel and eased onto the floor. She must have said something to send the men away, then she waited alone for Switha.

She did remember the boy sometimes groaning, and that she had wiped away the blood bubbling slowly from his lips. Her hands were sticky with it still. When Switha came she'd walked over here to the wall where she now stood.

It was her fault, she thought again while she watched the wisewoman's sure hands work their way down the boy's paralyzed body. If she had just left things alone. If she hadn't wanted to make everything perfect, he wouldn't have been up on that roof. He wouldn't have slipped. He wouldn't have fallen. He wouldn't have hit the watering trough and landed on the ground with God knew how many internal injuries and broken vertebrae.

There was nothing to be done. She couldn't pick up a phone and call 911. No evac helicopter was going to land and whisk him off to intensive care. He was going to die. It was going to take a long time, and it was going to hurt.

"It's all my fault," she said aloud.

She hadn't noticed anyone else in the room, but a girl's voice beside her answered softly, "No. It's God's will."

Jane turned her head and found herself looking into Lady Sibelle's eyes. They were a soft blue gray. For once there were no tears in them. Jane didn't understand. "What are you doing here?"

"Praying," the girl answered. "I followed you from the bower. I tried to stay out of the way." She bent her head. "I came to do the only thing I know how to do. It's our duty to pray for the dying."

Jane couldn't think of anything to say in answer, so she pried herself away from the wall and walked to where Switha was examining the boy. The chapel was small, a boxy little room off the main hall. A cross-shaped window above the roughly smoothed granite slab used as an altar let in plenty of light. A small room, but the distance across it seemed very long to Jane. She was light-headed and felt as if she were walking down an echoing tunnel. Sibelle followed close on her heels.

Switha rose as they came to her. Sibelle knelt in her place. Jane didn't bother with foolish questions. She asked, "Can you give him anything for the pain?"

Switha shook her head. Her expression was grave and still; anguish showed only in her eyes. There was blood on her hands as well. Jane recalled that a plague had taken many villagers' lives that winter. Switha must have had her fill of death by now. How many had she lost in childbirth? To simple infections? To stupid accidents like today's? Never mind the unheeded peasant deaths when the nobles fought out their petty squabbles, using the countryside as though it were a playing field.

"I'm so sorry," Jane told her. She apologized not just for Oswy, but for all of history where the poor and powerless died without any help.

Switha acknowledged her understanding with the slightest of nods. Then the Saxon woman knelt beside the Norman girl. Sibelle was cradling Oswy's head in her ample lap. Switha put a hand on the girl's shoulder. "My lady?"

Sibelle looked up at Jane. "I'll take the death-watch," she told her. "Send Marguerite and Alais to me."

"I'll stay as well," Switha said. "There's nothing we can do but wait for his spirit to leave his body."

"If only we could have a priest here for the last rites," Sibelle added sadly. "Poor lost soul."

Switha placed a comforting hand on Sibelle's

shoulder. "We will pray. To the Lord, and the Lady Mother."

Jane watched them exchange a quick, understanding glance. "Each in their own way," Sibelle agreed.

It was the only thing left to do. Jane said, "I'll be back."

But when she had walked stiffly from the chapel, she realized she wasn't sure she could go back. She marveled at the women she'd left behind. She had thought Sibelle was just a fat, snively kid, she reflected in confusion. Maybe there was more to her. Obviously there was.

She found the serving women by the hearth and sent them to the chapel, then stayed by the fire herself, trying to get some warmth into her chilled bones. A few minutes later Marguerite and Alais came back into the hall again. They stopped Bertram, and after a short conversation oil lamps and linens and various other things were gathered and carried back into the chapel. Jane watched the activity with numb detachment. It all seemed well practiced, so commonplace. She'd thought she'd understood the reality of this era. Now she was beginning to realize she didn't know anything.

She didn't return to the chapel. She sat on the dais step with her hands propping up her chin, staring at the glowing embers in the hearth for hours instead. She sensed Bertram hovering nearby, but he left her alone.

She didn't let anything disturb her until Sir Daffyd entered the hall, his spurs and mail jangling with the rhythm of his stride. She rubbed her aching temples and stood, wondering irritably what the devil he was doing here.

He came and took her by the arm and led her to one of the carved chairs. He had beautiful hands; they covered hers comfortingly for a moment. "You don't look well."

She turned her pained gaze on him. "There's been an accident," she explained. "Someone's dying."

He nodded, understanding in his gold-green eyes. "Wine for the lady," he ordered Bertram. When Bertram brought two silver goblets, Daffyd handed one to her and ignored the other.

He took the seat beside her. "Drink deep." The wine tasted like vinegar—with a heavy kick.

"What happened?" he asked after she'd finished the cup. It should have made her head swim. Instead she felt more clearheaded.

"A lad fell from a roof. Broke his back. I should go to the chapel," she said, getting tiredly to her feet. "Sibelle's with him, but I—"

He rose in a swift, graceful movement to stand over her. He didn't loom; instead his large presence seemed like a protective shield. He touched her cheek with a callused fingertip and wiped a tear she hadn't noticed shedding from her cheek. It was the faintest of touches, but it heated her, not just her cheek, but fire raced to the very core of her being. She was shaken and confused as he stepped swiftly back to his chair and seated himself once more.

"Stay." He waved her back down, his deep voice not quite steady. "The little nun will be used to doing such a friend's service."

Jane settled back on the hard wooden seat. She gave a very small, very bitter laugh. "'Death hath no friend.'" The irony of her words could be understood by no one but herself.

He sat back in his chair. Tapping his beaky nose thoughtfully, Daffyd said, "I've heard that somewhere."

It was a quote from Guillaume le Marechal's biography. Something he probably hadn't said yet. More likely it was a common Norman saying. She looked down at the gleaming silver cup she was rolling on her palms. The same silver cup had been blackened with tarnish when she'd arrived. If only she hadn't interfered. If only she could interfere more.

"There's nothing I can do," she said softly.

"No," he said. "There isn't." His deep voice was troubled. As were the shadows in his green-flecked eyes. He gave a bitter laugh of his own. She got the impression he wasn't thinking about the dying boy.

"It's all my fault," she said. "I ordered the roof repaired."

"It was an act of fate," he countered. "The roof needed fixing?"

"Yes."

"Then you made no mistake. It was no deliberate act of negligence on your part. Don't be hard on yourself, lady. Don't eat yourself up with guilt. It'll eat you up inside." He sounded as if he were talking from experience.

She found herself wanting to find out just what sins were causing haunted shadows in the depths of his eyes, but she didn't know him, and it wasn't her place to pry. He didn't look like the sort to exchange intimate confidences with womenfolk, anyway.

"What are you doing here?" she asked instead. "The outlaws?"

"They're nowhere nearby. Probably feasting on the king's deer in the forest as we speak," he said.

"In truth, I came to convey greetings to the new lady of Passfair." The look she gave him must have contained more skepticism than she intended. He gave her a crooked, and totally cynical, smile. "Perhaps you did not know the lady's a kinswoman of the king. Her father's a by-blow of one of King Henry's lemans. Being the king's man, it does me no harm to speak soft and fair to his family, no matter how loose the connection."

It occurred to her that the Welshman was a landless knight, his only support coming from the favor of King John. Most such knights were always on the lookout for an estate to hold as their own. It reminded her of her resolve not to be attracted to him.

Perhaps he hadn't been quite honest when he'd said he preferred a pretty face over a rich dowry. Sibelle was a considerable heiress. She was also still an unmarried virgin, with her protector doing his best to put a great many miles between them. What if Sir Daffyd had heard of Stephan's absence and had showed up to sniff around the honey pot a bit? Or to kidnap the prize outright, as Hugh of Lilydrake had tried to do?

Well, he wasn't going to get the chance to steal Sibelle away as long as she was in charge of Passfair. Stephan's treatment of the poor girl was shabby enough, but at least he'd never do anything to harm her. This gold-maned *male* probably never even bothered to take off the at least forty pounds of chain mail he wore.

She swore silently at the perfidy of all men. And almost laughed when she noticed that the colorful language rolling through her mind wasn't English. In just a few days' time she was beginning to think in

Norman French. She wondered inanely if her accent was improving as well.

Such speculation did nothing to alleviate her immediate problems. Suddenly wary of Sir Daffyd, she wondered if she should call DeCorte into the hall. Not that Raoul would be any match for the formidable younger soldier. Raoul and about a dozen guards might even the score considerably.

She rose and said, "Excuse me."

As she stepped off the dais, Switha and Alais came out of the chapel. She changed course to go to them. "It's over," Switha told her.

Jane gave an almost relieved sigh. At least the boy was out of pain. She crossed herself before she realized she actually meant the gesture. "His family?" she asked.

"They died of the fever. I'll see to the burial."

"Thank you. Sibelle?"

"Praying in the chapel," Alais answered.

Jane nodded. The light coming in the windows was beginning to fade. The tables would be set up for dinner any minute now. Then the guards would wander in without any need to call them. She would speak to Bertram and DeCorte. They had to protect Lady Sibelle, but there was no need outright to offend the man who commanded the king's force in this part of the countryside. She could get Stephan in trouble if she wasn't careful. She fingered the dagger on her belt. It wasn't much protection, but there was also strength in numbers.

"I'll join Lady Sibelle at her prayers," she told the women. She gave a quick glance over her shoulder. Sir Daffyd was lounging comfortably on his chair, one muscular thigh thrown casually over the sturdy armrest. The carved lines of his face reflected a somber mood, his eyes seeing into an inward distance. For a moment she thought she saw something familiar about the brooding cast of his features.

She shook off the urge to go to him and ask what was wrong. He wasn't a lamb who'd strayed into her keeping. Sibelle was. And he was the strongest contender for the wolf who could snatch her away.

The day, she thought, had been one damn thing after another. She turned her back on Daffyd and went in to Sibelle.

9

It was no hardship for Jane to fast through the dinner hour. From her place kneeling before the empty altar she could hear the sounds of the household at dinner, but she couldn't understand how anyone could find an appetite. Marguerite and Alais came and went and came back again as the long hours wore on. She and Sibelle remained. She hoped her mind would go numb, as numb as her body gradually became.

The stones beneath her knees were hard, the chill of the unheated room seeped through the layers of clothing and into tense muscle and bone. Early in the vigil, Alais placed a lit candle on the altar. Jane marked the time by watching the small spark of light eat its way through the fine beeswax. The scent of wax and honey spread out on the chapel air, lingering after the light died away.

Jane endured the hours with stubborn stoicism. This was proper. This was expected. This was what she'd been sentenced to. Once she entered a convent there would be regular prayers five times a day, fasting, and the narrow rules of the order. And there'd be many more long hours on her knees through all hours of day and night for saints' days and penitence and holy days and vigil for the dead and dying. This was her future, her life. After a few hours she thought she was going to go mad.

The older women stirred occasionally, easing tired bones. Sibelle simply kept her eyes on the altar, her lips moving in silently whispered prayer. While the faint golden light of the candle remained, it shed a warm glow over the girl's fine pink complexion. Sibelle's expression was serene with prayer. Her large eyes focused with intense concentration. Glancing at the overweight girl out of the corner of her eye, Jane made a startling discovery: Sibelle's face was actually quite pretty. After the light went out, Jane, who had no prayers in her, considered this new bit of information.

She had no idea how long it was before Alais and Marguerite came to silent agreement and rose ponderously to their feet.

"Come, my lamb," Marguerite said, touching Sibelle's shoulder. "Time to rest now."

"But—" Sibelle began.

"No prayers can help the poor lad, anyway. He died in sin. There's nothing even the blessed Mother can do to save his soul."

"Come away, my lady." Alais added her urgings as the girl hesitated reluctantly.

Jane waited on her knees, unwilling to rise, if her numb legs would let her rise, until Sibelle acquiesced to her women. She kept her mouth firmly shut. No era was a good one to argue religious philosophy. An era where torture and execution awaited those who didn't follow the current party line or the right pope was an especially dangerous place to voice an opinion. So she kept still and fumed over the notion of eternal damnation for anyone who didn't receive the sacraments. These people believed it; that was what made excommunication such a powerful political weapon.

Sibelle didn't hesitate for long. She crossed herself and let Marguerite help her up. "Kings and priests shouldn't bring God into their arguments," she complained, expressing an opinion of her own.

"Come away," Alais coaxed. "You're cold, my love. Let's get you to bed."

Jane waited until the other three left before climbing to her feet. It took a few minutes of stumbling painfully around the dark chapel before she got enough circulation back to attempt the walk up to her room. She picked her way silently through the sleeping forms in the main hall, managing to find her way up the stairs and into her bed without any light. Berthild didn't seem to be anywhere for her to trip over as she passed through the storeroom. The dogs were already comfortably curled up on the fur bedcover.

Once in bed, she thought it would be easy to find sleep. The day had gone on forever, and she was wearier than she'd ever been in her life. But sleep didn't come, although she gradually grew warm and relaxed, and the image of the dying boy didn't haunt her as she thought it would. The regret was there, but not so sharp and immediate as it had been. Perhaps the hours in the chapel had done something to alleviate her sense of blame. But still she couldn't sleep. The events of the day had been too overwhelming, and the realization that she was trapped forever in an alien culture was hitting her with the force of a blow.

She didn't toss restlessly, just lay on the straw mattress and listened. To the roar of blood in her ears, to the dogs' breathing, to rodents skittering among the storage barrels. She made a mental note about bringing in some hungry cats from the tithe barn. Sometime, very late, the storeroom door creaked open. She assumed it was Berthild until she heard the unmistakable, soft clinking of chain mail. She started up with a terrified gasp. Her hand grasped the hilt of the dagger she made a habit of leaving under her pillow. Melisande whuffed gently and got up to investigate, in no hurry to attack the intruder.

Jane started to slip out of bed, not sure whether to hide, call out, or follow the dog into the storeroom. She was saved from having to decide by the sound of Berthild's voice whispering words Jane couldn't make out. The girl must have tucked her sleeping pallet somewhere out of the way. Berthild's question received an equally soft answer. There was a muffled giggle, then sounds of chain mail and clothes being shed. Jane waited stiffly in the dark. Melisande bolted back into the alcove as though someone had shoved her through the curtain. It would seem that Berthild's guardsman lover had arrived. He must have waited until he thought the chatelaine deeply asleep before venturing in.

She wondered if she should throw him out or let the couple be. She valued her privacy, which was hard to come by in the communal atmosphere of the castle. She would lose it forever when she entered the convent. She supposed the pair in the storeroom valued privacy as well, and they got less of it than she did. She waited tensely on the edge of the bed, indecisive. She put the dagger away. She expected sounds of lovemaking to follow the man's undressing, but nothing but silence came from the outer room.

She crossed her arms and frowned in puzzlement. How could she throw somebody out on his ear for fooling around with her maid when he wasn't fooling around? Maybe they just wanted to cuddle up together and sleep. Rather sweet, she thought, and lay back down.

Must be nice to have someone to cuddle up with, she thought. Nice not to be alone in the dark. Someone warm and comforting to just be with, never mind the rest. Though the rest would be nice, her wistful, lonely thoughts ran on. She'd never really been in love. There had been too much to learn, too much to do. She had given all her energy to the excitement of research, hadn't thought about love at all. Not the share-your-life-with-someone-forever kind of love, at least. She had thought there'd be time later. Dammit, she was getting maudlin. It was just sleep deprivation making her depressed. Life was so fleeting, though. So often wasted.

To get her mind off melancholy speculation of might-have-beens, she searched her thoughts for another subject to consider.

The cook wanted fresh eels. Bleah. Could they fish for them in the Stour? Perhaps she should point out to him that she was from the Middle East, where the trendy delicacy was sheep's eyeballs. No, it was better not to give him any ideas. She didn't want him trying to impress Lady Sibelle with his artistry. That girl did not need to be impressed with anybody's cuisine.

The girl needed a strict diet and plenty of exercise. And . . .

Jane sat up straight in her bed. She could almost see the light bulb—or blazing flambeau—going on over her head. "The girl needs . . ."

She settled back down slowly, her mind suddenly buzzing with ideas. What did Sibelle need? Well, a husband, for one thing. She wanted Stephan. What girl wouldn't? He was handsome and brave and charming and nice. Well, he was nice to everybody but Sibelle. Poor kid. What could she do to change that? Jane wondered.

Should she? She wasn't supposed to change anything. There was nothing she could do.

Why not?

Don't give me "why not," she argued with herself. History. She couldn't do anything to change history. What if Sibelle and Stephan were supposed to loathe each other throughout their lives? What if they were supposed to be childless?

But, just by living here in the Middle Ages, Jane was altering history. A boy had died, because she had ordered him to fix a roof. The course of events had been changed. Well, if she could change things for the bad, maybe she could change them for the good as well. She hadn't been able to help the boy.

"Maybe I can help the girl," she whispered into her pillow. Without revealing any secrets of my great technological age. Sibelle didn't need to know how to work a computer. She needed a little help with her socialization, some skills training. Surely Jane could manage that much without making any great changes.

She rolled onto her back and laced her fingers together across her stomach. Staring into the darkness, she considered just how to deal with the situation. Though not for long. Now that she'd made up her mind to do something, she finally drifted off to sleep, before she could figure out exactly what it was she was going to do.

She woke up with a cunning plan.

She also woke up because she heard Berthild moving around in the outer room. The door opened. The dogs jumped down and followed the servant out. Jane sighed happily, waiting in bed for Berthild to bring back a couple of buckets of warm water for her to bathe in. She'd asked her to do that the night before. She was stiff all over; a bath would do her a world of good. She checked the window. The darkness was just barely beginning to turn to gray. She had plenty of time before she had to be up and very, very busy.

So much to do, so much to talk about. First to Switha, then to Sibelle, and the cook, and a nice, firm lecture for Marguerite and Alais. So much to do before Stephan got home. She chuckled happily and waited under the soft warmth of the fur cover. The room grew lighter as the sun climbed into the sky.

After a while she heard footsteps and Berthild's voice directing a couple of helpers she'd brought with her to empty the water in the tub. Good, Jane thought with pleasure. She could have a proper, fully naked, soaking up to her chin, hot bath. Berthild shooed the menservants out the door and left herself. Jane got up and, keeping the cover wrapped around her for warmth, threw back the curtain.

The first thing she saw was a broad, naked, masculine back and small, muscular buttocks leaning over her bathwater.

The first thing she said was, "Get out of my bath-tub!"

The first thing she thought as the surprised Sir Daffyd turned to face her was, *He does take off his chain mail.*

Then she looked at him. She couldn't very well help it, since every gold-furred inch of him was on display: his soaking wet golden head and his strong throat, the brown rings of nipples nesting in the darker blond hair that veed down to the flat stomach, the manhood flanked by powerful thighs, the bare toes curled on the cold stones of the storeroom floor.

Jane went hot and cold all over, then stayed hot. She couldn't seem to make herself stop staring, though. She was rooted in the doorway, her heart thudding frantically in her chest as the erotic dreams she'd had about this stranger chose this moment to replay through her mind in vivid detail.

She supposed anyone who constantly carried around the weight of all that armor had to be strong; she'd felt how muscular he was when she rode with him back to the castle. It just hadn't occurred to her working mind that the hard-muscled body would be this beautiful. His flesh was so, so perfect, the lines perfectly proportioned. Her fingers began itching to trace the outline of his upper arms and pectoral muscles. To follow the curve of his chest down to . . .

She gave a hard swallow and cleared her throat.

He didn't seem particularly embarrassed. He was, in fact, smirking in an insufferably self-satisfied way. He was perfectly aware he was gorgeous. It made her want to kick him.

Annoyance helped her recall her dignity. "What,"

she demanded a bit belatedly, "are you doing here?"

"I was going to take a bath," he replied instantly.

"How did you get in here?"

He glanced at a pile of clothing in a corner. It suddenly occurred to her that he'd been the soldier who'd come in during the night. Of course, it couldn't have been anyone else. She'd heard chain mail. No mere man-at-arms was equipped with such expensive armor.

"Why did Berthild let you in here?"

He shrugged. She really wished he would cover himself. She really wished she could take her eyes off him.

"I always sleep here when I visit Passfair. Actually"—he put his hands on his narrow waist and looked her up and down—"I've always taken the bed in the alcove before."

Her skin went hot all over again. It was a heat that began and concentrated most fiercely in the deep core of her. The look in his eyes was enough to start a sensual prickling along her nerve endings. She gripped the fur tighter around her body. She suddenly felt vulnerable and far too much alone. She was a giantess to all the others, but near Daffyd ap Bleddyn she felt small and vulnerable. If he took a step toward her, she didn't know what she'd do. She didn't know what she wanted to do.

"Get out," she said, her voice ragged with tension.

The smirk turned into a full-fledged leer. "The water's nice and warm." He gestured to the tub. "Care to join me?"

"Get out!" she repeated, louder this time. "You have no business being in my quarters, Sir Daffyd."

"You didn't seem to mind a few moments ago." He

took the step forward she'd been fearing. "What's wrong now?"

She stood her ground, though she wanted to duck around him and run down to the hall. She'd be safe there, surrounded by people who listened to her when she gave them an order.

"I'm not interested in any dalliance," she told him fiercely. "Not with you!"

"Who do you have in mind?" his deep, chocolate voice rumbled sarcastically. "With the lad gone there's not much else of interest available." The leer turned into a very seductive smile. "I'm available."

"I'm not," she snapped angrily. "I'm going to be a nun."

"You weren't looking at me like any nun I've known." The superior smirk returned. "At least not at first."

"I'm a widow," she pointed out hastily, refusing to show just how much he was both embarrassing and infuriating her. "I know what a man's for and how to look at one. I was comparing you to my dear, late lord." She drew herself up haughtily. "And believe me, Sir Daffyd, I found you wanting."

He shrugged again. "Suit yourself, lady." He turned toward the bath. And climbed in while she stood sputtering in indignation. As he sank into the water, he added, "I thought you were the one who was wanting."

He then proceeded nonchalantly to scrub himself while she fled back into the alcove. She dressed hurriedly, then marched through the storeroom, head held high, eyes averted. His deep laughter followed her all the way to the hall.

She was barely calm enough to face him by the

time he came sauntering down the stairs, fully clothed at last. She finished her conversation with the cook while the Welshman grabbed himself a breakfast of bread and cheese. Even though he was at the table, and she was half a room away from him at the hearth, she was far too aware of his every move. After the cook went back to his duties, Sir Daffyd approached her.

"You are leaving this morning, aren't you, Sir Daffyd?" she inquired with chilly politeness as he came to the hearth.

His hazel-green eyes were bright with wicked amusement. "After I speak with Lady Sibelle, yes."

"Lady Sibelle is indisposed. I'm afraid she won't be able to see you. In fact," she added, "Lady Sibelle is going to be too busy to see anyone for some time to come."

He crossed his arms, the amusement in his expression turning to skepticism. "Busy? Doing what?"

She had to tell somebody. She was dying to tell somebody. This arrogant Welshman would just have to do. "She will be busy being turned into the sort of bride Sir Stephan wishes. It's a lady's duty to please her lord, after all," she added in justification of her plan. "My duty is to help her."

"Help her what? I hear the girl's a witless, fat lump."

"Not witless. And lumps can be rearranged. It just takes a little work."

"I doubt it can be done."

"How do you know? You've never even met the girl."

"I would if you'd give me the chance."

She discovered she and Sir Daffyd were standing

nose to nose, their hands-on-hips stances mirroring each other. She took a step back. "The lady is indisposed," she repeated.

He gave a frustrated growl, but before they could resume the argument, DeCorte and two men in black surcoats similar to Sir Daffyd's came hurrying into the hall.

"Sir Daffyd," DeCorte boomed out. "News of Sikes."

Sir Daffyd deserted the hearth to speak to the men. "Where?"

"A group of merchants were attacked on the Canterbury road. Five miles west of the town. Two dead."

"Damn! I thought the outlaws were holed up in Blean; instead they've circled around behind us. How many men did you bring from Reculver?"

"Ten."

"Fine. Let's ride." He glanced at DeCorte. "Have someone saddle my horse."

"Lady Jehane already ordered your horse saddled."

"I see." He threw an annoyed glance over his shoulder. "Out," he ordered his men. He waited a moment after they'd gone. "Lady Jehane?" His voice dripped with honey.

"Yes?"

"I'll offer you a wager about the girl."

"Oh? What is there to wager about?" Somehow she felt up to any challenge the man could offer.

"I'll wager there's no improving the girl," he dared her. "I'll give you two months to prove to me I'm wrong. What say you?"

Jehane remembered her bags full of silks and gems and spices. They made her a very rich woman. She was thoroughly annoyed by his complacent certainty. "All right," she agreed.

He fingered the heavy gold hoop in his right ear. "This might look well on you."

As if anyone would ever see her earlobes. Still, it was very nice. More important, she'd know she'd won it from the disdainful Sir Daffyd. Fair and square. "I can match its value," she confirmed.

He shook his head slowly, his face taking on a sultry expression as his eyes caressed her from head to foot. His voice was a seductive purr when he told her, "I don't want your gold."

He didn't want gold? "Silk or spices?" she questioned.

Another negative shake of his head. His eyes caught hers, and Sir Daffyd smiled. It wasn't the smirk she'd seen before; this was a sensual curving of the lips. His gold-flecked eyes glowed heatedly. It set Jane's blood racing. "I'll have you, lady," he told her.

Jane's breath caught in her throat. For a moment she was frozen, half in surprise, half in hope. Then he laughed softly, and outrage took over from other stunned senses.

He turned on his heel and was out of the hall before she could find anything to throw at him.

Just as well she hadn't tried to kill him, she fumed after he was gone. The man was too dangerous to provoke physically. She would never, ever give him an excuse to touch her. Besides, she added, more angry at herself than the Welshman, she should have seen that coming.

It was just a joke, wasn't it? He wouldn't . . .want to . . . you know . . . bed me, as they say in these parts.

She had two months to find out. Two months. But

it wasn't Sir Daffyd she should be worrying about. Who knew how long it would be before Stephan returned? She had to have results by then.

She grabbed her cape and hurried to the village to talk to Switha.

10

As Jane expected, she found Sibelle in the bedroom, on her knees, head bent in deep prayer. Neither Marguerite nor Alais had hassled her about coming into the bower this time. In fact, the women seemed happy to see her. After poking her head briefly into the bedroom to check on the girl, Jane drew the older women aside.

"Do you want your mistress to be happy?" she asked.

"Oh, yes," Alais answered fervently.

"More than anything!" Marguerite echoed her sentiment with a decisive nod.

"Good. So do I."

"Why?" Marguerite asked suspiciously, very much the dragon ready to defend her young.

Jane knew she could just order the women back to Sturry if they balked at her plans. She'd rather have their help. They'd probably been with Sibelle all her life. She seemed fond of them and they of her. It would be much better to have them encouraging and supportive over the next few months. There wasn't any overnight cure to Sibelle's problems. The more people she had around her to help, the easier it would be for her.

Jane sat down on the window bench and motioned the women to be seated on the long bench next to the disused loom. She tucked her hands in her sleeves and leaned forward. Speaking in a low, confidential voice, she said, "The sooner I can enter an abbey, the happier I will be."

Alais nodded sympathetically. "I do miss the life at Davington."

"As do I," Marguerite chimed in, but not quite so enthusiastically.

"But my duty is also to care for Passfair," Jane explained with wistful resignation. "And my dear, kind kinsman Stephan." The women's expressions got a bit dreamy at the mention of this paragon of chivalry.

"He deserves a good wife," Jane continued. "One who can serve him. One who can cheerfully make his life comfortable and pleasant and give him all a man desires. Since your lady will be his wife, her duty is to serve him as he wishes to be served."

"Of course," Alais agreed wholeheartedly.

Marguerite nodded.

"I think Sibelle will be happiest if she can serve him properly."

Marguerite's nod was thoughtful this time. "Yes. That only makes sense."

"It would be awful for her if she couldn't please him," Alais contributed. "She's a gentle thing. It would be dreadful for her to be beaten and locked away."

"And just because she doesn't really know how to please him." Jane shook her head sadly at the perfidy of the male race. "Sir Stephan is—rightly, of course— very demanding of his womenfolk. Very strict. There's so much she needs to learn before she can truly satisfy him. So much I would like to teach her before the day comes when I can take my vows at a house of prayer."

"Oh, do you think you can help her?" Alais asked eagerly. "My poor lamb knows nothing of the world."

"Nothing of men," Marguerite added tartly. "The monsters."

Jane clasped her hands together fervently. "I so want to try. Will you help me? I can't change her ways unless I have the two of you—her loving and constant companions and confidantes—to help keep her on the path that will bring her whatever joy a woman can find in this life."

"Oh, of course, Lady Jehane!" Alais breathed reverently. "Anything!"

Marguerite's reply was more fatalistic. "The rule of an order, or the rule of a husband, neither is any different as far as obeying goes. All a woman must do is give herself up to the command of her superiors, and pray for the strength to never waver."

"I knew you'd understand. Thank you," Jane said, rising from the bench. "We will have a long talk this afternoon. Then I will tell you what needs to be done. Now I must talk to Sibelle."

"Of course," Alais answered, dark eyes alight with fervor and affection. "Go in to her. Hurry. We'll await your commands."

Jane gave the women a grateful smile. She hoped her shoulders weren't shaking too much with suppressed laughter as she crossed the bower to the bedroom.

Sibelle was still praying, head bent and hands clasped tightly.

Jane considered her thoughtfully. The girl was fifteen years old, and she'd seen how she looked at Stephan. There was more on her mind than God. Even if she didn't exactly know what it is. She said, "Lady Sibelle."

The girl looked up immediately. "Lady Jehane." She crossed herself, then sprang up, agile despite her bulk. She stood uncertainly, all of five feet one, covered in more layers of mismatched finery than Jane could count.

Jane studied the nervously waiting girl with a dressmaker's eye. How much bulk was there, really? Thirty pounds? Forty? Hard to say. She was fine-boned. Toning up a lot of unused muscle would help. Spring or summer coloring. Strong pastels would look good on her. The shades from modern dyes in the silks Jane had brought would suit Sibelle better than the natural fiber dyes of the period. But she wasn't going to worry about clothes yet. Attitude adjustment first, wardrobe later. A reward for good behavior.

"Let's sit and talk," Jane said. Most of the small bedroom was taken up by the wide bed. There was a big clothes chest at the foot of the bed, a narrow window seat and a short bench near the door. Jane seated herself on the chest while Sibelle chose the bench.

"Word came from Sturry this morning," Sibelle said abruptly. "My father still lives, though he's coughing up great gouts of blood. I was praying for his recovery."

"We will all pray for it," Jane replied. "You're a dutiful child, Sibelle."

"My father's wish was for me to spend my life in prayer."

"I see. When did you enter Davington?"

Sibelle's fingers twitched, as though she were using them to count the years. "I was seven." Her expression brightened with fond memory. "I was sent to keep my granny Rosamunde company. She was very old, and a very great lady. She had such wonderful stories to tell." She bent her head and sighed. "While she lived I was happy. Then there was nothing but prayer."

"Which you're very good at," Jane commended her. "Still . . ." Sibelle's head rose in curiosity. "Still," Jane went on. "You're not under your father's command anymore."

"No." The idea seemed to take Sibelle by terrified surprise. Hand to veiled throat, she whispered hoarsely, "Sir Stephan . . ."

Jane nodded. "You must please him in all things."

"I want to try!" The girl's big blue eyes were shining with adoration.

"I know what he wishes you to do. How he wishes you to behave when he returns."

"You do?" The girl sprang up from her seat. Holding her clasped hands out dramatically toward Jane, she vowed, "I will do anything you say!"

Maybe this was going to be easier than she had expected, Jane thought with relief. "Good." She patted the bench. Sibelle came and sat beside her. "What do you know of courtly love? Of the rules of chivalry in courts like Eleanor of Aquitaine's? Have you heard of the Courts of Love and the songs of the troubadours?"

"I know Granny didn't like Queen Eleanor," was Sibelle's answer.

Jane ignored the urge to ask why. "Sir Stephan has been tutored in the ways of the Courts of Love," she said. "He will have his wife trained in all things gentle and amusing. A court lady must be knowledgeable in all the arts of pleasure."

"Oh!" The girl's cheeks were covered in bright splashes of pink. Her naturally large eyes were so wide, Jane was afraid they were going to spill out of her head.

She continued despite the girl's shock. "Pleasure of the senses, my dear. Not just of the flesh. You must learn to take pleasure in music." She just hoped there was somebody who knew how to play a lute at Passfair. "In the needle and the table. You must learn to manage a household so that its master is constantly at his ease. You must learn the pleasures of riding and the hunt. Can you use a bow? Can you ride a horse?"

Sibelle shook her head at both questions. "I can weave. A little."

"Good. I've been meaning to have the loom repaired. As to riding and archery, you can learn. Raoul DeCorte and I will begin your lessons this very day." Thank God for Girl Scout Camp and Mom and the Medievalist Society.

"But . . ."

"Can you read? . . . No. Well, I don't think we have any books at Passfair anyway. I grew up listening to the great poets who came to the court of Jerusalem. I will tell you all about Arthur, and Tristan and Isolde, and the feats of Guillaume le Marechal."

"Granny had lots of stories about King Henry."

Good for her, thought Jane. "And in order to start your training in running the household, I wish to ask a favor of you."

"Yes?" Sibelle asked with eager fervor. "Whatever you wish."

"The lady of a manor should know about nursing the sick."

"Oh, yes," Sibelle agreed. "Easing the suffering of the ill is so important."

"I thought you might think so. That's how I need you to help me."

"To nurse the ill?"

"Oh, much more than that, my dear." Jane took the girl's hands in hers and pressed them affectionately. "Switha is very wise in the ways of herbs and cures and distilling medicines. She knows every healing root and grass and flower in the area. Her apprentice died in last winter's fever. She needs someone to pass her knowledge on to. Who better to know the healing arts than the lady everyone must turn to for kindness and charity?"

"Me?"

"You."

"Do you think I could learn to be a healer?"

She could certainly give it a shot. It would give the girl something useful to do with her life. A career rather than sitting home with an embroidery hoop while waiting for Stephan to put in an appearance. More important, Switha had already agreed to run Sibelle's buns off over every inch of hill and dale in the neighborhood. Nice, healthy, hard exercise combined with a practical education.

"Of course you can do it," Jane enthused. "You must listen to Switha very carefully and do everything she tells you. Remember that she is your teacher and not just a peasant woman."

Sibelle blinked her big eyes in wonder. It seemed the idea of doing something besides praying her life away was sinking pleasantly into her consciousness. "I will work very hard. I promise."

Jane patted the girl's hands again. "I know you will. Now," she went on briskly. "There is one more thing I wished to consult you about. It's Lent, you know."

"Of course."

"Since we have no priests to care for our souls, I thought we might try to observe the season a bit more strictly than usual. To make up for the lack of spiritual guidance, you see."

Sibelle nodded slowly. "That might be wise."

"I'm glad you agree. I'm not thinking so much about services, since we can't have them anyway. I was thinking perhaps those of us at the high table should serve as an example of piety to those below. That we would limit our meals to small amounts of simple fare. And fast at least one day a week as well, of course."

"Fasting?" The girl sighed.

"For the sake of all our souls, my lady. I know how important the state of our souls must be to you."

"Yes. Yes, of course. When we fasted at Davington, Marguerite and Alais would sneak food to me. I knew it wasn't right, but I was sad and lonely. I prayed and prayed for a vocation, but the days were just so tedious and long. I will fast now. With you," she declared. "It will please the priests when they will hear our confessions again."

"I've already spoken to your women," Jane said.

"They will help you with everything. Now"—she stood, keeping hold of one of the girl's plump hands—"come along." She gave Sibelle a coaxing smile. "It's time for your first riding lesson."

11

It had been thirty-five days since Sir Stephan had absented himself from Passfair, Jane thought as she leaned against the paddock fence. She breathed in the warm smell of sun-heated straw with satisfaction. It was safe to say life at the castle had changed for the better in his absence. She chuckled. The kid didn't know what he was missing.

It was a beautiful day, a well and truly spring day. A groom was walking the horses she, Sibelle, and DeCorte had ridden in from the fields a few minutes before. She watched the animals' fluid movements with approval. Stephan certainly kept fine horseflesh. She was especially glad the sidesaddle hadn't been invented yet. Women could look forward to at least two hundred more years of riding astride when they got the chance to ride at all. The morning was getting on. She supposed she'd had enough of dallying in the shade of the stable and had better get herself off to her duties. It had been a good, brisk ride over the flowering countryside. The exhilaration of it left her full of energy for facing another busy day.

There were bluebells blossoming at the bottoms of the fenceposts. She plucked one, entranced by the beauty of the long row of tiny, purple-blue flowers as she walked through the outer bailey toward the guard's training area. Archery targets were set up at the far end of the grounds. A few apple trees in full bloom shaded the edge of the grounds. Marguerite was seated beneath one of the trees, her fingers busy with a piece of embroidery. The freshly planted herb garden was nearby as well. Sibelle had worked very hard to help Switha transplant the seedlings from spots all over the estate. Switha was skeptical about taking the plants from their natural settings, but Sibelle's idea was to see which would be able to stand the transition from the wild. Sibelle, it seemed, when given half a chance, was just brimming with ideas.

Right now Sibelle was standing next to the guard sergeant, her bow in one hand, watching with rapt attention as he showed her something. She was loyally applying herself to every task Jane set for her. She kept apologizing because she wasn't progressing as quickly with hunting skills as she did with gardening. Lady Sibelle, it turned out, was a bit nearsighted. DeCorte was patiently teaching her some tricks to help overcome the problem of not being able to see what she was aiming at. He seemed confident it could be done. Jane wished him luck. Luckily Sibelle didn't seem to be too nearsighted.

She had been nearsighted herself, unable even to wear contact lenses. It was lucky she'd had laser surgery just before she ended up in the thirteenth century. In fact, she'd only just returned from sick leave when the argument with Wolfe had occurred. She remembered the thick, clunky glasses she'd always worn before that. As a teenager she'd been so embarrassed, she'd go out on dates without them. Half the time she hadn't known what her boyfriends even looked like. As an adult she'd been more philosophical, but she'd always felt as if her real self had been hidden behind those glasses. And they certainly would have been difficult to explain in the Middle Ages.

As Sibelle raised her bow and took aim, Jane studied her figure critically. And smiled. Getting there. Definitely getting there. Sibelle was definitely tying her belt tighter. Her face was thinner, too. So were her hands. Getting muscle tone. She had to have lost ten or more pounds since this started, which was mostly Switha's doing. Switha had kept Sibelle busier than Jane had thought was possible. Jane's smile grew hopelessly fond. It was time to give Sibelle a treat.

She waved her bluebell like a magic wand before going, humming something Disneyish, into the castle to get some help with the fairy godmother bit. Alais, Berthild, and several other castle women were working on the household's spring issue of clothing in the bower. She commended them for their hard work, inspected a few seams like a good, dutiful chatelaine, and then shooed everyone out but Berthild and Alais. To them she gave orders to be carried out immediately. Having set things in motion, she hurried back outside happily.

When she spotted the tall, gold-haired figure looming over Sibelle, large hand on her delicate arm, an instant of pure terror shot through her. Her first thought was, *I was right!* The monster had come to spirit her darling lamb away! She belonged to Stephan. No landless knight would ever lay a finger on her for the sake of a barony. He wasn't going to have her! Not as long as she was chatelaine here.

She'd protect the girl with her life if she must! Adrenaline fueled, she ran as fast as her legs would carry her down the length of the outer bailey. Four pairs of curious eyes were turned on her as if she were mad by the time she came to a panting halt at Sibelle's side. Four pairs. Sibelle's, Daffyd's, DeCorte's, and Marguerite's. DeCorte and Marguerite, Jane realized belatedly. The sergeant of the guards and a fierce old mother dragon. It wasn't as if the girl were left alone and unprotected.

It didn't matter. She refused to be embarrassed. She didn't trust Daffyd ap Bleddyn. Especially not in the presence of a tender maiden. "What," she demanded between ragged breaths, "are . . . you . . . doing . . . here?"

His eyes laughed down at her. Every green glint in them sparkled with amusement. "I?" he questioned, hand touching his breast gently. "I, good Jehane FitzRose, was speaking to the lady of the manor. What were you doing, running like the hounds of hell were after you?" He smirked familiarly. "Did you miss me so badly?" He drew her hand up and kissed her palm.

"I didn't miss you at all!" Which wasn't true, exactly. Not that her uncontrollable dream life was any of his business. She snatched her tingling hand away. She'd tried not to think about him in weeks. But it seemed as if the man had haunted her from the first day she'd arrived at Passfair. She'd only been with him a few times, yet every encounter was more intimate, more exasperating. More . . . exciting. She'd fumed about him a lot, her imagination had run off on wild tangents when she wasn't keeping a firm grasp on it, but that wasn't the same as missing him. It was impossible to miss someone you didn't know and didn't want to know and knew it wasn't safe to know. She took a deep breath, mentally and physically. Calm down, woman!

She deliberately ignored him to speak to Sibelle. "Finish your lesson, then go to the bower. Alais is waiting for you. Sir Daffyd," she said after Sibelle nodded her acquiescence, "come with me." She marched purposefully away from the training ground, leading the disreputable knight toward the gate.

"I suggest you leave the girl alone," she told him as he matched his strides with hers. She had to look up to speak to him. So far he was the only man besides Sir Stephan she didn't tower over. It was almost refreshing to have someone to look up to.

For some reason he put his hand on her elbow. She tried to shake it off, but there was no budging those strong fingers. She didn't like being reminded of his size and strength, even if she enjoyed not feeling like a giant herself around him. She didn't like being close enough to catch his aroma of sweat mixed with lavender. She didn't like the way the light caught the wheat-and-honey highlights in his thick yellow hair.

"Go away," she said. "Please." She wasn't sure when they stopped walking and started standing very close, face to face.

"Should I let go of you first?" his deep, satiny voice questioned. He leaned closer, his breath brushing across her cheek. She caught the scent of cardamom.

Softly and seductively, he continued, "Or should I drag you off with me? To where, Lady Jehane? Some deep, moss-covered bank in the woods? Would you like that? To lie down with me somewhere soft and fragrant?"

Abruptly, before she could draw breath to answer, he jerked away from her. Before she even knew what her answer to his seductive suggestion would be, he took his hand away. He stepped back, his face gone distant and unreadable.

"My apologies," he said stiffly. "A small joke. I didn't mean to frighten you."

The hot, melting sensation running through her blood and stirring the secret parts of her had nothing to do with fear. Not much. His words sent cold after the heat. His hot and cold actions made no sense. Nothing he'd said made any sense. She struggled to get her equilibrium back. She discovered she hadn't stopped being angry with him. "You don't frighten me."

Which wasn't true. He did frighten her. Not with his size or the threat of violence in the warrior way he carried himself. He frightened her because she was attracted to him. How could she be attracted to this warrior? She knew she was and she didn't understand it. Was she mad? What was it that made her nurse a secret longing for this man when no macho jock from her own time ever held any appeal for her? Perhaps, she explained to herself, trying to ignore the sheer sensuality he exuded, it was because his being a soldier gave all that dangerous strength purpose. He was strong and he was purposeful, and, she reminded herself of the harsh reality, he was a mercenary. This was no time for her to start believing in chivalry herself. People like Stephan and Sibelle, with their secure places in the scheme of things, could afford to act out games of chivalry. She was a dependent, an outsider. She had to remain a realist. She didn't dare be attracted to anyone. She had to live her life alone. She had to play the role David Wolfe had exiled her to. David. Daffyd. She was bedeviled by men named David!

She had to play the religious widow, the nun. There was no other place for her, not at Passfair or in the years ahead. She dared not jeopardize her position with something as foolhardy as lust. Not for any man. Especially not a Welsh mercenary who would only use her to ease a momentary attack of passion.

"You're trembling," he pointed out. His hand cupped her cheek for a moment, then sprang away as though it were burned.

"It's the wind," she told him, though the breeze stirring her veil was gentle and warm.

"Of course. Your bruises have healed, I see."

"Yes."

"You're a beautiful woman, Jehane." His brows lifted sardonically. "Too beautiful for me, I think. You had better give yourself to God before some man snatches you away."

"God's waiting on the king," she answered tartly. She tried to stomp on the part of her that had latched happily on to his calling her beautiful. "What are you doing at Passfair?" she questioned. "Still chasing outlaws through Blean Forest?"

"We've hanged a few not too far from the castle," he responded. He seemed all business now. "The rest are elusive. I've come to ask DeCorte for a few men to help root out some more. There's a village I want to search and I need help."

"What village?"

"Lilydrake. Sir Hugh's gone to Normandy, so I thought I'd pay his holding a visit. Will you loan me the men?"

"Discuss it with DeCorte," she said. "You have my permission if he agrees. How many men does Sikes have?" She looked back toward the training ground. Sibelle was gone, so she started walking toward it, with Sir Daffyd by her side.

"About twenty, I think. There'd be less if Hugh didn't let them have the run of his lands. And all the while he protests he knows nothing of bandits in the area."

"So you only came on business?" she questioned, remembering his hand on Sibelle. The memory sent a hot shaft of jealousy through her, for just a moment. She denied the feeling and waited for his answer.

"And to see the Lady Sibelle."

It wasn't the answer she wanted. She wanted to shout for him to stay away from Sibelle, but not for her original protective reasons. "Oh?"

"I told you before, I needed to talk to her."

"About what?"

"A private matter." He set his jaw stubbornly, and she knew she'd get no more details from him. "You've done wonders with her," he conceded. "Or perhaps she wasn't as bad as I'd been told."

"A bit of both, I think," Jane responded. She stopped near the inner gate leading to the courtyard. "I'll leave you to speak to DeCorte."

He gave an acknowledging nod. She turned to leave, but his rich voice called her back. "Lady Jehane?"

Hearing him speak her name sent a shiver down

her spine. She turned, but didn't retrace the five steps or so she'd taken. "Yes?"

"I think you've won the wager."

She smiled. "So I have." She held out her palm. "Hand over the earring."

He tugged on the gold hoop in his ear. "Isn't it too worldly an ornament for a nun? Who'll see it beneath your veils? Actually," he went on, "I think it would be best for us to forget the wager ever happened. It was a joke, Lady Jehane. Nothing more."

He stood before her, all tall and muscular and handsome. He wasn't a young man. Sunlight shafted down on him, catching the harsh lines around his eyes and face, pointing out the small, intriguing crookedness at the bridge of his hawk nose.

A joke? As he stood there in his armor, most of his attention on chasing down outlaws, he was every inch the barbaric warrior. Completely alien. She still thought him the handsomest man she'd ever seen, and he was telling her his wanting her was nothing more than a joke.

She should be relieved.

It broke her heart.

"A joke. Of course." She tucked her cold hands neatly inside her sleeves. "A joke on my part as well. DeCorte just stepped out of the privy. I'm sure he can talk to you now."

She hoped fervently, as she tried to walk instead of run into the shelter of the thick walls of the castle, that she never saw Daffyd ap Bleddyn again.

12

"What did Sir Daffyd want to talk about?"
Jane demanded as she walked into the bower. She
stopped in her tracks, totally surprised at not only her
words, but the harshness with which she'd spoken.

Sibelle peered at her, round-eyed, over the length
of peach silk she was holding up to her face. "Sir
Daffyd," she said from behind the bunched-up veil of
material, "is a very strange man." She held the cloth
out before her, then spun around with delight, the
silk streaming airily behind her. "Wherever did you
get this beautiful cloth?"

"I brought it with me from Jerusalem." Jane took a
dozen calming breaths, then stepped forward carefully. There was material spread all over one side of the
bower. There was also a tub of hot, scented water
steaming next to the loom. She made her way to
Sibelle, mindful of both. Alais and Marguerite stood
by the window, while Berthild knelt on the floor, lovingly running her hands over the many-colored
mounds of cloth.

Gently she pried the peach material from Sibelle's hands. "Here, let's get you ready for your bath. I thought you'd be done by now. What do you mean, strange?"

"He asked me a great many questions about Davington Priory. May I have a kirtle of this?"

"Yes. We're going to make you several new costumes. Stephan will be very happy when he sees you dressed in summer silks, your hair unbound." She touched the girl's closely veiled head. "You do have hair under there, don't you?"

Sibelle giggled. "Of course I do. I've never worn my hair loose. At Davington—"

"You're a maiden. It's perfectly proper for a maiden to wear her hair loose about her shoulders. What did Sir Daffyd want to know about Davington?" Jane gently unfastened the veil from where it was pinned to the thick barbette chin strap. "Bring a comb, Berthild."

"About the women there," the girl answered. "He wanted to know if I knew where the older ones went when they were turned out. But I don't know."

"Oh." Baring the girl's head, she discovered that a pair of thick, greasy braids had been tucked up under the veil. "Perhaps we'd better wash it first." She began picking at hairpins. "Why would he be interested in the older nuns?"

"He said he was looking for a kinswoman he thought might have been at Davington. He said she would have been there for about fifteen years."

Marguerite came forward to help with the unbraiding. Jane stepped back and let Sibelle's woman finish the job. Sibelle's hair turned out to be nearly to her hips, of indeterminate color at present.

"Concern for a relative. I see. That's not so strange. Off with your clothes now."

"No. But when I told him the only Welshwomen who were at Davington came with my granny Rosamunde, he said his kinswoman wasn't Welsh. And when I spoke Welsh to him—I always spoke Welsh with granny Rosamunde—he didn't act as if he understood me. What sort of person doesn't speak his own language?" Sibelle inquired suspiciously. "He laughed and said it was my accent, and that he'd been among the Normans too long. I just think he's very strange." She didn't comment further, as Alais and Marguerite began lifting her voluminous dresses over her head.

When the girl was down to wearing only a thin, threadbare linen shift, Jane, who'd been standing out of the way and digesting Sibelle's comments about Sir Daffyd, took the opportunity to walk around the nearly naked girl.

Sibelle's head followed her as she moved. "I know I've lost weight," she said, smiling. "It helps with all the walking I have to do. My feet don't hurt all the time anymore."

"I'm glad you've lost weight," Jane told her, patting her shoulder affectionately. "Sir Stephan will be delighted."

Melisande and her half-grown pups wandered into the bower and began sniffing curiously at all the silk laid out on the floor. Berthild pushed them away, then gathered up the material in a heavy armful and carried it into the bedroom, firmly shutting the door on any intrusion by the deerhounds.

Sibelle looked at the tub full of water, then undid the strings fastening the neck of her undershift,

sighed like the bravest of martyrs, and let the shift fall
to the floor.

She still wasn't perfect, certainly, but her body
with its full breasts and girlish ungainliness was
showing promise at last. She was going to have a tiny
waist by the time Jane was through with her. Jane was
willing to bet her hips, even without the extra flesh,
were always going to be femininely rounded.

Jane helped her step into the tub. Her women proceeded to bathe her thoroughly and wash her hair
while Jane went to pick out a bolt of silk to start the
first dress with. Sounds of splashing and laughter
came from the bower.

She was pleased with the girl's enjoyment but also
felt detached from the activity. For some reason a
wave of homesickness was washing over her. Maybe
it was just touching the silk. The weave of the cloth
felt foreign to her, very different from the hand-
loomed cloth she'd been helping the women work
with for the household clothes. Maybe it was brought
on by the sudden craving for a taste of popcorn.

"Or angel hair pasta with alfredo sauce," she murmured with whimsical longing. "Where are Columbus
and Marco Polo when you need them?"

Maybe it was Sibelle's curiosity about Daffyd ap
Bleddyn's not remembering his native language.
Maybe he wasn't what he claimed. She understood
about people not being what they claimed. She
wouldn't put it past him to really be some peasant
boy who'd stolen a dead knight's armor and identity
so he could make his own way in the world. She
didn't blame him for that; the higher on the food
chain, the better the chance of survival.

Maybe it was her own language she missed, the

knowledge that if she spoke English there was no one in the world who would understand what she said. Not even the Saxons down in the village would be able to make out more than a few English words. Maybe none; she was having trouble learning their dialect.

She could hardly manage to think English anymore, she admitted. Someday she was just going to forget about it altogether. Jane Florian didn't exist. There was only Jehane FitzRose left. Perhaps it was better if she didn't think about home. This was the place where she had to survive. But she did miss a place where she was able to live with her own identity, on her own terms. A place where she was in control of her life. She missed that more than she did coffee.

She didn't cry. She did stand for a while with her fists clenched so tight the nails dug into the palms of her hands. She didn't know how long she remained in this tense position, but by the time the sad mood passed and she came back into the bower, Sibelle was finished with her bath.

The girl was dressed in a fresh shift, standing before the window, while Marguerite worked diligently at combing out her long hair. It was drying quickly in the spring breeze wafting into the bower, stirring gently about her head in soft, honey-gold tresses.

Jane felt a slow grin lift her features. Pleased amusement lightened her heavy heart. The diet and the cute little button nose and the big blue eyes were all irrelevant. Once Stephan got a look at that hair, he'd be hooked. Blond. Honey. Apricot. Gold. Men went for the blondes every time.

She gave a wicked little laugh. *Stephen, my boy, just wait until you see what I've got waiting for you. Frankly, you don't deserve her. Bring home a dragon carcass immediately, then we'll talk terms.*

She came forward and took the girl affectionately by the shoulders. "Sibelle, my dear, you are beautiful. Such hair!"

Sibelle leaned forward into her embrace. She whispered confidentially into Jane's ear, "Granny Rosamunde said I got it from my great-grandfather Geoffrey. His grandmother was a witch. That's why I don't mind learning from Switha. It's in the blood." She kissed Jane on the cheek, and asked, "May we make a kirtle now?"

Jane was delighted to do some sewing. Never mind if the sewing machine wouldn't be invented for hundreds of years. She didn't need a sewing machine; she had a household full of women with busy fingers willing to work to her direction. She drew designs with charcoal on the bower walls, measured with knotted string, cut with primitive scissors that she kept having to send back to the blacksmith for sharpening.

They cut out and sewed three new combinations of lightweight summer shifts and overdresses in peach and salmon and apple green for Sibelle. For herself Jane made summer overdresses in royal blue and bright yellow. The stronger colors suited her dark complexion. Her face was tanning quickly to a bronzed glow from no more than the lightest exposure to the spring sun.

When the dresses were done, Jane brought out some of the embroidery thread in her bags. The women were as amazed by the jewel-bright colors and varied textures as they'd been with the silk cloth.

They were enthralled by the wonders and marvels brought from the paynim East. She handed out multiple skeins of perle cotton thread, and busy fingers set to work once more.

One afternoon, as the sun grew long through the high bower window, she and Sibelle sat together, sharing the width of the round, floor-stand embroidery hoop as they worked on different sections of skirt decoration.

Into the companionable silence, Sibelle suddenly asked a question. "What will you do with all the goods in your bags? Other than make dresses for me?"

"For which you may repay me with many thanks when you're baroness of Sturry," Jane replied, needle poised thoughtfully as she tried to remember if the chevron stitch she'd just blithely taught Sibelle was in use yet. She decided it was too late to worry about it now and went on embroidering.

"I will indeed."

"Good."

"About the other goods?"

She stuck needle in cloth and looked at the girl. Sibelle's eyes twinkled with amusement. She'd lost more weight, and it was showing in her face. Her cleft chin was becoming a prominent and attractive feature; cheekbones were starting to emerge, adding a hint of elegance. Her hair was hanging in two thick braids, the ends covered in embroidered casings Jane had finished just the day before. She'd added a few garnet beads to the pattern worked onto linen-backed silk and was satisfied the girl was dressed in the height of the era's fashion. She just wished Stephan would come home so he could appreciate it. And she was glad Sir Daffyd hadn't paid a visit to Passfair lately so he couldn't. She'd asked DeCorte to keep track of any news of the Welshman. She had Sibelle's welfare to think of. Never mind her own.

"Well?" Sibelle asked after a considerable silence from Jane.

"What am I going to do with my goods? I'm not sure."

"You've spices and jewels and gold besides the silk. I'm sorry I looked, but I was curious. And you don't lock the room. You're very trusting."

"The key's lost, and the blacksmith hasn't made a new one yet."

"Oh. But what will you do with it all? Did you bring it all from Jerusalem? Why?"

"Yes, I brought it with me from the Holy Land. We had no more wealth in land, but my husband and father left me with wealth in rare and precious things. I have no idea what to do with them. Trade them for gold somehow, I suppose. Use the gold to pay my entrance into a convent."

Sibelle nodded her agreement with this strategy. "But you need merchants in order to trade. Merchants come from London to Canterbury. And traders come to Dover and to Reculver on the coasts. We need a way to make them all come here." She smiled brightly. "We could hold a fair."

"A fair?"

"All the big towns have summer fairs," Sibelle pointed out enthusiastically. "If we had a fair here, and did it every year, Passfair could become a big town as well. Which would make Sir Stephan far more prosperous, and that would be good for everyone."

Jane sat back on the bench, leaning against the cool stone wall. "A fair?"

"It could be arranged," Sibelle said with confidence. "It wouldn't take long to send word to Canterbury. Or to Dover and Reculver. If the traveling merchants know there's nobles—Sturry and Passfair and Blackchurch for certain—looking for fine goods, they could be persuaded to come. And Sir Daffyd's soldiers would come also if there were wine and weapons merchants."

"Who have you been talking to?" Jane asked, looking at the girl through narrowed eyes.

"Bertram."

"I thought so." She tugged thoughtfully on her veil. It wasn't a bad idea. Not a bad idea at all. It would be good for the villages. Why not bring modern commerce and culture to this little corner of Kent?

"Very well," she agreed. She stood and straightened her dress. "We'll see if we can arrange it for sometime this summer."

Sibelle gave a complacent nod. "Bertram has it all planned out."

"I'm sure he does." Jane had great faith in Bertram. "He and I had better talk right away."

13

"Why, today of all days, did I have to fall off my horse!" Sibelle complained from the grassy spot where she'd tumbled. Her horse, probably more surprised by the girl's sudden fall than she was, had shied over to the far side of the orchard. It remained there, peering at them almost accusingly, as Jane and the groom helped Sibelle to her feet.

"Are you all right?" Jane asked, patting the girl for signs of broken bones.

"I don't understand how it happened," Sibelle went on as if she hadn't heard Jane. "Perhaps I wasn't paying proper attention. I suppose my mind was on the fair. It's such a lovely day for it. The merchants' tents and carts look so bright and colorful spread out across the pasture. I must have forgotten what I was doing."

"Are you all right?" Jane repeated the question louder.

"Oh, yes. Ow! No. I must have twisted my foot under me." Sibelle let out a dramatic wail. "I will not miss the fair! Jehane, you mustn't tell Alais and Marguerite! If they think I've been hurt, they won't let me go to the fair. You know what they're like. We can sneak off to the fair now and—"

"The merchants haven't even set up their wares yet, love," Jane answered. "It's barely dawn." She knelt in the grass while the groom helped steady Sibelle. "How bad does it hurt?"

"Not at all. Don't touch that! Hardly at all."

"A bit of swelling. Can you walk?"

"Of course."

"Well, try."

"You're so demanding."

Jane raised her eyes to see laughter mixed with pain on the girl's face. Sibelle was very changed from the frightened girl Stephan had brought home only two months before. Jane really couldn't see any of the old Sibelle in the svelte, shining-haired, good-natured young woman who now shared her days.

"It's not so bad," she told her. "You'll make it to the fair. Go back to your room for a while and soak your ankle in cold water. That should take care of most of the swelling and soreness. By this afternoon you'll be able to come down to the pasture. I could send the merchants up to the castle with their best wares if necessary, but it wouldn't be as much fun. Not on such a nice day."

Sibelle's eyes were alight with inspiration. "Couldn't I have the peasants carry me from booth to booth in a chair?"

"You could, but you'd look damned silly." Jane rose to her feet. "Fetch the horse," she directed the boy. "Lean on me for a moment, dear. The fair will be there tomorrow, too, you know," she reminded Sibelle, just in case the muscle strain proved to be worse than she thought.

"I will be there today," Sibelle declared stubbornly. "I will rest this morning, though the waiting will be awful." She sighed dramatically, complaining as the groom returned with the horse, "I've never been anywhere or done anything, Jehane." The boy lifted her up, and she grasped the reins firmly. "What's it like to have adventures?"

Jane stood among the sweet-scented boughs of the apple orchard and looked at the girl in crossed-armed consternation. "Ask Sir Stephan," she advised.

"But you've seen so much of the world. What's it like?"

"Uncomfortable. I think I've told you too many romances," she added, a smile softening her lips. She patted Sibelle's mount's flank. "Go home and soak your foot. I'll see you at the fair."

"All right." The girl turned the horse's head, and she and the groom rode off.

Jane remounted and rode slowly toward the village. It was a long time before she could get to the fair as well. She wanted a new fence built for the paddock, so she had to talk to Cerdic this morning about having some straight young timber felled from the coppice.

"Why," she wondered aloud to the birds and beasts of the field, "is there always something else that needs doing?" She made her trip to the village, where Cerdic was as eager as she was to get the details taken care of so they could get on with enjoying the holiday on this bright late-April morning.

Riding back along the track leading up the hill, she

passed the pasture wedged between woods and castle and village where a tent and timber village had sprung up overnight. The merchants and traveling entertainers had actually been arriving for three days, though in fact there were only half a dozen traders, two jugglers, a seedy minstrel, and a couple of lady friends who traveled with the minstrel. Not much, really, as culture and commerce went.

But not bad for only a month's preparation, Jane congratulated herself.

Back in the castle courtyard, she turned the horse over to the waiting groom and hurried up to her room. It was the full light of day, and everyone from Passfair and Hwit and other outlying areas were gathering in the pasture below.

Jane had carefully selected a few of her precious possessions to offer the merchants the night before: some spices and strings of freshwater pearls and lapis. She was beginning to have an idea of what to do with her wealth, but she wanted to get to know the men she traded with before making any concrete plans.

She took her small bundle in hand, said, "Come along, Berthild," and left the castle with the red-haired girl, this time on foot.

On the walk down the hill she considered her plan, hoping it wouldn't be too complicated to pull off. She'd spent a great deal of time thinking about the possibilities life might have to offer her.

For the sake of preserving this society, Jane knew she had to live apart from it. The only acceptable seclusion where she would be safe and fed and completely anonymous would be as just one more of a group of black-dressed, praying women. She hated her fate but accepted its necessity. Gradually, however, she'd come to the conclusion that she held the power in her hands to make this fate far more pleasant than the dreary life she'd first envisioned. It had nothing to do with a sudden discovery of faith. It had a lot to do with remembering Wolfe had sent her back here with a great deal of wealth.

She couldn't think of anything more proper and acceptable in this religious age than for a rich widow to found her own order of nuns. It was only right for her then to administer the order as the abbess of the establishment she founded. An abbess was law unto herself in her own house.

If she had to live by the rules of the order, she reasoned, she wanted to be the one who made them up. An elegant solution to a tricky problem.

All she had to do was get permission from whatever bishop first poked his head up after the interdict was lifted, get herself some land, get some peasants to work the land, build the abbey, and get herself some volunteers. She could name it Saint Elizabeth's, after Mom. Or perhaps Our Lady of West Point. No, she didn't think a militant order of nuns would be quite the right approach. Too bad there weren't any teaching or nursing orders yet. Doing something useful would have been a nice way to pass the time.

The pasture was bustling with every inhabitant of the nearby villages by the time she and Berthild arrived. It was not just the traveling merchants with products to show; local people were busy trading their own wares. Someone was selling little dried fruit pies. A vintner was hawking ale, while his partner was dickering with the cooks from Passfair and Sturry over the price of his better wines. Children and young people were gathered around the entertainers. Groups of men clustered together discussing the weather and the crops and the sad state of the world. It was quite a turnout. She estimated at least seventy people spread out among the carts and tents and tables.

Seventy people, Jane thought as she walked with Berthild from one merchant's stand to the next. She stopped to finger some moss-green muslinlike fabric at the cloth merchants. She bought a length of it, secretly planning on making a new dress for the red-haired Berthild.

The silversmith from London said he'd brought only his third-best wares to this tiny fair. She showed her string of freshwater pearls to the jeweler, got his opinion and an asking price, smiled prettily, and moved on.

She'd worked her way to the edge of the pasture where the potter was showing dishes with pretty blue glazing. She picked up one of the larger pots. Its texture and substantial weight felt good in her hands. She was turning to call to Berthild, who was lingering to haggle over a string of glass beads, when she saw the group of men emerging from between the trees. She thought nothing of it for a moment, assuming they were just some more villagers come to enjoy a day's holiday. She opened her mouth to call her servant but voiced no sound as the sudden tension in the air registered on her mind. Where there had been much talk and laughter only a moment ago, suddenly there was silence.

Then she noticed there must be at least twenty hard-faced, filthy strangers spreading out in a long line as if to circle the encampment. They were moving at a swift lope now, long bows slung across wide backs, staffs, rusty broadswords, and sharp daggers held poised and ready. For a long instant the stunned crowd remained paralyzed, staring in frightened silence while the bandits bore down on them.

Then a woman's shrill scream pierced the air. Someone yelled, "Outlaws!"

There were castle guards patrolling the fair, of course. They rushed forward to meet the advancing outlaws, forming a thin shell of protection as the villagers began running from the attack. But there were only five guards. And although they were trained and well armed, they were only five against at least twenty. The rest of Passfair's men were still at the castle. The king's guard from Reculver was expected but hadn't yet put in an appearance. The five castle swordsmen didn't slow the armed and vicious attackers for long.

Jane watched the fight. She had no weapon, she had no training, and she was terrified, but she just couldn't bring herself to run away. People milled around her. She was responsible for them.

She grabbed a woman by the shoulders, ordered, "To the castle," and pushed her toward the hill. The woman snatched up a child and ran, calling other folk to join her.

There was a deafening crash as one of the merchant carts was turned on its side. Several of the outlaws began pawing through the remains. A woman cried out as she was pulled to the ground. The air was filled with screams and begging and the iron smell of blood. The last of the guards went down with a trio of arrows in his stomach. Jane saw a flash of red hair and Berthild's flailing arms and legs as the girl was grabbed around the waist by a big man with filthy yellow braids. She started to run forward to help the girl but was cut off by a pair of leering outlaws, both with daggers clutched in bloodstained hands. She registered greasy hair, grime-encrusted features, hungry, pitiless eyes.

One of the men lunged forward to grab her, and Jane danced backward out of his reach. The other moved closer. She threw the heavy blue pot in her hands at his head. She turned and ran, hearing a crash and cry behind her. She also heard the other one hot on her heels.

She ran up the hill, her heart racing, her fear laced with revulsion as she caught the heavy reeking odor of the man so close behind her. Her legs pumped. Suddenly every steep step of the hill track seemed unfamiliar, the footing uncertain. She gave one quick glance up at the castle, caught a glimpse of the gate. There were castle men there, guarding the entrance and helping the steady stream of visitors inside. Archers were perched up on the wall, ready to shoot at any invader coming too near. She caught a flash of peach and gold: Sibelle was up on the wall with a bow, ready to defend her land and people.

Jane ran harder, hoping to get within arrowshot of the castle before the man behind her dragged her down. She felt the rush of air as he reached for her. She ran harder, feeling her breath sobbing, her ribs and calf muscles aching from the effort at speed.

She felt the man's breath. He laughed in her ear. So close. His hands grabbed again, snatching a handful of silk, pulling her backward, pushing her down.

She writhed on the ground beneath him, frantic to get away. She tore and clawed and kicked, actions driven by blind panic. He laughed. Laughed and brought his filthy mouth down hungrily on hers. She screamed and tasted blood from her own cut lips. He held her down, ripping away her silken dress. His hands moved obscenely over her half-naked body.

She prayed and cursed as his laughter and grunting sounded in her ears. Her head pounded and the earth beneath her pounded, shaking like the strong hoofbeats of a charging horse.

The outlaw's hand moved roughly between her legs, prying them brutally apart. She opened her mouth and screamed again, continuing to scream as the man was pulled backward. Off her and onto the ground.

The outlaw lunged forward with his dagger. A booted foot kicked it out of his hand. Jane climbed to her knees. Her eyes registered chain mail, an arrogant, hawk-nosed face beneath a conical iron helmet. Chain mail. A sword held tightly in a large gloved hand. A gray horse breathing heavily somewhere in the background. Daffyd ap Bleddyn.

The outlaw sprang up off the ground, attacking the knight barehanded. Daffyd ap Bleddyn, his face cold as death, smiled just a little and gutted him.

The man died holding his insides in his hands. Daffyd turned to her without a backward glance at the man he'd killed.

14

Jane was on her hands and knees, retching uncontrollably, when Daffyd ap Bleddyn reached her. She looked up at him. The horrible smile was gone, but his eyes as they swept over her were hard and intense. He had put away his sword and was reaching for her with gloved hands.

She screamed and slithered backward, still on hands and knees. "Don't touch me!"

He came closer. She tried to rise, tripped on her torn skirt, and rolled farther down the hill.

She had to get up! She wasn't that far from the gate. She had to run before he touched her. But her limbs wouldn't obey her. There was a sharp pain in her side. She clutched at it, trying once more to find her feet. She made it this time. She struggled to run up the rutted hill track.

The gray horse loomed up in front of her, its dangerous hooves flashing near her head as she stumbled, almost falling into the animal's path. She screamed, just barely recovering her balance. The horse was too close. The man's shadow fell over her. He leaned from the saddle, reaching with a muscular arm. He grabbed her around the waist, hauling her up before him.

Jane tried to pull away, but she was quickly pressed to his chest, her arms pinioned. He said something. The words were soft but they were just sounds to her, drowned out by the screams and laughter filling her mind. He smelled of blood. Her bare flesh was pressed to unyielding armor. She squeezed her eyes shut, all fight going out of her. He held her tightly, urging the horse forward. She held on, her fingers digging into the heavy iron mesh covering his shoulders, sobs shaking her.

There was more shouting, and the sound of running feet. Jane ducked her head lower, trying to hide, to curl up into a tiny ball. But she was caught in the man's iron grip. There were more hands, and voices. She was pried away from the man and lowered to the ground. So many hands touching her!

"How badly is she hurt?"

"I don't know! She's hysterical. Someone get her inside!"

"Did the bastard . . . ?"

"He didn't have the time. Care for her. What about the others?"

"Where were you and your men? This wouldn't have happened if you—"

"We were stopped on the road by a messenger from the king. I'm sorry. My men are still chasing the bastards. I've got to go."

There was a loud clattering of hooves. Many voices surrounded her, some warm and soothing. Jane latched on to the comforting sounds. She was wrapped in some rough cloth, helped to walk. There were stairs, then a bed. Wonderfully cool, wet cloths washed her. A cup was held to her lips; its warm contents smelled of chamomile.

Jane opened her eyes, recognized Switha bending toward her, holding the cup to her lips. Beyond Switha was Sibelle. Marguerite stood gravely in the doorway, the alcove curtain held back with one hand.

"Berthild?" Jane asked.

Switha just shook her head. A look passed between her and Sibelle. "Drink," the wisewoman urged.

Jane opened her mouth and gulped the liquid down. She dropped her head back on the pillow and closed her eyes once more.

When she woke it was night, but a lamp had been left burning, placed on a small upturned wine cask. The familiar weighty warmth of the dogs surrounded her feet. The panic was gone. She knew she could think if she wanted to. But she didn't want to think. She didn't want to be alone. She didn't want anyone near her, either. She knew she never wanted to stir from what little safety this place offered. She hurt. She was bruised all over, outside and in. The whole world was tainted with fear.

She didn't want to remember. She couldn't help but remember.

In her memory it all happened slowly. Especially the laughter, and the screams both distant and her own. She fell asleep again to the memory of screams.

She woke next at the sound of footsteps moving closer. She heard the chink of mail. Terror was like bile in her mouth as her hand flew under her pillow. The curtain was shoved aside. She kept her eyes on

Daffyd ap Bleddyn as he walked softly into the room.
His face wore the mask of a smile. She stiffened with
fear, waiting without moving as he bent over her.

Before he knew what was happening she had a
handful of his soft, golden hair twisted in her fist. She
pressed the sharp tip of her dagger into the unprotected flesh at the base of his exposed throat.

"Don't touch me!" she hissed.

The man lifted his hands out at his side. He spoke
quietly, his deep chocolate-and-cream voice infinitely
reasonable. "I won't touch you."

He moved his head slowly, pulling against the
pressure on his hair. He managed to bend his head far
enough so they were gazing eye to eye. He ignored the
dagger point even though a tiny line of blood trickled
from the mark where it punctured his skin.

"You don't have to be frightened," he reassured
her. "The man who hurt you is dead."

"I've had enough," she told him. "I want to go
home."

"You can't," he said. "Jerusalem's a very long way
away. You're safe now. Safe here. This is your home,
Jehane."

He couldn't understand.

"What are you doing here?" He wasn't going to
touch her. She wasn't going to let any man touch her.
Never again.

"I was concerned, my lady. I wanted to make sure
you were all right. You're obviously still upset."

She almost laughed. How could she possibly ever
laugh again? But it was funny to hear a man she was
holding at knifepoint calmly tell her she was "upset."

"Yes. Smile," he urged. "It's good for you."

She hadn't seen his hands moving, very slowly.

She'd been looking into his eyes. Strong fingers suddenly clamped onto her wrist, pulling it down and away. A quick twist and the knife was in his hand now. Daffyd jerked his head back, freeing his hair from her loosened grip.

He stood and handed the dagger to her, hilt first. "Very wise to keep this within reach," he commended her. He touched his throat. "But I prefer some small expression of gratitude to a death threat." It was a gently spoken, though sardonic, reminder that he'd saved her life.

Jane's eyes suddenly filled with tears. She wasn't sure she had anything to be grateful about.

"It's all right," he soothed from the distance of the doorway. "You're not ready to talk to anyone yet. The man who attacked you," he went on anyway, "was named Pwyll. One of the leaders of the outlaws."

"I don't want to know his name!"

She didn't want to give that animal an identity. She didn't want to talk. She didn't want to think. Pwyll. She'd heard many stories about Pwyll since arriving at Passfair. The peasants feared him more than they did Sikes, the outlaw leader. Pwyll's temper was unpredictable. He preferred torture and killing to simple robbery. It was said he hated the Normans for killing his own wife and children, that he had a reason for hating.

He'd so enjoyed taking his hatred out on her.

Her stomach lurched painfully. The drink Switha had made her swallow came up out of her stomach. Daffyd was holding her head when she stopped vomiting. He wiped her mouth with a cloth.

"It's all right," he soothed. "You're strong, Jehane. You're going to be all right. You're never going to be quite the same, but you will be all right." He moved back by the doorway.

She was beginning to feel something other than fear and the memory of fear. Remembering the stories about Pwyll reminded her of the people who'd told them to her. "The village?" she asked. "How many were hurt?"

"The five guards were killed, two others besides."

"I'm sorry."

"The merchants lost most of their goods. I don't think there'll be a fair here next year."

"What happened to Berthild?" she wanted to know. "My maid," she added in case he didn't know the serving woman's name.

"Switha's sister?" He gave a curt shake of his head. "They took her with them."

"No. Oh, no." The words came out a tired whisper. "You have to find her."

Daffyd ran his hands through his shoulder-length hair. He looked tired. "When I find their camp, I'll find her. I hope. But I can't mount a massive search for one peasant woman. If I could . . ." He gave a fatalistic shrug. "That's not the way the world is run, Lady Jehane."

"You won't look for her?"

"It's no use."

His flat-out refusal infuriated her. No, of course that wasn't the way the world worked. He wouldn't do anything. She couldn't. Chatelaine she might be, but DeCorte would laugh at her if she tried to get his men to search the forest for one village girl who'd been dragged off to serve the lusts of an outlaw band. What difference did it make? There were plenty more peasant girls where she came from.

No one had any value if they weren't born into the noble class. Nobody cared about the life of one expendable peasant woman. She looked at Sir Daffyd with loathing, hating him and all his kind.

She didn't argue. She wanted to, but she couldn't find any words. The ones she knew, like equality, and justice for all, might be known to him. But her meaning and his would not be the same. She wanted to shout and to rage and to defend Berthild's rights. But the man was an alien. Their minds simply couldn't touch. His comprehension was so different from hers that it might have been easier for her to communicate with a being from another galaxy. Too much time and change separated them.

She didn't say anything to him. She just lay down and turned her back to the door. The dogs had gone away while she'd slept. She missed their warmth and companionship. She heard Daffyd as he stood in the doorway for a while, his breathing, the soft *shoosh*-ing of surcoat rubbing against chain mail. She could almost feel his eyes studying her. She ignored everything. Eventually he went away. Yet when he was gone, she wanted to call him back.

She sobbed into the pillow—crying for herself and Berthild, and the world she'd never see again and the world where she'd thought she could belong but never really could—until eventually she cried herself to sleep.

15

By dawn, Jane felt better. Or at least able to cope. She didn't want to be alone anymore. By mid-morning she worked up the courage to dress and step from the alcove to the storage room. She moved slowly, stiff with bruises. Her awareness was a fragile thing. She felt insubstantial as a soap bubble. Or trapped behind a wall of glass, perhaps.

A woman who was not Berthild was waiting for her, seated patiently on the sleeping pallet. She stood when Jane came around the curtain. Jane ignored her. The woman dutifully followed her down to the hall.

Sibelle came to her as she approached the hearth. The girl's face had changed since yesterday. There was more strength there than Jane remembered seeing before. She flinched as Sibelle's arms came around her but appreciated the warm embrace and returned it after a moment.

"I was so worried," Sibelle told her. "But Switha said it was best to give you time alone. That you would come to us when you were ready."

"Switha was right," Jane acknowledged tiredly.

"You don't look well."

"I'm better."

Sibelle crossed herself. "At least you're alive. We buried the dead this morning." She gave a sad shake of her head, and her braids swung gently. "We're going to have to pray very hard for an increase in births to rebuild our hearts and our losses. Come." She lead Jane to a chair. "Rest today. I will deal with what has to be done."

Jane didn't argue. She didn't care. Passfair could fall down around her ears and she wouldn't care. Her new servant brought some sewing and took a seat on the floor beside her. Bertram came in from the pantry. He and Sibelle went off together. Other people came and went about their duties. No one paid much attention to her. Jane watched, feeling as though she weren't really there. She tried to pretend she was back at the Time Search Project, observing with equipment that provided video instead of the energy readings she'd painstakingly learned to interpret.

After several hours the hall began to seem small to her. It was a cloudy day outside, the light coming in the narrow windows above the table was thin and uneven. She found herself wanting to instruct the lights to turn on. Her lips twisted in a sour smile: in her up-to-date town house, talking to the appliances was standard operating procedure. Here telling the light to shine was blasphemy. Possibly witchcraft, if it actually worked. Or a miracle if the situation was politically correct.

I want out. She squeezed her eyes shut hard in

frustration, hands bunching into fists. *I want out so bad!*

She'd been resigned. She'd been content. She'd played happy housekeeper and fairy godmother and fooled herself into thinking she belonged in this horrible place. Well, yesterday reality had reminded her of just what was really going on here. She wanted out.

She got up and walked out of the hall.

It was better in the open space of the courtyard. She stood on the castle steps, drinking in great gulps of mist-laden air. Much better. The cool breeze was reviving. The world out here was alive. Full of everyday sights and sounds. There was smoke coming from smithy and kitchen. Children were playing near the gate, lunging back and forth, using sticks as swords. The goosegirl was chasing after her charges. They'd somehow strayed as far as the inner bailey this time. Her little brother was toddling after the geese while she kept calling for him and them to go home. It was nice to know the children were all right. It was good to hear their shouts and laughter. They were so *alive*.

The adults she saw went more somberly about their duties, but no one seemed to be hiding away today but her.

She walked away from the castle, down the hill to the village, passing guards patrolling near the gate. Along the way she deliberately stopped at the spot where she thought she'd been attacked. Rain had washed away any hint of bloodstains. She didn't want to know what had happened to the body. She did kick at a muddy clod of earth.

"It's over," she told herself. "It happened. Don't let it haunt you. You can't let it haunt you if you're going to survive. The people here live with disaster, day in, day out. Maybe they're stronger than you. Learn from them."

The feeling of being an observer lingered. She didn't know if or when it would fade. She knew there was nothing she could do but go on. So she straightened her spine, tried to put confidence in her walk, and went down into the village. She spoke to no one, disturbed none of the women working near the huts, but she was very glad to see them. Glad they were alive and unharmed. She made a quick tour of the village, then headed back up the hill.

The guards at the outer gate were peering attentively into the distance as she finished the climb. "What?" she asked. Fear grabbed at her, but she pushed it back. Turning, she looked where one was pointing.

"Riders," he said, though she could clearly see the line of horsemen from this vantage point. One of the men disappeared. A minute later Raoul DeCorte was at the gate, and a group of archers were on the platforms at the top of the wall. Jane was relieved to see the precautions being taken since yesterday's attack.

Not that they mattered, of course. By now the big black stallion and tall, thin rider leading the line of horsemen were clearly recognizable. It seemed that without word, without warning, Sir Stephan DuVrai was coming home.

DeCorte went forward to meet his liege before he reached the gate. Jane followed after. She scanned the group of riders. Stephan had left with only a groom and a few guards. He'd returned with a few extra people in tow. Several servant types were bringing up the rear of the column. Up front, riding abreast with

Stephan, were two well-dressed strangers.

One was a scrawny boy of about ten, with a round face and masses of brown curls, straddling a horse someone had probably told him he'd grow into. He was looking about him with a combination of curiosity and eagerness. His gaze kept returning expectantly to Sir Stephan. She guessed Sir Stephan was bringing home some noble's son to train as his squire. The other new arrival sat his horse with long-limbed ease. His yellow hair was cut unfashionably short. A sky-blue, hooded tunic covered a powerful form. A well-worn broadsword sheath hung across his saddlebow, and one arm supported a round, crested shield. The device on the shield was of a mailed hand grasping a gold ball. Their eyes met, and he gave Jane a pleasant smile. She quickly focused her attention on Sir Stephan.

Stephan's dark eyes took in the guards and the tensely waiting DeCorte. He got down from the stallion. "What news?" he asked, towering over his guard sergeant.

Jane tucked her hands in her sleeve, grasping her elbows tightly, as DeCorte explained about the fair and the outlaw attack.

The young man's fine, pale skin flushed with anger as the story unfolded. "Such pickings were bound to draw the brigands out," Stephan pointed out. "Why only five guards on patrol?"

DeCorte ran a hand through his short gray hair. "Three of my men were hunting poachers who've been taking deer in the forest. I didn't want to leave the castle defenses short of men."

"Quite right," Stephan acknowledged with a short

nod. "What about Sturry? And where was the Welsh Wolf and his men?"

"The patrol from Reculver was delayed by a messenger," DeCorte explained. He went on to add a part of the story new to Jane. "Sir Daffyd returned after chasing the outlaws until nightfall. He had news of Sturry's men. They were waylaid at Stourford. Riders set on them at the river crossing. They drove the attackers off, but turned back to Sturry Castle with their wounded. The riders wore no device, but Sir Daffyd assumes they were from Lilydrake."

"A diversion while the outlaws attacked the town?"

"Just so, my lord."

Stephan rubbed his long jaw, which was stubbled with a day's growth of dark beard. His wide mouth was set in a hard line. "With Hugh getting a share of the spoils? I should have killed the man the last time we met."

DeCorte nodded. "The castle," he went on, "was never in danger. It was Lady Sibelle who first noticed the outlaws. She was just going down to the fair, but ran back with word of the attack. Ran like the wind despite having hurt her foot earlier in the day," DeCorte added for emphasis.

Stephan looked at the guard sergeant in astonishment. "Lady Sibelle? My Lady Sibelle?"

"Yes, my lord. It was the lass who got the archers up to the walls as soon as we knew there was trouble. And she was up on the walls with us," he went on, praising the girl enthusiastically. "She's turning into a fine archer. And fierce in protection of her lord's lands," he concluded, throwing a quick, conspiratorial glance Jane's way.

She was grateful for the sergeant's fervent praise of the lady. Stephan clearly didn't know what to make of DeCorte's words. Instead he turned to her. "I'm glad to see you well."

"Thank you." She thought it was better not to tell him she was anything but well. Besides, how could she be completely unwell when a smile was threatening to erupt at the consternation she saw on Stephan's face?

The lad and the knight got down from their horses. The solidly built man was about her own height. The boy was small for the age she estimated, probably undergrown even for this time.

Sir Stephan introduced them. "My good friend, Jonathan Citrom, and Michael of Wilton, here to begin knightly training. My chatelaine."

"The nut-brown Jehane," Jonathan said with a winning smile. "Stephan has praised your name to me all the way from Striguil."

Oh, yeah? she thought. "Welcome to Passfair," was all she said.

"Michael," Stephan said, one hand resting lightly on the boy's thin shoulder. "Listen well to Lady Jehane."

Michael ducked his head shyly. "I will, my lord," he answered.

Stephan called for grooms to see to the horses. The group started through the bailey on foot, the two men side by side, Michael loyally dogging Stephan's steps. Jane followed a bit behind, beginning to feel a warm glow of anticipation mixed with hope. Stephan was home. His lady was a heroine. Maybe things were going to work out.

They came through the inner gate, and the castle

steps came into view across the courtyard. Jane glanced toward the castle door as Stephan faltered to a halt in front of her. He looked back at her in puzzlement. She just smiled. He blinked and turned to stare.

Waiting demurely on the top step was a delicately lovely girl, dressed in gracefully draping silks of peach and green. She held a silver cup clasped to her rounded breasts, a tribute of wine to welcome home the lord of the manor. Her thick gold hair was unbound, flowing about her like a river of wheat and honey.

Good move, Jane thought at this maidenly sight. Always hit 'em with your best feature. Sibelle had been listening to all those love poems she'd been reciting. She almost wished she'd been in the hall when news of Sir Stephan's return was brought to the castle. Witnessing the quick change and primp act in the bower would have been priceless.

Jonathan bent his head close to the dumbfounded Stephan's, whispering a quick question.

Close enough to overhear, Jane had to suppress a delighted laugh. Jonathan spoke in the flowery language of the troubadours. But what he said could loosely be translated, she decided, as, "Who's the babe?"

16

Stephan looked as if he were in a trance as he took the goblet from the girl. Sibelle's soft blue eyes were shining up into his through the veil of her long lashes. Her lower lip trembled, her cheeks were colored with agitation. Stephan took a sip, the politeness seeming more automatic than conscious, then held the cup awkwardly, perhaps not even remembering it was in his hand. Jane, staying firmly in the background with Jonathan and the boy, looked on with detached amusement. She did not rush forward to relieve the lord of the manor of either his silver or his embarrassment.

The two young people stood transfixed, discovering each other with their eyes, until those around them began to shuffle restlessly. Marguerite finally came forward from where she and Alais stood near the door. She pried the goblet from Sir Stephan's hand while murmuring some words into Sibelle's ear.

"God be with you, my lord," Sibelle recited timidly. "Welcome to your home."

He leaned forward, his impossibly long black lashes almost touching the girl's face as he peered closely at her. "Sibelle?" he asked, their noses—his long and pointed, hers upturned and pert—almost touching.

"I am Sibelle, my lord," she assured him in soft, gentle tones.

He straightened, squaring his narrow shoulders. He turned in a slow circle, eyeing Jane curiously in passing. There was a glint of pleased gratitude to her in his glance. Then he forgot her and concentrated on Sibelle. "Things—you've—changed."

Sibelle ducked her head demurely, but there was an upturned hint of a smile playing about her lips. "If it pleases, my lord."

Jonathan gave Jane a curious look when she made a small, smug sound and crossed her arms.

He leaned close and whispered, "You have the look of one satisfied with their labor, Lady Jehane."

"If I've done my duty to my liege, I am content," she replied primly. Besides, she added to herself, it was Sibelle who did the work. She just had a little stage management.

Stephan came up the two steps to stand beside Sibelle. His fingers briefly brushed through her hair. He offered her his arm. They made a strikingly contrasting couple, one so tall, slender, and dark, the other small and gold and lushly curved. After only a moment's becoming hesitation, Sibelle breathed a happy sigh and placed two delicate fingers on Stepan's wrist. She swayed close to him as they entered the hall together.

Mentally giving Sibelle a perfect ten for her performance, Jane prepared to follow. Jonathan Citrom gallantly offered her his hand, but she smiled politely at him and kept her hands tucked under her arms.

Stephan led Sibelle to stand beneath the dais windows. Jonathan grabbed the back of Michael's tunic to keep the boy from following after the couple. Jane was grateful for the man's amused tact. He and the boy lingered by the hearth. Melisande and her pups, with no knowledge of tact, came bounding into the hall, making a raucous beeline for their master. Stephan and Sibelle ignored them completely. After a few minutes the dogs came down to the hearth. They began weaving in and out between the legs of the people standing by the glowing embers, shamelessly fawning for attention. Both Jane and Jonathan began automatically to rub rough coats and heads.

Jane called for ale for the guests. When Bertram brought the full tankards she caught his eye, tilting her head significantly toward the pair standing close enough to share a sunbeam falling through one of the narrow windows.

The old man's wrinkled map of a face lit happily for an instant. Then he gave Michael a serious look. "New page?" Michael nodded. "Good. Come along. We'll start with teaching you how to serve at table."

Michael gave Jane a wretched, hopeful look. He reminded her of one of the puppies. He was little, and tired from a long ride. The longing in his eyes told her he was lonely as well.

"Perhaps Michael can join us at table tonight," she said, placing her hand on the boy's curly head. "And start his duties in the morning."

The boy looked at her with gratitude that told her he was hers forever. It couldn't hurt to spoil a kid a little, she thought. Bertram sighed disapprovingly and shuffled off. Michael slipped away and began curiously to explore the mysteries of the dimly lit room. Melisande peeled herself away from where she was leaning against Jane's thigh, and followed after the boy.

"You're kindhearted, lady," Jonathan said. "Stephan said you were."

Stephan knew her well enough to know she was softheaded, she thought tartly. Whether that was the same as kindhearted, she wasn't sure.

"Practical," she responded. "I didn't see any reason why everyone at Passfair should be miserable. The solution wasn't hard to find."

He glanced significantly at the young couple. Jane found herself wondering at this man's age. He had a great deal of presence and an air of authority. She found herself comparing this knight with Sir Daffyd.

Jonathan was tan beneath his yellow hair, his skin weathered. She thought the lines around his clear blue eyes might be from good humor and laughter. It was a very different face from the brooding, hawk visage presented by Sir Daffyd. What was it Stephan had called him? The Welsh Wolf? Hawk or wolf, the man was a dangerous hunter.

She wondered what brought Jonathan Citrom back to Passfair with Stephan. He was smiling at her amiably, but she didn't feel it was her place to pry into the business of her liege's guest. As long as he didn't get in the way of the romance, she didn't begrudge him a place in the castle.

After an eternity of about an hour of gazing limpidly into Sibelle's eyes and having her return his gaze with equal adoration, Stephan seemed to recall his duty. He led Sibelle down to the hearth and introduced her formally to his guest.

Jonathan gave her a charming smile. "We hear you were very brave yesterday," he complimented her. "It seems Stephan's found himself a beautiful lioness to guard his home."

Sibelle's pink cheeks took on rosy spots of color. Her eyelashes fluttered. Stephan's adoring sigh was audible.

Jane took several steps back into the shadows, covering her mouth with her hand. This morning her world had been nothing but gray ashes. Now she was fighting not to laugh. Perhaps her reaction was as much lingering hysteria as it was relief at Stephan's response to a pretty girl. She knew the fear was still part of her, lurking beneath her daily concerns, but she took fierce joy in knowing she could laugh. Perhaps she appreciated laughter more today than she had yesterday.

You're never going to be quite the same, but you will be all right. Who had said that? Then she remembered. Daffyd ap Bleddyn—the Welsh Wolf—had come to her room to comfort her. She shook her head in confusion. First the man killed, then he showed concern. What was he?

The tables were being set up. DeCorte came in with several of the guards. He joined the group by the hearth as Stephan was saying, "I didn't know you knew how to use the bow."

"She's a quick student," he asserted before Sibelle could answer. Jane thought the girl looked relieved to have someone do the talking for her. She didn't blame Sibelle her shyness. She didn't think it would last long after she got to know Stephan a little better. And for now Stephan was certainly finding her maidenly diffidence charming.

"She's learning to ride as well," Jane chimed in, happy to help laud the girl's virtues. Happy to get her mind off her own confusion.

"An Amazon," Jonathan said. He eyed Jane with speculative amusement. "Is it true there are Amazons among the infidels, lady?"

Only the ones they import, she thought, reminded of her mother's two tours in the desert theater of operations. "Oh, no," she said. "Their women are kept completely in seclusion."

"You must tell me all about the Holy Land," Jonathan urged her.

She gave him a stiff smile. "Yes. Of course." She considered looking for something she could supervise.

Stephan drew reluctantly away from Sibelle's side. He gathered up Michael with a look, and the two of them went upstairs. Jane made for the kitchen, returning only after the cook informed her furiously that she was interfering in his artistry. The kitchen smelled of onion and lamb and the first green vegetables of the summer. She discovered she had an appetite.

When she returned to the hall it was to find everyone still waiting on their young lord. Fortunately it was only a few more moments before he came bounding down the stairs, shaved and wearing a fresh tunic. Jane caught a distinct scent of rose oil combed into his blue-black locks as he passed her to reach Sibelle's side.

"This is truly serious," Jonathan murmured to Jane

as they took seats side by side at the high table.

Michael was given the chair to her left, the blond knight on her right. Stephan and Sibelle sat close together, sharing one trencher, one wine cup, dipping their fingers in one washing bowl.

"Serious indeed," she agreed with the visiting knight. She picked at the meat and vegetables on her own trencher, sipping slowly at a cup of ale, eyes on her plate but her attention on nothing.

Jonathan ate in silence for a while. "You've been a widow for how long?" he asked, startling her out of her thoughtless reverie.

"I'm not—" she managed to catch herself and end, "—exactly sure. Much of the journey to England after Geoffrey's death is unclear in my memory."

He nodded understandingly. "A brave journey." He concentrated on a large portion of lamb and onions for a while. Then he looked up and gave her one of the most winning smiles she'd ever seen. "Stephan doesn't think you were meant for the abbey. I've told him I'd offer him my opinion on the matter."

For a moment Sir Jonathan's startling words made no sense to her, then she felt her eyes go wide as she stared at him in shock. She gulped. Her mind was full of tumbling thoughts, but her tongue was completely frozen. Jonathan just gave her a benign nod and went back to his dinner.

Her own meal was forgotten. She stared at the meat congealing on her wooden trencher while nervously picking a hunk of heavy bread into tiny crumbs. She didn't notice what she was doing. Jonathan was a warm and solid presence beside her. A presence she wanted very much to go away. She was tempted to run, but running simply was no solution. She'd found that out the hard way with Pwyll chasing close on her heels. Men in this society took what they wanted. There was no running away.

She had thought she was exempt from the iron will of men that circumscribed women's lives. She had thought her choices were her own to make. She had thought her status of widow and chatelaine was a safe haven. She knew now it was a trap. She'd ridden into it pillion on the back of a black charger.

She'd accepted Stephan's protection and given him her service. She was a woman under his command; he was her liege. By law, if he wanted to bring home a friend for her to marry, she had no choice but to marry that friend. It was up to Sir Stephan DuVrai, hardly more than a boy himself, to decide what was best for her good. She was only a woman, after all. It was his duty to take care of her.

She was also a marketable commodity, just as much a piece of propertied goods as little Sibelle. She had wealth; she could bear offspring. Her body and belongings would make a perfect reward for anyone Stephan chose to favor. Sir Jonathan Citrom, perhaps?

She was being ridiculous, she told herself firmly after the speculation had buzzed in her head long enough to give her a headache. Stephan wasn't going to just give her away. He might be thinking about it, might have brought Jonathan home to see if they'd both be interested. But he wouldn't just throw her into any man's bed. Would he? She could talk him out of it, she was sure. She wouldn't worry just yet. But what did Jonathan mean about "offering an opinion"? She decided it was best not to think about it.

Stephan waited scarcely a moment after the meal was ended before rising from his chair. All eyes turned to him, speculation and ribald amusement on many faces as he once more offered Sibelle his hand. There was only one bedroom in the castle. Sibelle slept there, but the room belonged to the lord of the manor. So did Sibelle. She was his formal betrothed, living under his roof. She belonged in his bed if he chose to take her there.

It was a simple matter of property rights, Jane thought acidly, but her opinion softened as she gazed at the couple. Stephan was looking at Sibelle with almost reverent tenderness. Sibelle's eyes on him held the same awe as when he brought her, a maiden rescued from a monster, to Passfair Castle. To them law and custom and formality no longer had any meaning. They wanted to be alone together. To discover each other. To make love as a man and woman.

Sir Jonathan rose. He called, "Stephan?"

Stephan's eyes left his lady's long enough to answer his friend. "Yes?"

"I see you plan to exercise your conjugal rights before your wedding day."

Both Sibelle and Stephan blushed to the roots of their hair, pink and pale skin going almost identically red. The hall filled with ribald laughter as the young couple exchanged a quick, furtive glance. Stephan's arm came protectively around the small girl's shoulder.

"The lady is my betrothed," Stephan announced proudly. "I would wed her this moment if—"

"Such haste is not possible," Jonathan cut him off. "As long as you honor the lady, I will be content. But

I did promise Lord Guillaume and the baron to remind you of your duty." He bowed toward Sibelle.

Stephan frowned at his friend but nodded. "I understand your concern, good Jonathan. I will make Lady Sibelle LeGauche my wife."

He tilted her face up to gaze in her eyes.

"Tonight," he said, loudly enough for all to hear, but obviously speaking only to Sibelle, "I will make you my lady love."

Sibelle took Stephan by the hand, not the delicate touch of fingertips to wrist, but warm palm to warm palm. Smiling, shy but unafraid, she let him lead her up the stairs. They left to the sound of laughter and applause.

Jane breathed a hearty sigh of relief as the noise died down. She, Marguerite, and Alais shared triumphant looks. She was also tempted to share high-fives with them but supposed the hand-slapping gesture would only confuse them.

She rose from her chair, full of enough leftover benevolence to wish Sir Jonathan a sweet "Good night."

"God go with you," he replied, also getting to his feet. "I think I will spend some time praying in the chapel before I find sleep. Would you join me, Lady Jehane?"

Pray? Was it really prayer he was interested in? She eyed his pleasantly inquiring expression suspiciously. "I think not, Sir Jonathan. I say my evening prayers alone," she added.

"Solitude is not a common practice in the abbey."

"True," she agreed hastily, "but it is my habit, and will remain so until I may enter an abbey. Good night," she said again, and turned toward the stairs.

Nikki and Vince joined her as she started up. She looked back to find Melisande stretched out on the rushes next to Michael. The boy had an arm thrown over her back. Her head was on his shoulder. Jane smiled at the dog and boy.

"You take good care of him," she whispered to the dog. "Poor homesick thing. Looks like maybe he's the runt of the litter. Come on," she added to her canine companions, who bounded quickly after her.

17

Jane woke in the last stretch of darkness before dawn and lay on her back, eyes tracing the thick lines of rough wooden beams supporting the low ceiling. She knew she'd dreamed of Berthild, reliving the sight of the outlaw dragging the struggling girl away. She'd dreamed of other things, too. She didn't want to try to catch the disjointed images just waiting to jump up to bedevil her waking thoughts. Some of them managed to flit to the surface despite her efforts to ignore them. She'd dreamed of Daffyd ap Bleddyn. She'd often dreamed of Daffyd ap Bleddyn, but never before had he been holding a gun.

The incongruity of the weapon he held on the would-be rapist in her dream was enough to take much of the horror from the situation for her. She couldn't help but see the dream image again: the half-clothed outlaw, the armored fighter holding out a weapon. Instead of a disemboweling sword stroke, a silent shot was fired. Then Daffyd ap Bleddyn blew on the smoking barrel of the gun and holstered it in his sword sheath. It was completely ludicrous.

It was just her technologically oriented subconscious trying to help her put the trauma in perspective, she told herself. It was just weird. You'd think she'd be more prone to a wake-up-screaming-with-rivers-of-sweat nightmare than to weird, almost funny, images. Still on her back, she shrugged.

The movement reminded her she'd been bruised and mauled. Some of the marks were still sore. But whatever had happened to her, she recalled grimly, was nothing compared to what Berthild was going through. She wished there was something she could do to find her. Maybe she could talk to Sir Stephan. Get him to help Daffyd hunt down Sikes, perhaps.

She rose from her bed, determined to talk to the young man as soon as possible. She should have thought of this yesterday, she chided herself sternly as she pulled on her shift. The servant was up and gone from the outer room already, but there was a bucket of water left for her. Jane bathed quickly, then finished dressing while chewing on a hazelwood twig. Sibelle had told her it was a Welsh trick for cleaning teeth taught to her by her granny Rosamunde. Jane was grateful to dear Granny Rosamunde for such helpful household hints.

It was barely light when she came into the hall, but all the servants were up, ready to make the most of the longer hours of daylight. Sir Jonathan was seated at the high table alone, dipping his fingers into a bowl of cheese curds. He watched her come across the rushes, a welcoming smile lighting his square-jawed face. He gestured her to the seat beside him. It would have been rude to make a run for the open air of the courtyard.

She settled onto the chair, bidding him, "Good day, Sir Jonathan."

"God's blessing on you," he returned. "You don't look as if you slept well," he told her after studying her face for a few moments. "A lady as beautiful as you should never have to look so sad."

Jane's lips twitched up shyly. "I slept well enough."

"But for the dreams," he added for her. The look in his eyes was one of gentle understanding. She looked away, a knot tightening around her heart. "Stephan and his lady won't be joining us this morning, I don't imagine," he went on conversationally. He gave a low chuckle. "I'm glad now I came on this visit. Not that my hosts will be much company. You'll entertain me, I trust, Lady Jehane?"

She turned back to him. "I'm not very entertaining," she answered stiffly. She didn't know if his words were meant as teasing or as ardent courtship. She didn't want to find out. "I have a great deal of work to do."

"Stephan thinks you're especially clever," he went on, oblivious of her response. "And I agree. I've seen it myself. Look at how you managed with the maiden. The way Stephan dragged his heels back here, I was certain there would be no wedding for years. Yes, very clever," he repeated, sitting back on his chair and crossing his arms across the wide expanse of his chest. "But will you make a good nun?"

She gave an exasperated sigh. "It is my only choice," she told him. "Therefore, I will make a good nun."

"Stephan doesn't think so." He tilted his head to one side. "Looking at you, I think I might be inclined to agree. You're far too lovely to take the veil without any vocation."

"I'm not lovely," Jane snapped. "Sibelle calls me an ugly giantess." And Daffyd . . . Daffyd doesn't. What was she thinking about Daffyd for? As if that arrogant pig's opinion mattered!

Jonathan's eyes roamed gently over her form. Though he didn't touch her, she wanted to shudder and run away.

"You are quite beautiful," he told her. "A slender form of graceful and proud carriage." She sat and listened with her fists balled into hard knots as he one by one described her features. "Eyes brown as peat and deep as the forest, with bark-brown hair to match, if those high arched brows are any indication. Such expressive eyes! So full of all the joys and pains of life. You have a woman's face and form, Jehane, not a girl's. So slender, yet so alluring, a tall, willow-woman's body. Your lips are wide and full, smiling easily. Lips to make a man wonder if they would open as generously beneath his touch as they open to give kind words and comfort. Your skin has a sun-ripened seductiveness. It looks so warm, so earthy. The fine, strong lines of your jaw and shadowed hollows of your cheeks speak of strength and vulnerability. You have great beauty, Jehane."

Jane found herself gradually relaxing as his words reminded her of her femininity. He was reminding her of a part of her life she knew it was best to forget. She had to abandon the flesh. She wanted to. Didn't she? The flesh was too easily hurt. Too easily humiliated. Yet his words brought her no pain. She wasn't flattered. Or offended. She was just . . . reminded.

She looked at him, a film of tears obscuring her

vision slightly. "Why are you saying these things?"

"Because I think it's wrong to enter the religious life without a vocation," was his answer.

"It happens all the time!" she protested. "Unwanted women thrust into a life they don't want. It nearly happened to Sibelle. At least I am making a choice."

"Without a vocation." He peered at her intently. "There is another honorable way to serve God, Jehane."

"No! I don't want a husband," she snapped. He couldn't understand, but for some reason she wanted to tell him. Jonathan Citrom seemed to be the sort of man it was easy to confide in. So instead of telling him what she must do and why she must do it, she told him her plan instead.

"I am going to found an order of nuns." It should be cloistered, walled aloofly away from the world, she knew. Instead she heard herself saying, making the decision even as the words came out, "A charitable order. One that will work among the victims of war. There's so much violence. I can't stop it, but perhaps I can help those who suffer from it." Perhaps it was wrong. She might do something to change history. But she was no longer so sure changing history was such a bad thing.

"I commend your charitable spirit." His eyes looked thoughtfully into hers. "But are you sure you prefer good works to the secular joys of marriage and motherhood?"

She pressed her lips together in a thin, tight line. After a few seconds of angry silence, she said, "I'm not going to marry you. No matter what Sir Stephan commands me to do. I'm not marrying you, or anyone. I'm going to be a nun."

Far from being annoyed, or even shocked by her willfulness, Jonathan gave her a delighted smile. "Your obedience and humility, sister Jehane, are less than perfect. Don't worry, sweet Jehane," he added, patting the spot just beside where her right hand now rested flat on the splintered surface of the table, "I'm not here to marry you. I'm here to marry Stephan and Sibelle."

She stared at him in confusion. "What? They're marrying each other."

"Not without a priest they're not." His square face was wearing a very satisfied expression, amusement filling his bright blue eyes. "I," he concluded, "am a priest."

She continued staring hard at him. She eyed his unfashionably short hair. "I don't see any tonsure."

"I let it grow out on my travels." He put a finger to his lips. "Seems a bit more political, times being what they are. Though my order has no quarrel with either your king or the archbishop who pronounced the excommunication."

The man was a knight. He carried sword and shield openly. He looked every bit as hard and capable and deadly as Stephan or DeCorte or Daffyd ap Bleddyn. "What order?" she demanded.

A glint of fervor showed for an instant in his blue eyes. His answer held both pride and modesty. "A brother of the Temple of Jerusalem. I think you know my order's reputation, being from the Holy Land yourself."

"A Templar," she answered immediately. A Templar. A member of the greatest Western paramilitary force ever to wage holy war. One of the few, the proud, the fanatical, who took the term *onward, Christian soldiers* quite literally. Wow.

He didn't seem like a fanatic. He seemed so genuinely nice as he watched her out of mild blue eyes. "A priest," she said. "You're a priest. A Templar priest."

"I am a priest."

"But what good will your being a priest do if you can't perform any of the sacraments?"

His faint smile widened. "I told you my order has no place in the quarrel. We are not subject to Canterbury. The archbishop may frown, he may thunder, but there are a few of us not subject to the English church, who go quietly about our business without being afraid of the thunder. I agreed to come to Passfair with Sir Stephan to perform the marriage. Actually," he went on, "the idea came from my lord Guillaume's wife. The countess dotes on young Stephan, but she wouldn't let him tarry too long among her women when he had a lady at home waiting for him. He kept using the interdict as an excuse. The baron of Sturry kept sending messengers asking when he could expect to be a grandfather. Finally, the countess had a word with me." He spread his hands. "And here we are."

"And here we are," she repeated.

"Fortunately the work you did while Sir Stephan was away saved my having to drag the man bound hand and foot to the ceremony. I do thank you for that."

She tapped her fingers on the table. A wedding, she thought. There was going to be a wedding. "When can you perform the ceremony?" she asked.

He cocked an eyebrow at her. "As soon as they can be dragged out of bed, I suppose. But I think the girl might like a bit more celebration after her long wait."

"You're absolutely right," Jane said with an emphatic nod. She stood, full of determination and plans. "I have so much to do. Please excuse me, Sir—Father—Jonathan."

"Of course, Lady Jehane." He waved her on with a wooden spoon. "Gather the women, inform the cook, do whatever you must. And when you are all done, I will be waiting in the chapel to say mass and hear your confessions."

"Yes, Father," she said, pausing before hurrying away to bend her head with as much obedience and humility as she could muster.

18

The steps to the top floor were still wet from Michael's latest accident, Jane noticed as she started up. It had been an incident with a water bucket this time. She pulled off her shoes; the rough, wet stone felt good beneath the soles of her feet as she made the ascent to the bower. Sibelle, with Marguerite and Alais, loaded down with toweling and fresh undershifts, followed quickly in her wake. The men were finished with their bath; now it was the women's turn.

Michael, she thought, splashing into a small puddle on the top step, was proving to be a menace: a very dear menace, but a menace. He was the despair of Bertram and Raoul DeCorte. The older men agreed the boy was amiable, biddable, and hardworking. They were also frightened that every task they set him would turn into a disaster of biblical proportions. Jane, they said, spoiled him. She did. She didn't care.

The boy could play the lute; he had magic in his

fingers, fire in his soul. He'd told her he'd been study-ing with a master troubadour in Guillaume's service since he was six. He was both sad and proud when his father had sent him with Stephan to learn to be a knight. He was eager to please his father, hoping someday to make him proud. But longing to please his father didn't stop him from missing his mother and his teacher. She thought that even at his tender age his heart was torn between love and duty.

So she let him practice his music far more than the older men approved of. She pointed out that when he was practicing the lute he wasn't breaking, stamped-ing, accidentally setting fire to, or tearing anything beyond repair. The men had to concede her point. Melisande was devoted to the boy. Sir Stephan was wisely staying out of his squire's education until he was "settled in" to learning the duties of a page. After a few years, supposedly under the civilizing influence of the ladies of the house, the lad would be turned over to him for further instruction.

It had been six days' settling in since Stephan's party arrived home. Even Jane sometimes agreed the old stones of Passfair might not be able to take much more settling. But Michael tried so hard—even while spilling buckets of water he was supposed to be car-rying up the stairs. Jane was grateful Michael hadn't been involved in wrestling the big tub up from the wash house.

If they'd lost the big wash vat, Passfair's laundry might never get done again, she thought as she reached the door. She waited for the others to join her. When they entered, Sibelle led the way. Inside waited three of the serving women and the tub full of fragrantly steaming water. Jane sighed happily at the sight, quite pleased to be taking part in the traditional wedding bath. It was customary for the bride and groom to share the bath with their friends, hence the need for a container large enough for communal bathing.

Sibelle had balked simply at using the wash house, insisting she needed the privacy of the bower. Stephan had agreed his lady was far too delicate to bare her lovely form in such crude surroundings. He'd decreed she should bathe where she always bathed, in the bower. It had taken Jane and the household staff an entire day to organize the proceedings, but now she decided the effort had been worth it. Communal or not, she always looked forward to a real bath. She hoped her orders to have the water changed after Stephan, Jonathan, and Raoul were finished had been thoroughly carried out. There had been grumblings among the staff over all this fuss with hot water.

The loom had been carefully pushed against the wall to make room for the tub. The room itself was full of containers of wildflowers placed on every possible surface. Switha and the other village women had brought in the flowers from woods and fields as a colorful, fragrant wedding gift for their lord and lady. Jane breathed deeply and drank in color and the wonderful blending of scents as her serving woman helped her undress.

When Sibelle saw her head bared, the girl's eyes widened. Jane's hand flew to the top of her head as Sibelle exclaimed, "Jehane, your hair's so short!"

She came forward to touch Jane's shoulder-length brown curls while Jane fluffed out the veil-flattened mass with her fingers. "I've seen curly hair and I've seen straight hair." She giggled. "But never hair that was curly and straight at the same time."

The other women gathered around to finger her curls and laugh at Sibelle's joke. She laughed along with them but shook their hands away. "I was sick with a lingering fever during my journey from the Holy Land," she explained. "Much of my hair broke off. And now it is growing in straight. It must be because of the fever." The salon where she'd had the now growing-out perm done had actually been called Fevre, come to think of it. Very trendy. Very expensive. A very long time from now.

The women murmured sympathetically as they adjourned to the bath. Jane sank into the water, immediately ducking her head to give her hair a good soaking. She came up and looked critically at Sibelle, who was letting one of the maids give her back a thorough scrubbing. Alais and Marguerite had been complaining that their dear lamb had barely touched a morsel since Sir Stephan's return. Jane suspected the girl was just practicing a little crash dieting. She was looking a bit thinner. Good.

Besides, weren't brides supposed to diet so they could fit into their wedding gowns? Even with the one-size-fits-all draping fashions of the moment, Sibelle obviously wanted to look as slender and delicate as possible on the big day. She had the whole neighborhood, as well as Stephan, to impress at the ceremony.

Jane gave thanks they'd started to work before Stephan ever came home on the sky-blue silk dress Sibelle would wear for the wedding tomorrow. Otherwise, they would never have managed the finishing touches in six days, not even with every woman in the place doing nothing but stitch on the eight-inch-deep bands of embroidery edging. She was also glad there had been enough silk left over to make up a tunic of the same shade for Stephan. The embroidery wasn't as fancy, but she had worked a few lapis beads into the pattern around the neck opening.

She leaned her head back against the edge of the tub and smiled smugly. The hot water was working its magic, relaxing all the days' exertions out of her muscles. Tomorrow there would be the wedding and a feast. All the local notables would be at Passfair for the celebration. She'd arranged it all. She was tired, she was frazzled, and she was very pleased with herself. Tonight was a time to congratulate herself and share in Sibelle's joy and anticipation.

She welcomed the hard work of the hasty preparations, really. During the day she was too caught up in details to think. In the hours after day and before bed, she concentrated fiercely on the music Michael drew forth on his lute. They taught each other songs. She was endlessly fascinated by how much she had to learn. She listened in amazement to the tunes he picked out to go with the words and avoided conversation with anyone but her young pupil.

She refused to brood. She'd been falling into her bed too tired to dream.

Six days. Was it seven or eight since the attack? She'd managed to pry Stephan away from his lady fair long enough to discuss Berthild. He'd frowned thunderously at learning one of his household was a victim of the outlaws and taken Jonathan out hunting in the woods, but no sign of Sikes's men was found near Passfair. Well, at least Stephan had tried. She sighed. There was nothing more she could do. She almost wished she could forget.

Around her the women were talking. Sibelle was giggly, and Marguerite, of all people, was making ribald jokes. The hot water was strewn with dried herbs and rose petals. Jane took deep breaths of the heady steam.

She opened her eyes and murmured placidly, "This is living."

"Oh, aye," Alais agreed. "The young men looked so handsome and refreshed coming out of their bath." Her eyes twinkled with merriment as she gazed at the blushing Sibelle. "I was mending the tear in your bed curtains, my lady," she explained. "Though how it got torn I couldn't say. Still, wanting the bedchamber to be perfect for Father Jonathan's blessing tomorrow, I kept working after the men came in. The door was ajar a little, but they took no notice of me."

"You spied on them!" Sibelle exclaimed, her eyes round as saucers. Far from overwhelmed with shock, she leaned forward and demanded eagerly, "What's Father Jonathan like? Is he as handsome and well made as my lord? Not that anyone could be!"

"Of course not, my lady," Alais hastened to assure her. "There's no fat on any of them. Good, firm flesh, with clean, honorable scars from many a battle. Father Jonathan's all shoulder and muscular thighs with a fine, strong back. But he doesn't compare to Sir Stephan, of course."

Then why was she licking her lips at the thought of him? Jane wondered.

Alais went on. "Raoul's a spindly-legged old warhorse with a great scar across his chest."

"It's what's between his legs you should be considering," Marguerite said tartly. "If it's marriage to the old *routier* you're thinking of."

Jane looked at the plump and prim Alais with a new light. Her and Raoul? She considered this coupling with a sardonic smile. It would seem Alais was adjusting well to life outside the walls of Davington Priory.

"I looked," Alais confirmed, her chin wobbling with an emphatic nod. "He'll do for as much as I'll need." She threw a sly glance Jane's way. "It's a pity Sir Daffyd sent word he couldn't be here for the wedding. Sir Stephan would have liked him to stand by him." She gave a deeply wicked chortle. "And I'd have liked to see what that golden cockerel keeps under his armor."

"Muscles," Jane said, the word escaping without thinking. She blushed from the roots of her hair to the tips of her toes. She was certain the heat she was generating raised the water temperature by several degrees.

Muscles covered in a mat of gold fur, she couldn't help but recall as images of Daffyd and another bath teased her memory. She swallowed hard, trying to banish recollection. She didn't know why the sight of him had been so—memorable. It wasn't as if she'd never seen a naked man before. Of course, compared to Daffyd ap Bleddyn . . .

And why was Alais looking at her like that? Berthild must have found out and gossiped about the little incident with Sir Daffyd and her bathwater. Not that it was all that . . . little. She made a small, disquieted sound. She didn't like thinking of it as a whimper.

"But why?" Sibelle asked in astonishment. "Sir

Daffyd must be nearly as old as Raoul DeCorte! And he never smiles!"

"Does he have to?" Marguerite questioned merrily. "He has a sultry way of looking that tells a woman he knows what to do with her. He's not old," she went on. "He's experienced. Experience has value, doesn't it, Lady Jehane?" Jane blinked stupidly, at a loss for any reply.

"My lord has all the experience I need," Sibelle said loyally. "I've heard how Sir Daffyd rides all over the countryside seeking out women."

He undoubtedly did, Jane thought sourly. How many gold-haired, green-eyed bastards did the man have running around Kent? Some women just couldn't resist a man in a uniform. Especially one with a knowing smirk and a chocolate-rich voice that purred in their ears like a big, sensual cat.

She thought perhaps the water temperature was rising again. Hers certainly was. She would not think about it—him, she declared firmly. It didn't help when Alais went on.

"Women with experience of their own," the woman elaborated, looking eagerly to see Jane's reaction. "He's the despair of all the pretty young maidens who long for him to turn his attention their way. It's not tumbling with just any skirt he seems to be after. Perhaps he's looking for someone special. Do you think so, Lady Jehane? He seems to enjoy talking to you."

Jane didn't know why the older women seemed to think she should be interested in contributing to their gossip. Or why they were interested in her conversations with Sir Daffyd. Her few encounters with the man had always been full of barbs and antagonism.

And a physical tension she couldn't deny.

She didn't want him, she told herself fiercely. She was grateful for what he did, certainly, but there was nothing else there. Just because he had saved her life, she didn't have to faint with longing tenderness over some big dude in armor who rode up and saved her hide. He hadn't even been riding a white horse.

She wasn't going to talk about it. About him. She didn't trust herself to express any opinion on the matter of Sir Daffyd.

Sibelle was looking at her a little oddly, too. "You're embarrassed, Jehane."

"No, I'm not," she protested quickly.

Sibelle was looking at her breasts. "Or cold, perhaps?" she questioned.

Jane glanced down, noticing for the first time that the tips of her breasts were tight and hard. She crossed her arms over them. "Yes. Just cold."

"Of course." The girl gave her a smile that was far too knowing. What had she and that boy been up to in here?

Sibelle rested her chin on her upraised knees and changed the subject. "Should I really wear my hair unbound tomorrow? I'm no longer a maiden."

Her statement set off another fit of giggles. There ensued a long and only occasionally serious discussion of propriety mixed with gossip and tales illustrating numerous acts of impropriety.

After a few confused and aloof minutes, Jane joined in happily, making up outrageous lies about court life in the beleaguered kingdom of Jerusalem. Eventually the water turned tepid, then cool, as did the spring breeze coming in the window, but the girl talk went on. Even as they donned undershifts and helped braid each other's damp hair, they continued to joke and tease each other. The subject of Daffyd ap Bleddyn did not come up again, though the memory of surprising him at his own bath replayed relentlessly through Jane's thoughts. She remembered how she'd longed to trace her fingers along the sharply outlined muscles of his arms and chest. She'd itched to play with the gold matted chest fur, to run her hands downward, stroking and rousing his blatantly displayed manhood. She hadn't actually realized at the time that was what she'd wanted to do. In retrospect she knew it was what her body had longed for even as she'd been lashing out at him in outraged anger.

He made her feel too much like a woman, she realized. She wished she'd met someone like him in her own time. Though she might not have noticed someone like Sir Daffyd in her own world. It seemed as if she'd only begun to notice her own sensuality since she got dropped into the persona of Jehane FitzRose. And little good it would do her, she also realized.

To keep her mind off all her own longings, she concentrated harder on enjoying the company, the conversation, and the bath. By refusing to dwell on her own homesickness she managed to push it into the background and ended up having a wonderful time.

It was only Stephan's banging on the door, demanding entrance into his own quarters and time with his dear lady in his own bed, that broke up the festivities.

Jane left with a smile, surrounded by a sense of fragile serenity. She felt as if she'd stepped into a little kingdom inside a bubble. It was full of laughter and love and dreams come true. It wasn't a real place, of course, and she wasn't really a part of it, but for now she was able to dwell inside the bubble, safely away from the terrors of the real world.

The sense of serenity helped her sleep through the night before the wedding without having to resort to complete exhaustion to keep the nightmares away. That night there was a great deal of splashing going on in her dreams, with love play and laughter mixed with soap bubbles.

19

"Lavender," she said as she woke. She sat up sniffing, but there was no scent of the flower anywhere in the room. Jane blinked and rubbed her eyes. "Must have dreamed it," she murmured as she got out of bed. As she combed her hair, she noticed it was still scented with last night's bathwater. Maybe that was where the lavender came from.

She was reminded of the day, and she smiled happily. "Beginnings," she said. She dressed hurriedly and even said, "Good morning," as she passed her maid on her way out the door. It wasn't the poor woman's fault she wasn't Berthild, and it had been foolish to try to pretend the new maid wasn't there. Today, Jane resolved, she would put both the past and the future behind her. No comparisons, no regrets. Today she would live only for the moment. She didn't want the magic bubble to burst.

The household was already abuzz by the time she came downstairs. Several of the guests had arrived in time for the evening meal the night before, finding bed space in chapel and pantry as well as around the hearth. Every landholder within a twenty-mile radius of Passfair was invited and had until high noon to arrive if they wished to witness the ceremony.

Jane was greeted enthusiastically by the earliest and most boisterous of the arrivals, Osbeorn of Blackchurch, a widower of substantial size. He'd arrived with his four offspring in tow and a gift of two barrels of French wine for the bride and groom. He was known locally as Osbeorn the Fat. Fat and Pickled, Jane thought, would be more appropriate.

He had tapped one of the barrels at supper last night and had been happily swigging, singing loudly to Michael's playing, when the women adjourned to the bower for their bath. From the looks of him this morning, rumpled, red-faced, and still boisterous, Jane didn't think he'd stopped celebrating all night.

He approached her with a flagon of wine in each hand. His smell reached her first. She blinked to keep her eyes from watering. "A good day to you, Sir Osbeorn," she greeted, taking the cup he held out.

"A toast to the happy couple," he proclaimed as his two adolescent sons came up to join them. He drained off his own wine while Jane took a tiny sip, then put the cup on the table.

Draping his arms around the boys' shoulders, he said, "Lady Jehane's a widow, lads. As sad and bereaved as we are. Such a sad thing not to have a good, stalwart lover in her bed." He peered blearily at her while the boys looked her over with less than boyish interest. "How you must grow cold at night," he elaborated. "Aching for a man's strength between your legs. Ah"—he sighed dramatically—"how I miss my own good woman." He perked up. "A toast to good women."

Jane backed away, smiling stiffly, happy to escape to her duties and leave Osbeorn the Fat to his celebrating. She was living for the day, she reminded herself as she stepped into the sweltering heat of the kitchen. But she would be happy when the guests went home.

Preparations for the feast were going on with frantic haste. The room smelled of cinnamon and cardamom and the ever-present onions. She stood in a corner, chewing on a warm, crusty piece of white bread just brought in from the ovens behind the kitchen building. Wonderful, great round loaves of bread had been stacked on one of the tables like a mound of gold coins. It was planchet, white bread made from fine milled flour reserved for the nobility, and was a rare treat after the coarse grain produced by Passfair's mill. There were also pigeons and dried-fruit pies and honey cakes cooling on the table. She'd sent a bag of silver, a small part of the dowry Sibelle brought to Passfair, to Canterbury for supplies for this feast. She'd also accepted some of Sibelle's silver in exchange for the spices used to flavor the dishes.

The cook was working at the chopping block in the center of the room, sweating profusely, bloody up to the armpits, using his cleaver to whack great hunks of beef into chunks for a savory stew. He was having the time of his life with this bounty. The scullions were busy stuffing chickens with a mixture of saffron, raisins, onions, and rice from her supplies. There were dozens of eggs boiling in a blackened kettle. Bowls of tiny strawberries were being cleaned by another pair of boys. There were suckling pigs and geese roasting on spits over slow, carefully tended fires. There would also be dishes of fish and eels and lamb.

And all this bounty was as much for the villagers as for the household and guests. The people of Pass-fair and Hwit had been talking of nothing but the upcoming feast for six days. It was more meat in one day than they usually saw in five years.

Nothing in the kitchen needed her attention, so she finished her bread and left. A group of riders was dismounting in the courtyard, two separate parties that had entered the bailey one after the other.

She'd never seen the thin, hatchet-faced man in the soiled gray and yellow surcoat who came with a half dozen men-at-arms trailing behind him. The device on his shield was a long, sinuous white dragon on a red field. Dragon, she thought. A dragon was a drake, if she recalled her heraldry. Lilies were white. Hugh of Lilydrake, then. So, he styled himself the White Dragon. White Snake would have been a more suitable title.

She turned her attention to the other arrivals, recognizing the colors of Sturry. She went to greet the man who'd ridden in while his groom took the horses to be stabled. He had brown hair liberally mixed with gray, and a slight paunch. He introduced himself as Yves, seneschal to the baron.

He looked around the bailey with sharp brown eyes, then said, "I commend your efforts here, Lady Jehane." His smile was both friendly and assessing as he looked her over head to foot. She was dressed in layers of bright yellow and white, trimmed in blue embroidery. She knew the colors flattered her tawny complexion.

"You are a widow, are you not?" he inquired curiously.

She wanted to cover her face with her hands and mutter, "Oh, God, not another one." Instead she gave him a polite smile and said, "I must greet our other guests."

When she approached Lilydrake, all the thin man said to her was, "You're DuVrai's spare woman. Fetch me some wine."

She could see why he wasn't popular in the neighborhood.

She bridled angrily beneath a fixed, polite smile and called for a servant to see to Lord Hugh's needs. She then went into the castle and sat in the bower with Sibelle and the other women until word was brought that all was ready in the courtyard. Yves came up to escort the bride to her lord. Jane, Sibelle, and Alais followed them outside. Jane was happy to note Sibelle's steps were firm and sure. Her head, hair flowing loosely, was wreathed in flowers.

They stepped out into the sunlight, halting at the top of the steps where Stephan, Raoul DeCorte, and Father Jonathan waited before a courtyard crowded with onlookers.

Jonathan took Sibelle's delicate little hand from Yves's and placed it in Stephan's. Jane watched, her joy mixed with curiosity as the wedding proceeded. It was very different from the ceremony she thought of as a wedding. First, Yves read the marriage agreement aloud. During the recitation, someone, she thought it was Hugh of Lilydrake, kept hawking and spitting on the flagstones.

Then Jonathan listened as the couple exchanged vows. He blessed them as Stephan then put not one,

but three rings on the fingers of Sibelle's right hand.
The last and largest ring was slipped onto her ring
finger while Jonathan murmured a benediction.

When Sibelle knelt and prostrated herself before
Stephan, Jane stiffened all over with shock. She felt
herself staring, a shudder going through her. She was
a historian, and medieval history was her specialty;
she knew as much about these people's customs as
had been recorded. She'd read about this bridal submission. Witnessing the gesture Sibelle made so easily shocked her to the core of her being.

I really am an alien here, she thought. *I could
never do that. I want out.*

Stephan helped the girl to her feet, smiling lovingly into her adoring eyes. The crowd cheered, and they
kissed while Jonathan's prayers rolled over them,
good Church Latin sealing the happy couple as man
and wife in the eyes of God and man. Jonathan eventually had to tap Stephan hard on the shoulder to
keep the kiss from turning into a more erotic specta-
cle on the castle steps.

"You should be ashamed," he whispered jokingly
to the young knight.

Stephan delicately touched a lovebite showing on
his long throat. "Me?" Sibelle rested her head on his
chest, shoulders quivering with unabashed laughter.
"Come, love," Stephan said to her. "Let's lead these
good people into the feast."

Her eyes sparked up at him. "Soonest begun, soonest done," she told him.

"My thoughts exactly," he agreed. He put his arm
around her shoulder. Holding his wife close to his
side, Sir Stephan led the way into his hall.

Sir Daffyd arrived just as everyone was seated at

the tables. The man did know how to make an entrance, Jane thought, watching him as he stood poised in the screen doorway, his sharp eyes scanning the faces in the hall. He gave the faintest of nods in Lilydrake's direction, and kept his left hand resting easily on his sword hilt. For once he wasn't dressed in armor, but for a party. Jane found herself gazing, mesmerized, at the strong sure hand, fingers curled loosely on his weapon. A shiver raced up her spine, and she forced herself to look elsewhere. She still couldn't take her eyes off Daffyd.

He was wearing a tight-sleeved black undertunic, which emphasized his long, strong arms. It was covered with a long, belted tunic of rich scarlet. Metallic gold embroidery trimmed the slit front, the short, belled sleeves, and the hem swinging around his calves. His long hair glistened cleanly to well below his shoulders, its thick texture and natural curl enough to make even Sibelle jealous.

He certainly cleaned up well, Jane conceded, as if by making flippant mental comments, she could ignore her racing heart.

After making his greetings to the bride and groom, Daffyd's eyes found hers. She was seated to Sir Stephan's right, between Jonathan and Osbeorn. She signaled for another chair to be brought. She didn't mean for Michael to squeeze the seat between her and the gently soused Osbeorn. Once it was done, she couldn't very well order the man be placed anywhere besides next to her. He came around the table and slid onto the chair.

"You're looking well, lady," he said in greeting. "Much better than when we last met."

She gave the Welshman a nod. His size and

masculine presence made her nervous. Vivid memories assailed her. The way he'd stroked her bruised cheek. His rich voice teasing her with a bet. His eyes roaming boldly over her while he stood naked before her. The smile as he killed her would-be rapist. Her flesh went hot, then cold. She turned her attention to the safe presence of the priest.

His blue eyes smiled gently into hers. She had to take a sip of wine to clear her dry throat before she spoke. "Citrom? It doesn't sound like a Norman name."

"It's not," he answered. "It's what I've been called since I was a lad."

"Oh," she encouraged.

"My family holds a stronghold on Sicily; I was born there. There are citrus orchards on the estate. Citrom is a pet name a Magyar slave gave me when I was young." His smile held fond remembrance. "I think it means 'lemon' in his rough language."

She was very aware of Sir Daffyd's hand reaching across the table to snatch a piece of bread, of his fingers slowly tearing the piece to bits. "Really," she said. "How interesting."

"How interesting," Sir Daffyd echoed mockingly beside her.

She kept her back half-turned to him and went on. "You've traveled far from Sicily. I was there once." She had spent a summer in college working on an archaeological dig. She hated to think the ruins of the Norman keep she'd helped painstakingly uncover might have been where the Templar priest was born. "After my husband died," she added.

"On your long journey to England?"

"Yes."

"Do you miss your husband much?" Daffyd asked,

the purr of his voice very close to her ear.

She was beginning to think Sir Daffyd's caustic comments were a play for her attention. Could it be he was jealous of her talking to Father Jonathan? No. Impossible. She too clearly recalled his remarks when he'd called off their bet. His interest in her had been a "joke."

Michael appeared, holding a clay jug almost as big as he was. He refilled her cup and Jonathan's, then turned, too quickly, to Sir Daffyd. Wine splashed out on the scarlet tunic. The man jumped in surprise.

Jane put out a protective hand, placing herself between the boy and the knight. Her hand brushed against the Welshman's in passing. The warm touch of flesh to flesh sent a searing shock of desire through her. She calmed herself with the stern reminder that she had the boy's safety to worry about. "He meant no harm," she said quickly, afraid the accident might rouse the man's temper.

He calmly brushed fingers over the damp spot, looking at her as if he thought she were mad. "No harm done," he said. "No need for wine, either, lad." He gestured Michael away. "I never drink anything stronger than ale, and never much of that."

Jane couldn't help but ask, "Why?"

"Because when I drink," he told her, "I think I'm God." Old pain haunted his eyes.

"I have news," he added now that he had her attention and before she could ask any more questions. He glanced briefly down the table to where Sibelle and Stephan were sharing their plate and cup, continually touching and whispering lovingly to each other. "It can wait for a while," he decided. His eyes held hers for another long instant.

Jonathan touched her sleeve suddenly. She jumped and turned away from Daffyd. "What?"

Jonathan was looking at her thoughtfully. "Something just occurred to me, my lady. Perhaps, if you're intent on entering the convent—"

"Oh, she is," Daffyd chimed in.

Both she and Jonathan ignored him. Jonathan went on. "You could travel with me when I return to France. I could take you down to Anjou, to Fontre—"

"I've been to Anjou," Daffyd cut in again.

She threw him a sour look. "I would rather found my own order," she told Jonathan. "Though perhaps I could do it in France as easily as in England. Easier, I suppose, since the Church is there to grant its blessing."

He nodded, then added with a wicked smile, "I still think you should marry." He looked around Daffyd to Osbeorn, whose attention had been caught by the word *marriage*. "Lord Osbeorn has need of a wife," Jonathan went on.

She felt herself blanching. "I—"

"And Yves of Sturry asked me about you after the ceremony. Another fine man willing to share the holy sacrament of matrimony with a good, devout woman. Wouldn't it be a shame to waste her beauty in a convent, Sir Daffyd?" Jonathan inquired of the Welshman.

Daffyd's face bore no expression. His rich voice was carefully controlled. "It's nothing to me if the lady wishes to give herself to God, or even Hugh of Lilydrake, for that matter." His eyes raked over her coldly. "It's nothing to me," he repeated, his voice softer this time.

She didn't understand the pain stabbing through

her at his repudiation. She couldn't understand what the man wanted of her, either. One moment his voice and eyes teased her with seductive promises, the next he pushed her cruelly away.

"Lilydrake?" Osbeorn said, suddenly somewhat alert. He peered at Jonathan indignantly. "I saw the woman first. Fine-looking woman. Bear fine sons. Lilydrake's got no feelings for children or anything else." He went back to his wine cup, mumbling, "Saw her first."

Jonathan's eyes sparkled with amusement. "He's a good father, at least."

"I don't want him," she said quietly but firmly. She raised her wine cup to her lips.

"What about Yves, then?" the priest persisted.

"King John," Daffyd spoke up over Jonathan's question, "will be arriving at Passfair with a hunting party in two days' time."

20

Jane's cup crashed onto the table. Her eyes flew to Daffyd's face. "You're joking!"

His lips twitched up in his customary smirk. "No." He jerked his head in the bride and groom's direction. "The news can wait for them until morning. But I thought you, as chatelaine, would need word sooner."

Then why hadn't he told her half an hour ago? He had her full attention now. His green-flecked eyes were full of triumphant amusement. "We have two days to prepare for the king?" she went on frantically. "What's the king doing coming here? Passfair's just a little keep, a minor holding."

"It borders on Blean Forest," Daffyd reminded her. "A royal forest where kings come to hunt."

She rubbed her temples tiredly. "Thank God the place is at least clean."

He gave a deep chuckle. "His Majesty travels with his own pavilions, so I'm told. He'll use the hall for feasting, and holding court, perhaps. He'll certainly require a great many of Passfair's provisions for himself and his attendants. Pray the harvest is a good one, Lady Jehane, if you don't want to starve after paying for the privilege of seeing a king."

He picked up his ale cup and shouted for quiet. His voice had power and authority enough to get the noisy throng's attention immediately. He used his expressive voice to make a flowery toast to the bride and groom while Jane sat in stunned worry.

"He should have been a herald," Jonathan murmured in her ear.

She didn't pay any attention to the priest. Or any attention to the toast to the happy couple Sir Daffyd offered in slyly amused, flattering words. There was a great deal of cheering. Jane stared at her hands, oblivious of the spilled wine dripping down from the table onto her pale skirts. I don't want the king to come here, she thought morosely.

She looked up and around the hall. Everyone was on their feet, laughing and shouting good wishes and hopes for many children. Switha and Cerdic were among the village folk given their own table in the hall. They had their arms tightly around each other's waists; Switha had flowers braided in her hair. Bertram was standing in his usual spot by the door, his broken teeth bared in a hearty laugh, but still alert as ever to the needs of those he served. Alais and Marguerite, and Raoul DeCorte were sharing a table with the guests' older children and retainers. Stephan and Sibelle were standing; voices urged them upstairs.

This had become her home, she thought unhappily. The king was coming here. King John. John Lackland. Why didn't he go to Sturry? A baron's castle would be a more appropriate place to house a king.

Because the baron was slowly and painfully dying, and John had a morbid fear of death. The historian in her head reeled off facts. The last-born and least-gifted son of Henry II and Eleanor of Aquitaine, he had been—he was! She knew too much, she thought desperately. What if she somehow, some way, did or said something around him that could change the course of history? Making small changes in a tiny corner of Kent was one thing, but anything to do with the life of a king was too risky. She had to get away.

Jonathan got to his feet, everyone else at the table following him. Jane moved with them automatically, her mind both numb and racing. Sir Daffyd was at her elbow. She was aware of his nearness, his overpowering presence. She was half tempted to reach out to him for support, to beg him to ride with her away from this place. She was feeling so desperate. He'd saved her once; a part of her believed she could trust him to save her again.

They were separated as all the people in the hall tried to mount the staircase at once. It was a friendly crush, noble jostling peasant in boisterous equanimity and getting jostled back cheerfully. Jane tried to step out of it then, thinking to make a run for the stables, but Cerdic grabbed her around the waist and pulled her along as he passed. She was halfway up the steps before she was able to disentangle herself. By then it was too late to turn back.

The bawdy, laughing crowd mingled together on the narrow stair. Jane flowed along with the mass up to the second floor but hesitated in the narrow hallway as others shoved and pushed toward the staircase leading to bower and bedchamber. She was unable to squeeze out of the way until she edged over to the wall at the bottom of the second-floor staircase. She waited there, pressed against the solid stone. She was in no mood to be a part of this bawdy, classically medieval bedding scene right now.

To her surprise, a tall figure stepped out of the passing throng, joining her in the shadows. She turned her eyes up to Sir Daffyd's face, half in light, half in shadow. The lines of his face and the shadowed hollows of his cheeks were starkly outlined by the flame of the nearest torch.

"What?" he purred, edging close to her as the last of the revelers straggled up to attend the blessing of the bedded couple. "Not anxious to witness the rest of the wedding?"

She could manage only a slight shake of her head.

"You're pale," he said, though she didn't know how he could tell in the dim light. "Could it be you're reminded of your own marriage bed?" He leaned closer. He wasn't so much taller than she, six inches, maybe. Why did looking up at him give her vertigo? "Could it be you miss the pleasures of marriage?"

What pleasures of marriage? What was the man talking about? She'd never been married. Why was he standing so close? Didn't he know the king was coming and she had to get away? Why did his lips look so soft and strong at the same time? How could lavender mixed with sweat smell so wonderfully masculine? His hands touched her waist. She felt the warmth and strength of his hands, the layers of her silk clothing sliding sensuously across her skin as he drew her forward against him. She tilted her head up to look him in the eye, her mouth opened to speak.

He whispered, "Jehane."

Growing suddenly weak with desire, she found herself melting longingly against him. Then his lips covered hers and she couldn't remember what she'd started to say. Then she didn't want to say anything as her lips opened hungrily beneath the questing insistence of his tongue. It was a demanding kiss, filling her with heat and pent-up need. The air around them seemed to burst into flame as she answered his hunger with her own. He cupped the back of her head with one large palm. The grip of his other hand on her waist grew tighter, pressing her closer. She clung to him, drinking in the pleasure from his mouth and his strong, muscular body. Her fingers sifted through the luxurious, soft waves of his hair.

He was stronger, more overpoweringly masculine, than she'd ever dreamed.

Dreamed. This wasn't a dream. The realization that this was very real brought Jane joltingly back to her senses. There was only a moment's surprised resistance from Daffyd when she tensed, then broke away from him.

"What are you doing?" she demanded shrilly, slithering backward along the wall just in time to avoid his hand grazing her cheek. She continued backing, crabwise, along the wall.

"Jehane . . ." His voice followed her. "Damn."

She turned her back on him, hurrying toward her door.

Where she found Hugh of Lilydrake waiting, lounging with arms crossed, next to the door. She'd recovered her composure by the time she came up to him. Far from being startled at the way he ran his eyes lasciviously over her form, she responded with an annoyed "What do you want?" She found herself repeating Daffyd's gesture as she fingered the small dagger on her belt.

He didn't take the hint. He took a step closer. "I'm going to take my pleasure with you, woman," he declared. "The boy won't be wanting you tonight. No need for you to be coy."

Before he could say or do anything that would have required her shedding blood, Daffyd came sauntering nonchalantly down the hall. "Hugh," he said cheerfully, stopping by her side. "I thought you were in Normandy."

"I'm not," the lord of Lilydrake answered shortly.

"Pity. Too bad you missed the excitement of the fair. No, you must have been back by then, surely."

"No."

"Then you wouldn't have heard about the ambush at Stourford?"

"No."

"No? With the news of it running all over the countryside?"

"I'm not interested in local gossip."

Something in the way Daffyd questioned the nasty little man reminded Jane of a police detective questioning a suspect. It reminded her that Daffyd was a policeman of sorts. What was his official title? Did he report to a sheriff or directly to the king? Whoever it was, she got the impression Daffyd ap Bleddyn was a law unto himself, whatever his place in the feudal hierarchy. Right now his stalwart presence was making Hugh of Lilydrake uncomfortable as they stood hostilely, toe to toe, before her door.

"I'm going to bed," she announced as the staring

match went on. "God's blessing on you both," she added, opening the door.

When she stepped through, Sir Daffyd leaned a stout shoulder on the wood and pushed in after her. He closed the door on Hugh's frustrated exclamation.

"Get out of here!" she shouted.

"And let Hugh in?" he countered. He bent an ear to the solid wood, putting a finger to his lips to shush her as he listened. "He's still out there pacing like a caged jackal. You must really inflame his passions, Lady Jehane."

She snorted derisively. "He'd do it with a dog." She covered her mouth with her hands, shocked at her own crudeness in repeating something the maidenly Marguerite had said the night before.

"More likely with his hand," Daffyd said.

Jane stifled a laugh. She came to the door and added her ear to the surveillance. She wasn't sure it was possible to hear anything through the thick wood. She certainly didn't hear anything now. "Caged jackal indeed," she muttered.

"Perhaps I exaggerated a bit," Daffyd admitted. She moved away from the door. He followed her to the center of the room. Her servant was gone with the others, but she'd left a pair of thick tallow candles burning on a barrel near the alcove curtain. On the floor next to the barrels Jane made out the shape of saddlebags. She wasn't sure if she was afraid Daffyd would kiss her again or afraid he wouldn't.

Rounding on Daffyd, she said, "Oh, no, you're not staying here!"

His sweeping gesture took in the whole room. "Where else? I have Sir Stephan's permission to occupy these quarters when I'm at Passfair. He hasn't revoked his permission," he pointed out in his cream-and-chocolate drawl. "Or I could offer to exchange places with Hugh if you like."

"That's not funny."

"Fine." He rubbed his hands together briskly. "You'll find me an amiable companion, as long as I'm not disturbed. Do you think your woman will be back tonight?"

"No," she responded, considering a moment after the word left her mouth that maybe she should have lied to him. She didn't want to be alone with him. Most of the time she didn't think he was interested in touching her at all. And then he'd look at her with a hunger that made her blood turn to molten lava. His actions totally confused her. She didn't know what to make of him. Right now he was showing no indication of approaching. He was being reasonable, if high-handed. She supposed she should try to be reasonable in return.

"I shouldn't share my quarters with a man," she went on sternly. "People will talk. I have my reputation to consider."

"Tonight no one will notice," he countered. He tugged the servant's pallet in front of the door.

So much for her half-formed plan to escape undetected from the castle in the middle of the night. He unfastened his sword belt, laying it near to hand beside the pallet. Then, smiling teasingly at Jane, he pulled off the scarlet surcoat. The tight-fitting black undercoat emphasized his wide shoulders and narrow waist. Beneath the knee-length undercoat his legs were encased in soft leather boots that molded tightly to his muscular calves. He began to peel the undercoat off next.

Before he could go any further she said hastily, "Good night," and disappeared behind the alcove curtain. Lying on her back, sensitized to his every movement, she tried to keep her nervous breathing as silent as possible. She tensed when his footsteps approached her doorway, only to gasp with shock when the candle flames were snuffed out. She heard the rumble of his chuckle as he moved away again.

"Sleep soundly, Lady Jehane," he called from across the length of the room. "I promise not to try to kiss you good night." She didn't bother to answer.

Soon she could hear the soft sounds of his breathing as he slept, and she thought with frustration, Men! Did he want to or didn't he? One minute he ignored her, then he acted as if he wanted to seduce her, then he ignored her again. Was the man who kissed her in the corridor the same one who was sleeping so soundly in front of her door? Her body was on fire and her nerves were just about shot and she was furious at him for being asleep when she was ready to go out of her mind.

Was he expecting her to crawl slavishly into his bed and seduce him? Did he want her, or had it been a momentary aberration? Did she want to crawl slavishly into his bed and seduce him? Yes, she admitted to herself. And no. She knew she wouldn't give in to the urge, even though it was close to overpowering her resolve for a few moments. Her senses felt singed, ready to burst into flame, but the chaste widow Jehane FitzRose was not going to compromise herself with a Welsh mercenary. No matter how much she wanted to.

Did she want to? Really? An image other than Daffyd's rose up out of the darkness to haunt her with a sudden stab of fear. She could see the outlaw clearly, smell him, feel him. The memory wasn't as painful as it had been even a day ago. It didn't make her want to scream with terror and revulsion, but it served to dampen the longing she'd been feeling. Maybe, she reconsidered, I'm not ready to make love yet, even if I think I want to.

So she lay in her lonely bed and turned her restless thoughts away from Daffyd ap Bleddyn.

Never mind him, she told herself as her anxious thoughts returned to her more serious problem. What was she going to do about John?

Obviously she had to get out of the castle before he arrived. But how? She could run off into the woods or try to flee by what passed for roads. Then what? Stephan would just come searching for her. Her disappearance would cause more fuss than her presence.

She could tell Jonathan she would go with him. Would he want to stay for the king's visit or avoid him as well? He was a priest, but not one involved in the religious quarrel. Perhaps she could persuade him that for the sake of her soul she needed to get herself to a nunnery, fast.

Her restless thoughts flitted to the image of Daffyd's beautifully muscled body as he stood only in his undercoat. She couldn't help remembering the time he had stood before her only in his skin. Her mind's eye wandered over every perfect inch of him. The memories tempted her to go to him now. The memories of Pwyll's rough hands and leering face kept her right where she was.

It wouldn't be lying to Jonathan to tell him she had to get away from worldly temptation, she acknowledged, although she didn't know if it was her soul, or history, or her sanity that was more at stake. But she had to get away from here, and soon. Jonathan's offer was the most sensible, the least suspicious route. She would talk to him first thing in the morning, she resolved.

She turned on her side and tried to sleep. She thought having a plan would ease her mind enough to let her get some needed rest. Instead she found her ears were tuned to every little sound coming from the storeroom. Her emotions were in a continued churned-up turmoil over the man sleeping by her door.

She was aching with need. All her arguments couldn't make it go away.

She hated admitting it to herself. It made her feel weak, and she didn't dare be weak. Not with Sir Daffyd, not with anybody. She'd already become too involved with the lives of these people. It would be the worst kind of folly to take a lover, to deviate one inch from the only safe course of action. She had to think of the future, not satisfying her own hopeless desires. One kiss *could not* make her change her mind.

She rolled and tossed and turned on the narrow straw mattress for hours. Sleep didn't find her until nearly dawn.

21

She was awakened by the sensual drag of a hot, moist tongue across the base of her throat. Strands of long hair tickled her cheek. Jane rolled her head languidly, making a soft, pleased sound, and opened her eyes. The eyes looking soulfully into hers were brown, long-lashed, and grinned at her above a long-nosed white muzzle. The dog was lying at her side, its head thrust toward her face.

"Nikki!" she scolded loudly. "Get off me!"

The dog, ignoring her totally, rested its head on Jane's shoulder, with a loud, snorting sigh that seemed to say it was happy to wait here with its mistress forever, but that it would really rather be fed now, please. Jane's hand came up automatically to pet the animal.

Jane's first reaction of chagrined annoyance faded quickly to faintly embarrassed amusement. What, she wondered, had she been dreaming to mistake the mutt here for, well, for, never mind. She shook her head back and forth on the pillow. She was very glad there hadn't been anyone else to witness her waking.

"I wonder if Sleeping Beauty really happened this way." she inquired of the dog, whose silky, floppy ears perked up at her words.

Sunlight streamed into the room from the narrow window high up near the ceiling. It warmed her cheeks; gold light bathed her eyelids. The mattress was comfortable, Nikki was a warm, friendly weight at her side. She drifted back into a languorous doze, only to be woken the next time by Vince, standing by the bedside, barking in her ear.

She sat up straight with a startled, "What!" She looked around frantically, "Oh, my God! What's the time!"

Why the devil hadn't Bertram or that useless serving woman woken her up! she railed angrily as she threw on clothes. Didn't they know the king was coming tomorrow? She had to talk to the cook. To Bertram. DeCorte. They would have to send to Canterbury for more flour. More everything. What was she doing staying in bed until the middle of the day!

Then household details were eclipsed as she remembered something even more important. "I have to talk to Jonathan!"

The dogs scrambled to get out of her way as she marched purposefully out of the sleeping alcove. She nearly tripped over Daffyd ap Bleddyn's saddlebags as she made for the door. She kicked them out of her way, then paused. What was he still doing here? Shouldn't he have ridden back to Reculver by now?

She ignored her annoyance at Daffyd's continued presence. She had more important things to think about. As she came out into the hallway, Sir

Stephan came clattering down the upper stairs. The slender young man was in full chain-mail shirt and coif. The iron rings practically danced from the speed of his loping stride. He came to a dead stop in front of her.

"Jehane. Good. I heard the news not an hour ago. That idiot Wolf didn't want to disturb me! I can bed my wife anytime," he went on pragmatically. "It's not every day I've got a king under my roof!" He patted her shoulder. "The demesne's in fine condition, thanks to you. All will be well. At least I won't have to send messages to all the other nobles to attend the king at Passfair. They're all still here, nursing their sore heads. I've got to see to the guards!"

He was off down the hall stairs without a backward glance. Jane stared after him, openmouthed, for several moments. By the time she recovered from his breathless vote of confidence—not sharing it, just recovered from it—Alais was at the bottom of the bower stairs, beckoning to her.

"My lady must see you," Alais said in tones of urgent distress. "The poor lamb's so dreadfully distraught."

Jane lifted her eyes pleadingly to heaven. All she saw were the low beams of the ceiling, still sooty from last night's torches. She figured she was on her own. "Coming," she said, lifting her skirts and starting up the bower stair.

She had seen Sibelle distraught. The young woman occupying the window seat, twisting her wedding rings nervously, was perturbed, but a far cry from the hysterical maniac Jane had been afraid she would find. She gave Alais a sour look before going to Sibelle's side.

"All will be well," she soothed, taking the girl's hands in her own. "It will only be for a few days. Think of the entertainment. Think of the honor our lord John does us."

The girl's tiny, bow-shaped mouth thinned in an unexpectedly hard line. Her blue eyes snapped. "You don't understand, Jehane. King John's my kinsman, with no affection between his line and father's. The Angevin blood in our veins comes through bastardy. But we are kinsmen. I know nothing about King John. He must have been very young, or not even born yet, when Granny Rosamunde was at court. She never mentioned him. Father didn't take part in those quarrels a few years ago with Arthur of Brittany. He stayed neutral and tended his English lands. I know he worried afterward that not siding with anyone made him suspicious to everyone." She looked Jane worriedly in the eye. "Will the king be an enemy or friend to my lord because of our marriage?" she asked. "Is he spiteful? Or does he judge each man on his own merits? Have I brought trouble to my husband?"

Oh, dear, Jane thought. She sat down beside Sibelle and continued to hold her hands comfortingly. She didn't answer immediately. She couldn't. She had to make a decision. The Angevin empire and the early Plantagenets were her special field of study. She knew more than she wanted to about the mean-spirited, spiteful, cowardly, lecherous, and treacherous king who was on his way to this out-of-the-way demesne. But she couldn't bring herself to explain anything about John to Sibelle, not even that he had a preference for young, lushly endowed women. She couldn't give Sibelle any advice because for all she knew the next few days might prove terribly important to the history of England. Just because she'd never come across a reference to Sir Stephan DuVrai or his lady Sibelle didn't mean they didn't play some pivotal role in some unchronicled power game. Not every day of a king's life was chronicled, after all.

"I hope everything will be all right," she said at last. "I know nothing of John, either. I was born in another land." She took her hands from Sibelle's. "I have so much to do. Excuse me, my lady."

She felt like a complete and total rat all the way through the hall and onto the hall steps. She took her mood out on the first deserving creature she saw as she walked out into the bright but cool day.

"Ap Bleddyn," she growled loudly at the man just putting his foot on the first step, "what are you still doing here?"

He gazed up at her, his mouth opened in stunned shock. Then he peered closer, squinting curiously, as if not quite sure who was speaking to him.

"Why aren't you in Reculver, or chasing brigands?" she demanded. "Instead of leaving your belongings all over my room?"

He bounded up the two steps. "Lady Jehane, you startled me."

"Tripping over your saddlebags was a startling experience for me as well."

"To answer your question," he went on, sweeping his arm to take in the whole of Passfair, "I brought my men here yesterday. And here we stay as extra guards for the king's household until he chooses to leave the dangerous environs of Blean. Our lord John," he added, "is a very careful man."

"Mmm," she mumbled. "So you'll be sharing my quarters for the duration?"

He gave her his most rakish smirk. "Does my presence disturb you so very much, sweet Jehane?" He lifted his fingers as if to touch her cheek, then seemed to think better of it. His hand dropped to his side.

She ignored the flirtation, if indeed that was what it was. "Will the king stay long?" She was mentally counting livestock and other supplies.

"As long as the game holds any sport for him," was Daffyd's ambiguous answer.

At least they'd have deer for the table. "Looks like those hounds will finally be earning their keep," she commented, glancing toward the kennel and dog runs she'd had rebuilt to hold the royal hounds Stephan was responsible for. She had two boys keeping the kennel now, making sure they were well tended.

"Perhaps not," Daffyd replied, following her gaze.

She gave him a puzzled look. "The king will be bringing his own hounds, I suppose?"

He nodded solemnly, running a thumb along his jaw. "The quarry he's come to hunt isn't deer, Jehane, but men."

She stared at the Welshman, profoundly disturbed. "What? What men?"

"Sikes and his outlaws. Who else? He's heard about our local problem and thinks to give his bored warriors some sport."

She swallowed bile. "A manhunt?"

"He's bringing Louvrecaire and his *routiers*."

"I've heard of Louvrecaire," she said grimly.

"A hellhound to chase a few starving outlaws." His

tone was as grim as hers, edged with bitter anger as well.

"I must talk to Jonathan," she said suddenly, speaking the thought aloud.

Daffyd's expression turned from revulsion to mere annoyance. "Whatever for, Lady Jehane? Seeking the most ardent and well favored of your many suitors, perhaps?"

"Suitors?" She gave him a pained look. "I don't want suitors. Besides, Jonathan's a priest."

He rested his hand on his sword, his whole manner casually unimpressed with the news. "I've known many a man whose father was a good priest," he said.

He had a point. "Jonathan isn't like that," she said, defending her friend. "Have you seen him?"

"He's in Passfair village, I think."

"Thank you." She hurried toward the gate. To her annoyance, Sir Daffyd ambled after her.

Before they reached the main gate two guards came running up, one in Sir Daffyd's colors, the other a Passfair man. "Riders approaching!" both men shouted excitedly.

Sir Stephan rode into view from the paddock. He stood in his saddle to get a better view of the road. "Riders," he confirmed. "DeCorte, gather an escort!" he called to the guard sergeant as he came running down from the platform circling the keep's outer wall.

"Yes, Sir Stephan."

Jane could just make out the large cloud of dust coming up from the road off on the horizon. Riders. Lots of riders.

She swung accusingly on Sir Daffyd. "I thought you said tomorrow."

"You coming, Wolf?" Stephan called.

Sir Daffyd shrugged. "I was wrong." He loped away, toward the stables.

Jane sat down on a bench near the inner gate. There was no getting away before the king's arrival. She considered crying.

22

It wasn't that bad, Jane repeated to herself from the farthest shadowed corner of the hall, where she sat with three of the serving women at her side. The girls kept throwing nervous glances at the lecherous group of a dozen or more *routiers* gathered nearer the hearth. The women were with her because their lowly station didn't allow them the relative safety of the bower. Nor could they run, like the village girls, to the haven in the woods Switha prepared for such occasions.

Besides the half dozen nobles and their thirty or more retainers, and all the servants it took to keep a royal establishment functioning, the king had brought the group of mercenaries now being quartered in the hall. The king and his court were enjoying the May air in the comfort of luxuriously appointed pavilions. The local nobles had been granted one large tent for their own use. This mark of royal favor helped clear the hall for the scum who'd settled in as if they owned the place.

It wasn't that bad, Jane silently asserted again, sparing a reassuring look for a girl with a large, purple bruise in the shape of a mailed hand covering one side of her face. The cause of the bruise had been the girl's unwillingness to be bent over a table and raped. One of Sir Daffyd's men had put a stop to the assault, but not before getting a knife cut across his arm for his efforts. So far, Jane couldn't see any difference between these notorious outcast mercenaries and the men they'd been brought here to hunt.

The women had come to her asking for help. Reasoning that there was safety in numbers, and hoping that her rank gave added protection, she'd kept the women by her side as much as possible for the last two evenings.

The men were lewd, filthy, and vicious, but she preferred their presence on the far side of the room to any sight of King John. So far she'd been lucky. He'd been at Passfair for three days and she'd yet to catch sight of him. She knew she was lucky to be a small fish in a small pond. Her duties were unimportant, her rank only that of a knight's widow. The chances were good there would be no interaction between herself and the king of England. Her fear of doing something to change the future was beginning to abate.

Stephan and Sibelle had been called to the pavilions the first night, along with all the other nobles staying at Passfair. The young couple returned very late. Jane sat in the bower waiting for them, telling herself there was nothing to be worried about. It was just a royal summons to exchange polite words. Very chivalrous, really. Stephan came in pale with suppressed anger. Sibelle's lips were swollen. There were unshed tears in her eyes. The couple didn't elaborate on their dinner with Cousin John, but Jane assumed he'd made a pass at the girl. Since then, Sibelle had kept to the bower, claiming illness. Sir Stephan was having an easier time of it with his wife tucked away. He had no trouble moving with confidence in the society of warriors and courtiers in the king's train.

Jane hadn't seen Sir Daffyd since just before the king's arrival. Rumor had it he was quartered, with a willing lady, in one of the pavilions. Irritably she thought that rumor could go hang.

She had not been able to talk Jonathan into leaving. He said he thought he might like to see a king. Like herself, the Templar stayed mostly in the background, spending some time with Stephan at the royal camp, but more time in Passfair and Hwit with the villagers. She limited herself to the castle as much as possible.

It wasn't so bad, she repeated to herself, bunching the cloth she was embroidering nervously in her hands. The supper tables were being set up; the noise from the men was getting louder. The hounds of hell, Jane thought, watching them through suspiciously narrowed eyes.

It *was* bad if you were an outlaw. The hunt was going well. Three outlaws had so far been brought in alive. It was thought at least two more had been wounded but crawled off to die in the forest. Jane felt sorry for the ones brought in alive. She knew what crimes the men were guilty of, but she didn't think their crimes were any excuse for the pleasure the hunters got from flaying the men alive. She'd heard a great deal of screaming from the camp. She was very glad she hadn't seen any of it.

She wished the dinner hour were over so she could take the girls out to the sleeping pallets she'd had placed in the kennels. The girls didn't mind sharing the dogs' vermin, and the dogs were proving to be very protective of their nighttime companions. The *routiers* had yet to discover the big deerhounds were about as fierce as Winnie the Pooh. At least they growled a good game, Jane thought. Maybe they would take on someone threatening one of their humans. She just hoped nobody got drunk and randy enough to test the dogs' limits.

She sighed as Bertram came to fetch the serving women. He gave her a regretful look, but there was, after all, work to be done.

Michael, Melisande shadowing him, came down the stairs carrying his lute as Bertram shepherded the girls away. Michael had been in the bower entertaining his lady. Now he'd come down to perform his duties in the hall. Jane wasn't too frightened for the boy around the fighters. So far none of them had shown any interest in young boys. He played lively music for them, and it didn't hurt that he had the large Melisande constantly at his side. The men greeted Michael's arrival with a cheer. His round face split in a wide grin at some of the crude words of welcome he received.

Jane stood, intending to retreat to the bower herself, but turned back at the stairs when a loud commotion erupted behind her. The emotion and noise level of the shouting changed abruptly. She turned, expecting to see another bloody fight.

Instead she saw a retinue of gorgeously dressed men and women entering through the screen. They were trailing behind a short, flabby, dark-haired man dressed all in shades of green. He wore a great many gold chains with medallions around his neck, and several rings decorated each hand. He was greeting the *routiers* with smiles and compliments on their hunting skills. They were loudly praising his might, on the field and in the bedchamber. Sir Daffyd and Sir Stephan were on either side of the man, both looking down on him warily. He was, of course, John, king of England, count of this, duke of that—most of it real estate in France he didn't own anymore thanks to his own bungling incompetence. And a little help from his cousin Arthur of Brittany and the king of France.

Jane's first reaction was to run up the stairs. She went with it.

"My lady," she said, bursting in to find Sibelle ensconced behind a big embroidery hoop, "the king!"

Sibelle jumped up, knocking over the embroidery stand. "Where?" She looked as if she thought he might be hiding under the loom.

And she was acting as if he might be, too, Jane chided herself. She waited for her racing heart to slow down a bit before explaining. "He just came into the hall."

"What's he doing here?"

Jane spread her hands before her. "Honoring your house with his presence?"

Sibelle looked unhappy. "I'm very honored." She helped Alais right the fallen frame. "As long as I don't have to see him."

"Poor lamb," Alais comforted her.

"It's Stephan who's the poor lamb," Sibelle retorted. "He must spend his days and most of his nights in company with the man. He's crude, and he's ugly."

"Calm yourself," Jane said firmly. She looked

around as as if to imply someone might be listening. "And mind your tongue."

Sibelle looked down contritely. "You're right, of course. I don't know what I'm saying."

As she finished speaking, Stephan entered. He came to Sibelle and took her hands in his. They kissed, then he said regretfully, "Since you are too ill to come to the king, he's decided to come to you at Passfair."

Sibelle's eyes widened with fear. "What?"

"I've told him you might be well enough to partake of the evening meal with him," Stephan went on firmly. He obviously wanted to get this little speech over with. And he didn't want to be argued with. "You will join us in the hall for dinner." He swept his gaze to Jane. "You and your ladies with you."

"My lord . . ."

He clasped the girl fiercely to him for a few moments, stroking her back and shoulders. "It's only for one evening," he assured her. "Smile and be silent at his flattering words. I will be beside you, and it is *I* who will bring you to our bed tonight. Tonight and every other night, my heart."

Jane witnessed this display of protective affection in a haze of chilling apprehension. Damn. Damn, damn, damn. She balled her hands into fists, wanting to beat the stones of the wall in frustration. She stood still as a statue, cold dread twisting painfully through her. It settled like a lead weight on her mind as the women cried out, then began bustling back and forth between bower and bedchamber.

"Lamb!" Alais cried, bringing Sibelle's blue silk wedding dress out of a clothes chest. "You must wear your best kirtle. You must go into the hall as proud and well dressed as any of the court ladies below."

Sibelle broke from Stephan's protection to round on her serving woman. "Nonsense!" she hissed angrily. "Beautiful is the last thing I need to be tonight. I don't want to hear murmurs of how much I resemble the fair Rosamunde, flower of his father's heart," she mocked in a high-pitched singsong. "He's no troubadour, our lord John." She grabbed the dress from the stunned woman's hands.

She rounded on Jane, a calculating look in her eyes. "Let me borrow your yellow kirtle. I can bunch the extra fabric up well enough with the purple belt."

"You look awful in yellow, lamb," Alais protested.

Marguerite came forward, touching Alais on the shoulders. "The point exactly, dearest."

Alais's troubled expression cleared. She threw back her head and laughed.

"The dress?" Sibelle asked Jane.

Jane pulled her thoughts from her own worries long enough to reply, "It's got a wine stain on the skirt."

"So much the better," Sibelle answered. "Marguerite," she went on, "do you think that if we fastened the barbette a little loosely around my chin, it might make it look fatter?"

Sir Stephan stood back, crossed his arms, gazing in proud wonder at his wife. "Hurry and get the dress, Jehane," he ordered his chatelaine.

Jane was loaded down with a sense of personal doom, but she could still appreciate the cleverness of Sibelle's efforts to frighten off a king. She gave Stephan a conspiratorial nod, then hurried down to her room.

Sibelle was ready to face the king a few minutes

after Jane returned with the stained overdress. Alais was right about the color not suiting the girl's pink complexion. Veiling covered her glorious hair, and her small face seemed rounder. She didn't look awful, not like the girl who'd come to Passfair not so long ago, but she didn't look great, either.

"You'll do," Stephan decided when he saw the finished product. He stepped up to her and kissed her forehead. "And I love you," he proclaimed in front of the other women. He shook a teasing finger at her and gave her his amazing, wide smile. "Just don't look like this after the king's gone."

"Never," she promised, eyes shining into his. Then she lowered them demurely, holding out her hand. "I'm ready now, my lord."

Jane trailed behind, the last person out of the room, the last person down to the hall. Stephan and Sibelle were already seated at the high table. The king occupied the chair in the center, Sibelle was seated to his right, Stephan was farther down, somewhere near the end of his own table. Jane was glad there were too many people of high rank present for there to be any room for her lowly self at the high table. She ducked her head and hurried to a place at a nearly empty trestle set up in the back of the room near the screen wall. It was just across from the *routiers'* table, but it seemed safer than somewhere closer to the king's sight.

As soon as she was seated with her back to the high table, she began to relax. From her shadowed corner, she could survey the crowded room without being noticed. Bertram, as usual, had the serving of the meal well in hand. The girls were assigned to the higher tables. Michael and another lad, the swine-

herd, she thought, were bustling around the *routiers'*
table, keeping them in meat and ale. Melisande and
her pups, grown to about half her size, were roaming
the hall scavenging scraps. Jane did not look up
toward the high table. She did, however, spare a fleeting smile at Sibelle's ingenuity. She figured the girl
was going to be okay.

"You're lovely when you smile," a chocolate-rich
voice said from her left.

She looked up and up. "And you're very tall when
you loom over me," she answered, still amused
enough by Sibelle's ruse to give Daffyd a friendly
answer. Besides, she was happy to see him. She
couldn't help it, and for once she didn't try to fight it.

He immediately threw his long legs over the bench
and took a seat beside her. "Better?" he asked, turning a winning smile on her. She nodded. "You seem
in good spirits. Enjoying the king's visit, lady?"

She gave him a sarcastic look. Bertram came by
and piled both their trenchers high with bread and
meat mixed with an unrecognizable greenish-gray
vegetable mush. It did smell strongly of onions.
What didn't? She poked at the concoction with
her spoon, then took a bite of coarse black bread.
She wondered what the high table was being
served.

Daffyd set to his meal with gusto. After washing
down a chunk of bread with a swig of ale, he
looked at her plate meaningfully. "You don't eat
enough," he complained. "Though I admit I like
you long and willowy."

She ignored the compliment. He'd been hanging out
with courtiers. They always talked like that. "And I must
admit I don't much like English fare," she told him. "I

much prefer the food of my own land." She pushed her plate away, then folded her hands before her on the table and looked up at him imploringly. "You wouldn't have any baklava with you, I don't suppose?"

He chuckled and shook his head. "I've heard of the sweet, though," he answered. "It's nuts and honey in a pastry, isn't it?" She nodded. He rubbed his chin thoughtfully. "Perhaps I'll have a talk with the king's cook."

She supposed he was joking, but the thrill of pleasure she felt at his thoughtful words was pleasantly undeniable. He was smiling, his eyes full of amusement and something unreadable. He reached out toward her face, his large hand stopping just short of touching her. "May I?" he asked, his rich voice quietly intent.

She could see the callused palm and elegant fingers from the corner of her eye, feel the warmth of his skin on her cheek. She moistened her dry lips with her tongue as she gave an almost imperceptible nod.

Instead of touching her, he flipped her veil back a single fold. "There," he said. "I'd almost forgotten what you look like. Sometimes it's hard to really get a good look at anyone in these dark buildings," he went on. His voice was chocolate and cream when he added, "I like you in sunlight more than in shadows, Jehane."

Jane felt his words as much as heard them. He used his wonderful voice to caress her, making her feel alive and beautiful and excited. She moistened dry lips again, almost wishing the touch came from his lips instead of her tongue. His hand moved to hover above hers as they rested on the table surface.

Stop this! Stop it right now, a stern voice in her mind demanded. *Think of where you are! Think of*

*who's here. This is no time to lose your head to a
skilled seducer. Get out of here. Right now. An affair
with a Welsh mercenary is the last thing you need.*

Oh, shut up, her heart and her body screamed
back at the voice of reason.

He leaned closer, and she didn't try to pull away.
She hardly noticed the shouting from the *routiers* at
the next table as they jumped to their feet, hardly saw
the green-clad figure suddenly moving in their midst.
But Daffyd did. As the group of ruffians gathered
close about the king, he pulled away from her. Spinning on the bench, he rose to his feet. Jane stared up
at the long form standing above her once more, so
drunk with his nearness, so bereft at this sudden
abandonment, that for a moment she wasn't aware of
what was going on around her.

It was Daffyd's fiercely whispering, "The king!"
that brought her back to her senses.

Jane almost jumped out of her skin at the shock.
The king! She bolted to her feet and tried to squeeze
herself behind Daffyd's wide-shouldered form as a
shield. He gave her an odd look but didn't try to move
away. Jane peeped out from behind his stalwart arm,
hoping the king wouldn't turn her way. She felt safe
enough behind Daffyd's sheltering form to risk a look
at the king.

What was he doing down here below the salt, anyway? She thought he was frowning furiously, the red
flush on his face from anger. Looking across the room,
she saw Sibelle was no longer at the high table and
decided that the lady of the manor had retreated to the
safety of her bower. Now the disappointed king of
England was looking for some low amusement with
about the lowest men of the thirteenth century.

He moved, laughing boisterously, and the hard men trailed him like puppies, toward the hearth. He had his arm around the *routier* commander, Louvrecaire. Louvrecaire made a comment and a lewd gesture, and the king laughed harder. Louvrecaire called for wine. Michael rushed forward with a jug too big for him to carry.

Jane knew it was going to happen. As she watched, the accident seemed to unfold before her in slow motion. The scrawny boy's foot slipped on some wet straw, he tumbled forward, trying desperately to keep hold of the wine jug. Dark liquid arced out of the jar's mouth as Michael fell flat on his face at the king's feet. The king's green surcoat was soaked from chest to hem with purple wine brought to Passfair as a wedding gift. The half-drunken *routiers* laughed, loud and long.

The sound must have been galling to the fat little man who held all their lives in his hands. He took it out on the prostrate boy, drawing back his foot and kicking him viciously in the ribs. The child cried out in pain. He curled up in a tight ball. The king kicked him again.

Appalled, Jane started forward automatically. Something hard as steel held her back.

It was Melisande who came to the boy's defense, rocketing forward through the crowd to stand, teeth bared and growling, hackles up, over the whimpering child as the king drew back his foot one more time.

In the room's sudden silence, the king drew a sword. One moment the dog was bravely defending Michael. The next she was a blood-covered heap on the rushes, struck down and forgotten. The king turned back to his crowd of cronies.

They were laughing again, but with the king, not at him.

23

The world turned red around Jane. Fire and ice came together as a terrible, killing rage rushing up to drown out her reason. The focus of her rage came nearer. She lunged for him, wanting only to scream and strike out and pay him back for the pain he so casually caused. She lunged but couldn't move forward. She was caught, tight bands of steel wrapped around her middle. She struggled in silent fury, flinging her head back against a mail-sheathed wall.

A voice in her ear hissed, "Stop it. Calm down, girl. There's nothing you can do." The words did nothing to soothe her. She kicked back at the leg of the man holding her. He didn't budge. He didn't release her. He just murmured soft words she didn't hear in her ear.

She jerked her head away, and as she turned it, her eyes met those of King John. Little, covetous eyes, she thought. Pig's eyes. They drank in the sight of her, and she almost spat at them. The king stepped closer, his hot eyes raking her head to foot. A slow smile spread across his bloated features. Jane tried to pull away from Daffyd again.

He hauled her into a tighter embrace. "Excuse my lady," he said to the king. "She was fond of the animal."

John came close. He took her chin in his fingers, forcing her head from side to side. He was little, but strong. The fingers touching her were greasy. Jane almost screamed. His fingers moved down to the base of her throat. "Your name—lady?"

"The Lady Jehane, widow of Sir Geoffrey FitzRose," Daffyd answered for her. "My betrothed," he added, as John's fingers reached her breast. He tugged her subtly away from the king's exploring hand.

She hauled her head around to stare angrily at Daffyd. "What?"

He shook her. "A difficult woman," he said, speaking around her to John.

"Fiery," the king said.

"A good beating will calm her," Daffyd said, his voice so matter-of-fact that Jane almost screamed with outrage. He gave a perfunctory bow, pushing her before him toward the stairs without awaiting the king's permission to leave. He had to drag her away by force. Ribald laughter followed them up the stairs.

Her anger was turning quickly to panic in the dark of the staircase. She hated this world! She didn't want to be touched! She struck out, fists and feet flying. Daffyd swore and swung her off her feet. He slung her easily over his shoulder and held her there as he marched into the storeroom.

"Out!" he shouted, and the serving woman fled. He slammed the door behind her, then flung Jane down.

By the time her knees hit the floor, Jane was start-ing to come back to her senses, but she remained where she fell for a few moments, doubled up and shaking, with her hands clutching her stomach. Reac-tion from fear and anger and adrenaline-driven hyste-ria was hitting her. Daffyd knelt beside her.

She turned her head to look at him. His eyes were snapping with anger, but he gave her the familiar smirk when he said, "I've never known anyone to panic like that to a proposal of marriage. Did Geof-frey have this much trouble with you?"

She blinked stupidly. Who was Geoffrey? "What?"

She sat back on her heels and covered her face with her hands. Her head was spinning, and it hurt, but the blood-red scene in the hall was coming back to her now. She peered hesitantly at him over her fin-gers. "What have I done?"

"Very nearly gotten yourself thrown across a table by the king of England with your dress flung up around your head," he stated bluntly. "With an audi-ence to cheer him on." He rose to his feet and paced the length of the room. She followed him with her eyes.

He spun around at the door. "Lord, girl, don't you know getting his attention was the worst thing you could have done?"

Getting John's attention was the last thing *she* had wanted, too. She'd been hiding for days, desperate to keep away from the king. Why had she tried to attack him? Why hadn't she remained calm in the midst of the ugly scene in the hall? Why the breaking point at this of all times?

"Why?" she said aloud, knowing the answer was because she couldn't stand idly by and watch anyone, king or slave, abuse a child or be cruel to a mindless beast.

"Why?" Daffyd raged at her, greenish eyes sparkling furiously in the candlelight. "Because he's a randy, rutting toad and you're just to his taste! Especially now the girl's proved to be a disappointment. Stay out of his way," he ordered. "Betrothed to one of his favorite captains or not, he still might try to bed you."

Jane got shakily to her feet. Daffyd's words were sinking into her brain. Detailed memory was returning. She rubbed her temples, pushing her fingers beneath the barbette covering them. "Yes. Thank you. It was clever of you to claim betrothal. Thank you for the lie," she said again.

He was looking at her with a sardonic tilt to his head, the angry glint still in his eyes. "It was all I could think of. And not a wise thing to say in front of the king and all those witnesses."

She stared at him while every plan she'd made for her life fell into broken shards around her. Stephan would be delighted. Jonathan would be delighted. There was no question of Daffyd's suit being refused by liege or Church. She was trapped. Daffyd held complete power over her. Why did this situation seem so familiar?

All she said, numbly, was, "No. It wasn't a wise thing to say." She lifted her head proudly and added, "I don't wish to marry you, you know."

He stepped close to her. "Jehane." He rested his hands on her shoulders.

"Don't touch me," she said tightly. He didn't let go. He came closer, until their bodies touched. Although he wasn't pressing close, she could still feel the power of his muscular body. "Please," she said. It wasn't a plea for her release. He nodded his understanding.

He put one arm around her and spread his fingers at the base of her spine. He lifted her chin with two fingers. It didn't feel at all the same as when John did it. He looked deeply into her eyes. He said, "Perhaps you need to be touched."

"Perhaps I do."

He put his hand on the back of her head, drawing her upturned face toward him. She was wide-eyed, full of trembling need. She couldn't take her eyes off his. His eyes spoke of trust and passion. Her lips opened, welcoming his kiss. It filled her with fire. The fire was cleansing, kindling passion, blotting out pain and loss and terror of the hours past and the days to come. Daffyd's hands moved over her, gentle and urgent at once. Her body responded to his touch as a lute did to a master player. She let his hands have their way, searching out her secrets through the layers of silk and linen, until his frustrated growl brought some sense back into her reeling brain.

"Touch me, woman!" he demanded.

She threw her head back on the arm holding her in a tight embrace, laughing joyously. Not without a can opener! she thought, but said, "You're dressed for war, my lord. Nothing's meant to get through all that armor."

He gave a snort of answering laughter. "True, love. But I thought you clever enough to contrive anything." He stepped away and began stripping off surcoat, mail shirt, and the quilted shirt worn beneath the heavy mail. By the time he was down to the black knit braccae covering his legs and loins, Jane was completely shed of her light summer wear. Her body was too warm and needing to shiver in the cool night air.

They looked at each other in the candle glow. His eyes danced over her, taking in every detail the same way she'd done in the same spot not so long ago. She reacted to the visual assault with the same bold abandon he'd shown then. She straightened, posed, turned slowly, throwing a seductive look over her shoulder.

He caught her to him as she finished the turn. His mouth took hers again. Their tongues entwined and slipped with hungry playfulness to trace the insides of lips and teeth.

She moved her hands across his torso, exploring his smooth-skinned, gold-pelted form as he'd urged. He purred like a big cat with each new stroke of her fingertips. She moved her mouth from his, leaving soft kisses down his strong throat, licking teasingly at each pink nipple half-hidden in a nest of gold chest hair. She'd never known this kind of powerful desire before. Need drove her, need to give and take pleasure, if only for this one night.

"This one knight," she said, laughing softly with her mouth against his throat.

"Only one Jehane," he answered. He swung her up into his arms and carried her to the bed. No one had ever done that before. She draped her arms around his neck and pulled him down on top of her, mouths pressed tightly together. This kiss sent her soaring. It was headier than wine. She gloried in it, crying out against his mouth when his hand covered her hard-peaked breast.

His lips moved to replace his hand, which moved down her body to rest at the juncture of her upraised legs. Her thighs opened willingly to the slightest of pressure. His finger began to tease and stroke her, while his tongue and lips played over her breasts. When he gently nipped the side of her breast she cried out, but not from pain. Her hand dipped down to the rigid maleness pressing up between them, closed around it, teasing and stroking to match the rhythm of his hand on her. His hips jerked forward in eager response. He caught a nipple to his mouth and suckled greedily.

The tight, hot pleasure grew unbearable. She was slippery with desire, aching to have him inside her. "Now, Daffyd," she urged.

His breath was coming in hard, ragged gasps, his fair skin suffused with heated blood. His eyes burned as they looked up into hers. She arched beneath his touch, begging for more.

"Daffyd!" she pleaded.

He took her mouth once more, a gentle touch, then covered her body with his. She welcomed him with a sharp cry, trembling and shaken with the power of her orgasm as he sheathed himself deep inside her.

White hot pleasure raced upward from the center where they joined. It was a lightning bolt, devastating her, leaving her hot and panting in its wake, yet still hungry for more as his smooth, hard shaft pierced her with deep, demanding strokes. Her hips pushed up to meet him, needing to take in all of him, to soar along with him as the pleasure climbed to greater heights. Climax took them together when it came, their bodies deeply entwined, breathing their cries of completion into each other's mouths.

They lay, melded together, for a few heartbeats while their racing hearts slowed and breathing calmed. Jane exhaled a soft moan. Daffyd collapsed on top of her with an exhausted "Umpfh!" Then he rolled to the side of the bed and drew her into his arms. He held her close, found her breast to use as a pillow.

She stroked the long hair away from his shoulder, running the blond silk through her fingers, and gazed up at the darkness outside the narrow window. She wondered at the time. She wondered what tomorrow would bring. She wondered why she was so happy when she'd just thrown all her carefully constructed plans to the winds of desire. She wondered if this feeling of newness and completion was what it felt like to be in love.

She no longer had to wonder if her erotic dreams of Daffyd ap Bleddyn would match the reality. She knew. She guessed her vivid imagination wasn't as vivid as she thought. Nothing in her dreams could compare to what had just passed between them. She told herself it didn't matter if it never happened again. He held her close. She wasn't alone. Tonight she could sleep without dreaming.

"I've wanted you," she whispered very softly into his riotously tangled hair, "since I first saw you." It didn't matter if he was awake to hear her words or not. It was probably better if he wasn't. To speak the truth as Jane Florian, even if she must be Jehane FitzRose in the morning, was enough. Being Jehane made it possible for Jane to meet and love this man. Jane could never have done it on her own.

After a short silence he sighed. He lifted his head from her breast to peer at her in the very dim light. "I've wanted you," he told her, "since the night the lad died. Or perhaps it was after that, when I saw how good you were for the girl. It wasn't your beauty I wanted, Jehane." He paused long enough to kiss her gently. "Though you are beautiful. It was the kindness that drew me back."

"Kindness?" Why wasn't she surprised to hear the word from the Welsh mercenary? But then, hadn't he been kind to her as well? He'd saved her life, made sure she was all right afterward, defending her from the king.

"Kindness. And knowing you wanted me." She didn't need to be able to see clearly to know he was looking at her with his usual smirk.

She tugged on his hair. "Insufferable."

"I can't marry you," he said. The words were spoken softly, but with bitter finality. "If I could take you from this . . . but I can't."

His words hit her like a blow, hurting her because she recognized the enormity of her mistake. For all her protests, for all the good reasons she had for living the rest of her life alone, she knew being alone was the last thing she wanted.

She'd fallen in love, and she didn't know how she could live without Daffyd ap Bleddyn after tonight. Just one night wasn't enough for her. She could never have enough of this man. How could she convince him they belonged together?

"I've been a soldier's wife," she told him, remembering Jehane's supposed history.

"I can't marry you," he said again. "Even if I wanted to. You couldn't live in my world, Jehane."

He didn't want to. He couldn't. He wouldn't. He didn't want to.

Why should he?

It hurt. Hurt enough to bring her back to her senses. She couldn't, either. Not really. Her brief vision of building a life together was just another foolish dream. Just another soap-bubble illusion burst by the cold reality of this awful place. She wanted to go home. She was as helpless as ever.

She still answered him angrily.

"Even if you *wanted* to? You claimed me as your betrothed," she reminded him.

"To save your honor."

"To save me for yourself?" she spat back. Tears scalded her cheeks.

"No! I . . ." He rolled out of the bed. "All right," he said coldly, looming above her. "Yes. It was just an excuse to bed you myself. It didn't mean anything."

"That's not true!" She leapt out of bed to confront him. "Don't lie to me. It meant something. I know it did!"

What was the matter with her? Why shouldn't she believe all he'd wanted from her was the sex? It would be easier to believe he was cold and uncaring. But she heard the pain in his voice. She remembered how protective he'd been. It was too late for her to hate him now.

His hands found her shoulders. "No," he agreed. "It's not true. It's more than lust. But . . . Why won't you let me leave you with only your pride hurt?"

"Because that would be too easy for both of us," she heard herself answer. "It's more than my pride that's hurting, Daffyd. If you must break my heart, give me a reason." *Please*, she begged silently, *don't let it be because he doesn't love me.*

"You don't know me," he told her. "I'm not the man you think I am."

She almost laughed. "You don't know anything about me, either. We could learn."

"Everything I would tell you would be a lie."

Without realizing it, he'd echoed her own thought. She didn't tell him so. "You're a landless knight who serves a hated king. I don't mind."

"You should. You deserve better. I will not marry you, Jehane." He took her in his arms. "But I want you more than any woman I've ever known. And I want you now."

In his embrace she didn't feel like talking anymore. She felt the peaks of her breasts hardening against the softly pelted muscles of his chest, felt the warm longing for his hardness begin inside her.

"You can't marry me and I can't marry you," she said, beginning to grow breathless with renewed hunger. "We can't be together after tonight."

She knew it was the truth, though the heady desire told her it was a lie.

She let him urge her back to the bed. She took his kisses and caresses, returning them with equal passion. She moved beneath him. They climaxed together, calling each other's names as they soared into a burst of light.

Jane came slowly back to herself to find Daffyd collapsed limply across her satisfied body once more.

He gave a gusty sigh, muttered, "You bit me," and was instantly asleep.

He was heavy, but she didn't try to move him off her. She was close to sleep herself. She held him tight, and thought, *Forget this "we can't be together" nonsense. I'm not giving you up. Not after what we just shared.*

I will have you, Daffyd ap Bleddyn. We can't. We shouldn't. This feeling is impossible. I don't care what you say, she vowed. *I will make you want me too much to ever let me go.*

24

Daffyd left her with a kiss before dawn. She clung to him for a moment, until she woke fully and remembered. Then she let him go. As she heard him dressing in the storeroom she reminded herself that she had to let him go. The night was gone. Just one night. She curled on her side and cried a little after the door closed behind him. She didn't feel like making puns. Then she remembered her vow before falling asleep: to make him love her. Not for just a night, but forever, somehow.

After a while she wiped her tears, got up, and bathed herself in a basin of cold water left from the day before. She dressed slowly, carefully, savoring the sensual memories of love play. Play? she questioned herself with an ironic little smile. It seemed pretty serious to her. She sighed.

She rubbed a sore muscle in her upper thigh. "Out of practice." Her step was light when she walked into the corridor. She told herself her insane decision was the right one. She felt confident and relaxed. It

helped her dodge the boy who came careening reck-
lessly up the stairs just as she reached them. She
turned to watch Michael skid to a halt, then pelt back
to stand in front of her.

"Lady Jehane! I . . . I was sent . . ." Pant, pant. "For
you."

His face was bruised and his eyes red-rimmed from
crying, but he seemed healthy enough. She grabbed
him to her in a fierce hug, and the memories of the
events leading up to her night with Daffyd came rushing back to horrify her. The boy. Melisande. The king.
Oh, God! The man she'd worked so hard to avoid
had seen her and touched her and spoken to her. He
knew of her existence. He—

No. She mustn't panic. She got tight control on her
fear. Nothing would come of it, she told herself.
Nothing happened to change anything last night.
Except her. And Michael. And perhaps Daffyd.

Michael wriggled out of her grasp. With his
breathing back to normal, he said, "Lady Sibelle
wants you in the chapel. She sent me to fetch you."
He danced nervously from foot to foot. "Please hurry.
It's important." He took off like a shot back down the
worn treads of the stairs. Jane watched him go, terrified the clumsy boy was in for another fall. Instead he
moved as if his feet had wings. She shook her head,
hoped no one of interest was in the hall at this hour,
and followed quickly after.

Sunlight pouring in the cross-shaped chapel window
gave the old stone walls a mellow glow. She found
Sibelle and Michael kneeling in a half circle near the
altar. They were looking down on something, not praying. Curious, she came toward them. Stretched out on
the floor was the bloodstained body of Melisande.

Michael shot to his feet and grabbed Jane's hand. "She'll be all right." It was more of a plea than a statement as he looked back at the hound's still form.

Sibelle looked up at Jane and nodded. "I think the wound will heal—"

Jane stared at Melisande. The dog raised her head slightly, looking at her with soft brown eyes. Her tongue lolled out ridiculously, but she let out a faint whimper of pain.

Jane sank gratefully to her knees by the dog's head, rubbing the gold-furred floppy ears. "You're alive, you silly bitch. You're alive." She kissed the warm black nose. She looked at Sibelle. "I saw the knife go in. I saw her fall. It seemed—"

"Michael and Bertram dragged her in here," Sibelle told her. "Bertram went looking for Switha but couldn't find her. So before first light, Michael came to me." She gave the boy a fond look. "I'm doing what I can. She's a healthy animal."

"What can I do to help?" Jane wanted to know. Melisande's head was lying in her lap, and she was drooling on Jane's dress. It was wonderful.

"I know Switha took some of the girls into the woods," Sibelle said. "She must still be with them. She said the Lady Spring, but she hasn't taken me there yet. Do you know the way?"

"Vaguely. She took me there in early spring. Cerdic could show me, I suppose." She wanted to find Daffyd, but this was more important at the moment.

"No! Cerdic cannot show you. No man can show you the way," Sibelle insisted in exasperation. "It's a *Lady* Spring."

Right. Of course. Sibelle's great-great-great-whatever-granny was a witch, too. Sibelle knew about such things. Jane got to her feet. "Then I'll have to remember."

"Hurry," Michael pleaded.

She looked straight at him. "Of course," she affirmed. "What else?"

And a nice long walk in the deep woods would keep her out of the king's sight. Not that he was going to remember her. Or that anything would happen anyway. Why was she so worried, just because this time travel business had got to be the stupidest thing that ever happened to anybody!

She took a deep breath. "I'll go now."

The men were out hunting outlaws again. When Jane checked with the guards at the gate, she was told the royal party was chasing their two-legged quarry in the opposite direction of where she needed to go. She breathed a thankful sigh of relief and set off as quickly as her feet would carry her through the village and onto the forest path.

She remembered the way as far as the ruined tower where she'd arrived. Once there, she stood in the clearing full of tumbledown structures and bluebells and turned slowly, taking in the massed ranks of trees. She didn't recognize the way Switha'd taken her. Everything looked different with leaves and flowers and butterflies cluttering up the scenery. She supposed she'd have to make a guess. Which way? They'd gone past lots of trees. It was a forest. Of course they'd gone past lots of trees.

She didn't know much about trees, and she didn't know much about British folklore. She knew one survey course on mythology in college didn't prepare her for dealing with real folk religion. "Trees," she said, racking her brain, trying to remember what the dotty old lady teaching the class had said about trees. "Oak. Everybody knows about oak." Oak . . .

"Oak, ash, and thorn," she said as the memory seemed to hit her in the back of the head. That was an oak there. Was that an ash? That's definitely a thorn. All in a row one right after another. All right! She could only hope it would work.

The row of trees led away from the stream. Although it was probably logical that the stream flowed out of the Lady Spring, she hoped she had chosen the right way anyway. She didn't remember traveling along the stream's meandering route the first time. She shrugged and plunged deeper into the forest.

It was cool under the trees. The air was still. Great boughs stretching toward the sky blocked out much of the light. She could hear birds high overhead, and her own breathing, and the bending and straightening of the undergrowth as she brushed through it. These faint noises seemed to be absorbed into the great, patient quiet of the forest.

She continued on determinedly for quite some time but was eventually forced to admit she had no idea where she was. There were oak trees all around her still, but no more ashes or thorns. She sank down on a moss-encrusted log and considered the situation. Looking around, she caught sight of a raven perched on a branch. It was eyeing her with its glossy black head tilted curiously to one side.

"Of course, you realize," she told it, "that I'm totally lost." It commented with a raucous croak and flew away.

She rolled her shoulders tiredly. She was hot, and

she was bruised and scraped from her encounters with the thick undergrowth. She supposed she had better try to find her way back to where she had last seen an ash or a thorn tree.

It took her at least an hour of finding and losing and finding again before she came to a spot she recognized. And she groaned in frustration. All her woodsmanship had gotten her was back to the very beginning of the path.

She stood at the edge of the clearing before the ruin of the old tower and swore at the uncaring stones for a good minute before she heard the sound of approaching hoofs. Several sets of hoofs. Coming from at least two directions.

She remembered the hunters. She'd been told they'd gone another way. What if the guards had been wrong? She remembered John's human hounds, filthy, barbaric, and lustful. The *routiers'* leaders were no better than the men they commanded. Forget chivalry. Pillage and destruction were the order of the day.

She could hear the horsemen getting nearer. The chink of mail and creak of leather reached her ears, carried on the clear breeze. Without further pause for thought, she headed, skirts flying around her pumping legs, for the shelter of the tower. She barely made it through the sagging doorway before the first rider entered the clearing.

25

Peering cautiously around the entrance, she had no trouble recognizing Hugh of Lilydrake. He rode with the reins held tightly in his gloved hand, and the expression on his narrow features was one of dark anger mixed with cautious cunning. It made Jane wonder what the troublemaking lord of Lilydrake was up to. She knew she didn't want to be caught finding out. As two other riders came into the clearing from the deep forest, she moved silently to the stairs and tiptoed up them as fast as she dared.

The three men were grouped together under the arrow slits by the time she reached the narrow openings on the second floor. She looked down on the trio, noting how well dressed the two strangers were and how fine the horseflesh was. She saw the arrogance and self-assurance in the men's body language. She got the impression these were powerful nobles indeed. She didn't remember seeing them in John's train, but she'd seen so few of the court that she knew her memory didn't matter. What were they up to? she wondered. There was a furtiveness to this gathering, sort of like a midnight deal to make a drug buy in a movie. What was up?

Maybe she should mind her own business, she countered. Maybe she didn't have a choice but to overhear them, was her immediate realization. It didn't look as though they'd agreed to meet here so they could then go somewhere else.

"You came," one of the strangers said. He wore a flat-crowned black hat. A dark blue surcoat covered a barrel chest. His nose was long and his lips thin.

The other man was dressed head to boots in chain mail, a white tabard embroidered in his coat of arms thrown over the armor. The device was a complicated concoction of gold circles, a boar's head, and flames. A thick sword belt girdled his waist. He leaned forward across the high saddle front, looking intently at Hugh. "We managed to talk the king into this manhunting you suggested. He's here, in your hand. The time will never be better. Will you do it?"

Hugh sat stiffly in his saddle. "I told you I'd get the outlaws to cause enough trouble so you could get him here. I never claimed I'd do the deed myself."

"You're a coward," said the man in the hat. He hawked, spat, then went on. "The idea sounded good enough when you suggested it to Lord Arthur. King Philip thought the plan fitting, having John die during the hunt like his ancestor William before him. These are known to be witchwoods, where no king's life is sacred. Besides, we have the outlaws and John's own bastard kin to blame. All that's left is to strike him down." He looked at Hugh with intently burning eyes. "Will you do it?"

"Arthur will reward you with land and power as he's pledged, when he is rightfully ruling the Angevin lands," the other man promised smoothly. His voice held all the insinuation of the snake in Eden.

Jane listened to the treasonous conversation half in shock. The other half of her mind was summoning up facts, easily filling in the gaps of place, time, circumstances, and personalities involved that must have brought these three men together to instigate the assassination of a king.

Arthur would be Arthur of Brittany, or a pretender, rather. The real Arthur was dead by now, probably by his cousin John's own hand. There had been several pretenders. The king of France, Philip Augustus, didn't discourage any of them. All the intrigue was to his advantage. He was busy chopping up England's French empire.

It seemed this particular false Arthur had allies among the king's closest cronies. Well, John was good at getting people to hate him.

She remembered Michael and the dog, the flayed-alive outlaws, Sibelle hiding in her bower, the girls terrified of the *routiers* kept on the king's own leash, his hands on her. She nodded grimly. Not a very lovable man.

Besides, the barons wanted power, she thought, putting personal experience aside. In a few years they would force him into signing the Magna Carta to curb his excesses. They would do it for their own selfish reasons, but it would turn out to be a first step on the road to rights and freedom for everyone. In the end John would do something good for England, though he would hate every second of it.

Unless, of course, John died first, before Magna Carta.

"All right," Hugh said. His voice had the shrillness of nails on a chalkboard. Jane shuddered at the sound. "I'll do it," he agreed. "After you make sure his guards are out of the way."

"We'll lead them into the forest," the mailed warrior promised. "No fear of that."

"Do it tomorrow," the other noble urged. "We've wasted enough time. Kill the king tomorrow."

Hugh's gulp was audible all the way up to the top of the tower. His face was totally colorless, his muscles so bunched with tension that he was quivering. "All right," he rasped out. He turned his horse and spurred it away, throwing his last word on the matter over his shoulder as he went. "Tomorrow!"

The nobles looked from him to each other. "It will succeed," the man in the hat said. "It had better. I hope the king doesn't notice our absence. He gets suspicious if a man's not constantly at his side."

The other nodded. "John will be dead by this time tomorrow. What matter if he gives us hard looks tonight? We'll find a wench or two to bed and claim the sport was too good to give up quickly." There was a snort of rude laughter from his companion. The warrior went on. "We needed to talk to Lilydrake. We needed to push him. His nerve's not as high as I hoped."

"It will have to do. Too late to worry now." They kicked their horses forward. The last words she heard before they reached the edge of the clearing were, "We'll spend the waiting time taking our pleasure."

Jane slid slowly down the wall to sit with her head propped in her hands. The scene she'd just witnessed was burned in her memory. Of all the complications besetting her life since she'd tumbled through time to this very spot, this was the worst. She was cold with dread and furious at fate for throwing this very unwanted knowledge her way.

This couldn't be happening! What was she going to do? What *could* she do?

She waited for a long time after the riders were gone, and it was getting close to sunset before she cautiously made her way down the tower stairs. Her mind raced, but her steps back to Passfair were slow. She didn't want to think, and she succeeded much of the time. She didn't want to make decisions. She kept thinking about *Richard II*. Not the king, the play. The line about sitting on the ground and telling sad tales about the death of kings kept popping into her brain.

And Richard's descended from John, she thought. And if John dies, Richard—who wasn't a good king, either, but had a great play written about him—won't be born and Shakespeare will probably end up as an accountant or schoolteacher or something and will never write about him, and then no one will ever think of England as a jewel set in a silver sea.

And it'll all be my fault.

The stars were coming out and the guards were getting ready to close the castle gates when she dragged reluctantly into the bailey. Receiving respectful nods of greeting from two of Daffyd's men posted at the inner gate, she nodded back and trudged on. Standing just inside the inner wall, she looked around, her eyes taking in all the usual sights. Stables and kitchen to the right and left of the courtyard, the other outbuildings ringing the square stone castle over a several-acre area of the hillside.

The light was almost gone. The sky was a rich, deep dark royal blue, jewel-dotted at the zenith, cut through with deep purple-and-orange ribbons of fading light at the horizon. All the usual smells and sounds assaulted her ears. Everything was going on as it had happened yesterday and the day before and should happen tomorrow.

Only she knew that tomorrow a king would die. Somehow the lord and lady—the bastard kin and her husband—would be implicated in the murder. This holding would probably fall to Hugh of Lilydrake as part of his reward for the assassination. The peasants would have a new master. Perhaps it wouldn't matter to them; one oppressor was much like another. She knew it would matter to some. To Bertram and Marguerite and Alais and Switha and Cerdic and Raoul. It would matter to Michael and the pets and to Jonathan. It certainly mattered to her.

It might matter to Daffyd.

She struck her forehead with her palm. Of course! Why hadn't she thought of Daffyd before?

She could try to talk to the king, but even if she could approach him, she doubted he would believe her. And she doubted she could even get to him. Maybe if he came back to the hall tonight. It might be possible then. But John might be more interested in bedding her than listening to her. She shuddered with revulsion at the thought.

But Daffyd, her mind raced on, worked for him. "High in the king's favor," was how Daffyd had put it. If she could get Daffyd to believe her, he could take word to the king. John would be safe. England would be safe. More important, Passfair would be safe. Daffyd might not want to marry her, but he'd always been there to help her before.

What did she mean, if he believed her? Of course he believed her. He had to believe her. She loved him.

She knew her reasoning wasn't exactly objective. But even if she tried to keep her emotions out of it, Daffyd ap Bleddyn still seemed the logical person to seek out with her information. She began crossing the courtyard with a new sense of purpose.

As she reached the stone steps, she heard Jonathan call her name. She looked up as he hurried down from the door to meet her. "What?" she asked, heart pounding with dread as the Templar grabbed her arm and pulled her aside.

"Don't go in just now," he advised, looking back at the castle entrance. "I'm glad I saw you as I came out."

She followed his glance nervously. "What's wrong? What's happened? Has the king been—"

"He's been asking about you. King John's been asking for you," he elaborated as she looked at him in confusion. Before she could ask any questions, a group of men came out the door and waited on the steps. The king followed after them.

"God's blood!" Jonathan swore in a furious whisper. "He wants you, lass." He pushed her toward the stables, away from the bloom of torches held by the king's party. "Try hiding in the loft. I'll see if I can divert him with talk of God."

"Jonathan!" she pleaded. "Don't get yourself in trouble over me."

She made out a flash of white teeth as he smiled. "All right, I'll talk to the king about gold. He's been seeking a loan from the Templars, and I was sent to negotiate it," he confided.

Jane stopped in her tracks. "What? You're a diplomat?"

The smile flashed again. "Saving souls is only what I do in my spare time, sweet Jehane." He kissed her firmly on the mouth, then pushed her toward the stables. She could hear the king's party crossing the courtyard. She was remembering what Daffyd had said about priests' sons. The light was growing closer. "I'm glad you decided on Daffyd," he added, then turned to approach the king.

She almost called him back to tell him about the assassination plot. Then she thought about how close John was. He'd been asking for her. John of the covetous eyes and grasping hands. She ran for the stable.

As she started up the ladder to the hayloft, she heard a horseman riding up behind her, heard the voice of a questioning groom, a grunted answer. She scrambled up the last few rungs and buried herself under a pile of straw just as the man led his horse in himself. She heard the chink of mail and peeped just a little over the edge of the loft. There was a torch set in a bracket next to one of the stalls, and she got a glimpse of the top of a conical helmet before easing backward out of sight.

Jane wondered which of the numerous guards quartered at Passfair was moving around below her. Friend or foe? If the king was looking for her, any guard who found her had to be considered a foe. It would be no more than duty for the man to take her to the king. She hoped he'd go away soon. The man set about grooming his horse.

Her worried thoughts kept buzzing restlessly while she waited for the soldier to leave. Perhaps nothing would come of the plot. John didn't die at an assassin's hand, she reminded herself. The nasty little twerp died of natural causes. Nothing was really at risk, she tried to convince herself. Hugh would lose his nerve. He'd get caught. No, if there was an attempt, it would have gotten chronicled.

Maybe it had and the record had gotten lost. Her century didn't know everything about the period. That was why she'd joined Time Search, so she could interpret new information in the light of previous records. But this little gem had never showed up in the data.

The man in the horse stall began crooning softly to his horse in a deep, rich-as-dark-chocolate voice. Jane jumped up. She knew that voice! Even if she couldn't hear the words and had never heard him sing, she knew the sound of Daffyd ap Bleddyn's voice when she heard it. She thought she'd know that voice if it was calling to her from the other side of the grave. It was calling, unknowingly, to her now. She took a step toward the ladder as the crooning turned into song.

She could hear the familiar words. She stopped, at first not understanding the language but troubled by the knowledge that she knew the song from somewhere. Welsh?

But Sibelle had said he didn't speak Welsh.

No. It wasn't Welsh. She didn't speak Welsh either. But she did speak the language Daffyd ap Bleddyn was using.

". . . day and night on our faces . . . living from moment to moment . . . we've no symbols left . . . of what was once . . . a year in black . . ."

Jane closed her eyes. Her head was spinning as the words penetrated her mind like some magic incantation. She knew that song. Of course she knew it. It was in the language she'd spoken all her life. A language she had never thought to hear again. It was a classic, a golden oldie. But not one from the thirteenth century. She'd known the song when she was a teenager. She wouldn't be a teenager for about eight hundred years.

Jane Florian sat down hard on the piled-up hay, her world crashing around her one more time. Below her, the man she loved went right on singing in a language he had no right to know.

26

What was he? Who *was he?* Where was he from?

Her head was pounding, her heart twisting and breaking. She remembered his touch, his eyes, his mouth covering hers, how perfectly their bodies melded together. She remembered him—abrasive, teasing, tantalizing, infuriating, brave, and protective. She remembered everything about him, but she didn't know him at all.

Eventually the stranger stopped singing. By then she was crying, great, silent sobs racking her. She heard his footsteps on the packed-earth floor below as he finally went away.

More important, she questioned, making herself think beyond her own sense of betrayal, what was he doing here? Think, woman! She tried to stop crying, to steady her breathing, to make her mind work.

All right, what were the facts? She had been sent there by a time machine. It was a prototype, a risky experiment. An experiment that worked. If one person could be transferred successfully, so could others. That's what David Wolfe must have been working for. Okay, so they had time travel technology back home. What were they doing with it?

If they'd had any sense, they would have dismantled it. But it was a government-funded project. Governments had this way of not having much sense. For all she knew, there were hundreds of time travelers, running around bumping off kings or handing out personal computers to their ancestors. It could happen. If one lone historian could be thrown eight hundred years into the past by a drunk kid, anything could happen.

But it had only been a few months. The sort of technology and organization needed for this paranoid fantasy couldn't have been developed in so short a time. *We're talking time travel here, Jane,* she reminded herself. The people involved in time travel might be from hundreds of years after the twenty-first century. They could have been doing it for a long time. They could have turned all of time into a battleground.

And Daffyd ap Bleddyn—whoever he was—was one of them.

What did she do about it? Ask him for a ride home, maybe? She chewed nervously on the tip of a fingernail, thinking hard.

"No," she whispered. Below her a horse nickered softly at the sound of her voice. "I can't trust him. He might be the person really behind the plot to kill the king. He's not my friend. He's not my lover. I'm going to have to think of him as my enemy and be very, very cautious from now on."

She didn't want to be cautious with Daffyd. She

wanted to run to him and shout at him and demand explanations. The deep hurt and sense of betrayal were almost impossible for her to control.

She had loved him, she thought. Not just for one night, but ever since he'd appeared out of the smoke on her first day at Passfair. She'd never seen anyone like him, so powerfully, arrogantly, primally male. Not a man from her own time, but a conquering warrior, secure in the strength of his sword, the surety of his place in his world.

Every bit of it was a lie.

She got up and cautiously made her way down the ladder. Moving quietly, ghostlike, disturbing neither the horses nor the grooms sleeping in the empty stalls, she went out into the courtyard.

The square of ground was white with moonlight. Clinging to the shadow of the building, then of the inner wall, she made her way slowly toward the gate. She didn't know why she didn't want to return to the castle, but the need to flee was strong. She had to get away from plots and politics and false lovers. She wanted to hide herself in the forest, where there were only wolves and brigands to worry about.

There was a group of men by the gate, gathered near a fire while they passed around a skin of ale. Whoever else was there, she would know all the guards from Passfair. She could command them to let her through. She peeled herself away from the safety of the shadows and boldly approached the group.

Only to be caught from behind by someone she hadn't noticed before. "At last!" a familiar voice shouted out. "I told you there was some sport to be had at this broken-down keep."

The man's breath smelled of stale wine. A hand hard as a brick began squeezing her breast. The guards at the gate turned to look but didn't run forward to stop the man. One called a question. One of the other guards pulled him aside.

"Help!" she called. "Stop it!" she screeched at the man holding her. She tried twisting and kicking, but he held her easily.

One of the guards started toward her, but another put a hand on his shoulder and said something to him.

"Leave me alone!" she shouted as she was dragged backward, farther away from the indecisive men at the gate.

A second man joined her attacker. "What's this?" he asked, voice slurred by drink. She knew his voice as well. She didn't know their names, but she knew who they were. She knew what they wanted. She'd heard their plans after Hugh rode off. They wanted a woman to use through the night, an excuse for their absence.

She had no intention of being gang-raped as part of their alibi. She remembered her panicked helplessness when the outlaw tried to rape her. It was only a memory. She felt no panic as the two men dragged her off, back into the darkness by the wall. She was sick of men doing whatever they wanted just because they were bigger and better armed.

She had a dagger of her own. She managed to work it out of its sheath while the two men jockeyed with each other, both trying to paw her at the same time. They both pressed themselves against her. One was in front the one holding her with one viselike arm was behind her. She could feel the man in front's erection poking at her thigh. That was where she stabbed him.

When the first man fell away, howling in pain, the other's grip loosened a little. She collapsed like a sack of potatoes, every muscle going limp, sliding to the ground and completely out of his grasp. She was hampered by her long skirts, which had twisted around her in the struggle, but she still managed to elude his grasping hands. She got up and ran, out into the moonlit courtyard.

Straight into another man's arms. He smelled of lavender and horse sweat.

"Let go of me!" she shouted as her attacker came running up. In the background, the man she'd stabbed was still screaming. Shouting guardsmen were heading toward the courtyard. At last.

"Give me the wench!" her attacker demanded, grabbing her arm.

Daffyd tucked her under his arm. He asked the man calmly, "What seems to be the trouble here?"

She could hear the strange familiarity of his accent now. Not even the lilting cadence of modern Wales. Somewhere else, somewhere she knew.

"The bitch stabbed FitzWilliam! I'll see her flayed. Give her to me!"

She stayed within the shelter of Daffyd's arm, though she wanted desperately to break away from him. Guards came pelting up; one held a torch to supplement the moonlight. "Sir Daffyd," one of the men said.

Another stared at her with bugged-out eyes. "Lady Jehane! It was you?"

"Yes, it was me!" she shouted back. "Why didn't you help me?"

"I didn't recognize you, lady, I swear. And it was Lord FitzWilliam and Count DeBourne taking their pleasure. How could we—"

"Give me the girl!"

The screaming man was carried past on a makeshift litter. Her assailant briefly followed the small procession with his eyes.

A guard she didn't recognize broke away from the group carrying the injured man. He came up to Sir Daffyd. "The woman did that, sir," he said to Daffyd. "Stabbed him in his privates."

"Good for her," Daffyd said in a lazy drawl.

"Sir?" the guard questioned.

"Give her to me, ap Bleddyn, or you'll die with her," the attacker threatened.

"You're quite the troublemaker, aren't you?" Daffyd said to Jane.

"Yes," she hissed back angrily.

He addressed the livid man demanding her death. "There are witnesses you and FitzWilliam attacked a lady of noble birth, intending rape. The lady of noble birth is the chatelaine of this castle. And my betrothed. Get out of here, DeBourne. Keep your mouth shut, and I might not challenge you to a duel."

DeBourne, red-faced and hard-eyed with hate and fury, glared challengingly at Daffyd for a moment longer. Only a moment. Then he got control of his temper and gave one sharp nod. "You'll pay," he threatened, his venomous look taking in both Daffyd and herself. "Soon." He turned and pushed his way through the crowd of guards, back toward the gate.

Daffyd barked a few orders, and the guards dispersed back to their duties. "Come along," he said to Jane after the men were gone.

"I'm not going anywhere with you," she declared, trying to pull away.

"Calm down, love," he soothed. "Nothing happened." He started to stroke her cheek, but she pulled sharply away from the touch. He sighed. "Stupid bastards," he raged quietly. "Always hurting people who can't defend themselves. You got the best of them this time," he told her, tone gentle and calm. "You didn't let them hurt you." She clung to him, shaking, as his arms came comfortingly around her.

She wanted very much to tell him he reminded her of Mr. Rogers. It didn't help her anger to know he'd probably understand what she meant. "Let go of me, Sir Daffyd," she demanded. Her voice was just as calm as his, but colder than ice.

"No, I won't. Let's go, love." She resisted, but he dragged her forward, up the stairs, past the gaping faces of disturbed sleepers in the hall, all the way up the stairs and into the candlelit storeroom. He let her go as they crossed the threshold. Momentum carried her to the center of the room. She spun to glare at him. She'd never felt anything as strong as the hatred for him that seethed inside her.

He closed the door firmly and leaned against it. He crossed his arms. "Now, what," he asked, "is the matter with you?"

Unintended, the words came out: "You lied to me! You lied to me about everything!"

He blinked in surprise. "I've never lied to you about anything."

She couldn't stop the anger from boiling out of her. She'd told herself she had to be careful, to be circumspect, not to give anything away, but she was

deeply shaken from the minutes spent in the courtyard in his embrace. A part of her had felt so safe, so
loved, so wanted, so protected. She'd almost laughed
at his calm handling of the situation, at the barbs he'd
tossed at both the attacker and herself. She wanted to
love him for the gentle understanding he'd shown
afterward.

She couldn't keep quiet, couldn't let it go. She
loved him and she hated him and she couldn't lie to
him about how she felt. "You trick me. You trick
everyone. What do you want?"

He spread his hands out before him. Big, competent, clever hands. "I don't want anything."

"Then what are you doing here?"

"I thought I brought you home so you could recov-
er. So we could talk."

"Not here." She stamped her foot. "*Here!*"

"Here here?" He looked as if he thought she were
mad.

Maybe she was. "You know what I mean!"

"Jehane, sweetheart . . ."

She took an angry step closer, dagger poised in her
hand. "Who are you really?" she asked. "Who are
you, Daffyd ap Bleddyn?"

"I don't know what you're talking about. I'm
Daffyd ap Bleddyn." He said it calmly, reasonably.
But she saw the dawning suspicion in his eyes.

"Who are you?" This time she asked in English. He
didn't answer. "Daffyd," she said. "Daffyd." The
sound struck a chord of memory. "Daffyd . . . David."
She looked into his hazel-green eyes. The face wasn't
the same. But the eyes. . . The voice . . . They were
similar. "David."

"Yes?" He took a step forward. She raised the dag-

ger a fraction of an inch. He said. "I won't hurt you."
He was speaking English to her now.

"Ap Bleddyn. Bleddyn." Stephan called him
Wolf. Wolf. Wolfe. David Wolfe? No. It wasn't
possible. David Wolfe was twenty years old. This
was a man in his mid-thirties. David Wolfe was a
shaved-head, scrawny, pale geek who wouldn't
know how to handle himself outside the confines of
his safe and sterile laboratory.

She asked anyway. "Does Bleddyn mean wolf in
Welsh?"

"Yes," he answered again. "Jehane."

"You're David Wolfe?"

He nodded. His eyes were searching her face, dis-
belief warring with surprise and she couldn't tell
what else. He reached for her, but she backed away
quickly. "Jehane," he said. "How do you—Jehane?
Je— FitzRose? FitzRose. Rose. Flower. Florian." He
let out a whoop. "Jane Florian! Thank God!" His
smile was like a burst of light. It was pure joy and
delight. He spread his arms as if he wanted to
embrace her. "I've been looking for you for fifteen
years!"

It was him. It was really him.

"I'm going to kill you, you son of a bitch," she
said, and lunged at him with the dagger.

27

"*Never,*" *David Wolfe instructed* sternly after Jane was sitting splay-legged on the floor and he held her dagger in his hand, "never warn someone of an attack. You're likely to get killed." He stuck the dagger in his belt and crossed his arms. "Or disarmed. Didn't your mother teach you anything?"

"What's my mother got to do with this?" she snapped angrily.

"Quite a lot, actually." He strode forward, offered her a hand up.

She ignored it and got to her feet on her own, surreptitiously rubbing her aching behind. She'd fallen hard. It had almost knocked the wind out of her. It had certainly knocked the killing rage out of her. She was still angry. Angrier than she'd ever been in her life. Angrier than when she'd discovered he was from her own time but didn't know who he was.

That wasn't anger, she knew now. It wasn't hate. It wasn't contempt or disappointment or betrayal. What she'd felt before had been nothing compared to the furious, contemptuous loathing she was experiencing now. She was trembling so hard with fury, she had to sit down on a nearby storage chest to keep from falling.

Wolfe walked past her, into the sleeping alcove. He came back with a small linen-wrapped square. He sat down cross-legged beside her and put the bundle in her lap. "Have something to eat," he suggested. His eyes caught hers. Impossible to look away from those eyes as he added, "Give me time to explain."

"Time? Time? Time!" she snarled at him. "I've been doing time, Wolfe. Hard time." Her fingers curled into claws, but she kept from launching herself at him this time.

"So have I, Jehane. Jane." He reached out to touch her cheek but wisely drew back. She was sorry she didn't get the chance to bite him. "Jehane's prettier."

"Why have you let me stay here?" she questioned. "You were here the first day I arrived. You saw me. Why didn't you tell me who you were? What kind of experiment are you running, Wolfe?"

"What do you mean, the first day?" he demanded in return, ignoring the rest of her questions.

"When you came to tell Stephan about Hugh trying to kidnap Sibelle," she reminded him. How long ago had it been? Three months? More? It seemed like a lifetime.

"You'd just arrived?" He sounded incredulous. "That was your first day? When I'd been hunting Kent for six months? Not to mention all the time I spent in Anjou and Brittany and Aquitaine and the Île de France. I've visited as many abbeys and convents and priories on the energy grid as I could locate. Only you weren't in any of them. So I started hunting out on the very fringe. It was habit to keep hunting," he went on, sounding more as though he were talking to himself than to her. "I didn't have any hope. There's only genetic tracings this far out. And they're so faint . . ."

"What are you talking about?"

"Time travel," he answered. "It's more complicated than I thought. So many factors to coordinate."

"Gibberish. Sheer gibberish. You make no sense. You've never made any sense. I used to sit in staff meetings thinking, This boy makes no sense. Why isn't he in a nice strict military school instead of running a multizillion-dollar research project."

"Because I got a Ph.D. from Stanford at fourteen, and was in line for the Nobel Prize for physics with that project," he answered tartly. "Credentials help, my dear. And intelligence."

"If you're so intelligent, why didn't you recognize me? And what happened to you, anyway? Time machine blow up in your face?"

"You could say that. And why should I recognize you?" Suddenly he blushed, his fair skin going deep scarlet. She could feel the heat from where she sat. He got up and paced the length of the room. From by the door he said, "Perhaps I would have recognized you if I had gotten a clear look at you that first day. But I didn't. The next time I saw you your face was bruised. I remember being angry because I'd thought the lad must have taken his fist to you for some reason. There're some things about this place I don't like," he added quietly. After a loud sigh he went on. "By the time your face healed, you were Jehane to me, with your own history and place. You were the lovely Norman widow I was attracted to. I couldn't let myself become involved with anyone from this century, so I tried not to think about you. But I kept coming back to you. Perhaps some part of me guessed. But I wasn't thinking with that part."

"You didn't remember what I looked like?"

"I was looking for an older woman," he explained hurriedly. "Someone about fifteen years older."

"Fifteen years?"

"That's how long I've been looking for you, Jane," he said. His expression was sad, eyes full of regret. "What I did to you was unspeakable."

"You could say that again."

"Anything for my lady." He tilted his head and repeated with the faintest of smiles, "It was unspeakable."

"I am not your lady." Tears stung her eyes. She looked for something to throw. The aromas of honey and nuts and flaky pastry were coming from the linen bundle. She lobbed it at Wolfe's head. He ducked, and it hit the door with a heavy splat. "You had no right doing what you did!"

"I know. Believe me, Jane, I know. It was unspeakable. I never meant to do it. Wouldn't have done it if I hadn't had a few glasses of champagne in me. What I had planned," he explained, "was to ask you to volunteer after I sent a few more test animals through and got them back. I knew it was too risky to try with humans yet. You wouldn't have gone alone. Or for long. I do remember thinking you'd be so eager to get involved that I had some supplies and costumes made for you."

"None of which you recognized."

"I never saw them. I ordered them and the supplies. They were delivered, and I used them the same day. I don't even know what-all was in those bags. I said, trade goods. Carlyle got me trade goods."

"Well, why didn't you ask Carlyle?"

"I couldn't. He got killed in the earthquake."

"Earthquake? What earthquake? The one that devastated Chicago and northern Illinois in the spring of 2002," she said, answering her own question. She looked at him in shock. "I just remembered. It's one of the things I saw when I got a look at the future. I'd forgotten all about that. I saw so much so fast. And you wouldn't listen to any of it."

He nodded. "I know. If I had, maybe some of the disaster could have been prevented. I certainly wouldn't have spent my life the way I have." He spread his hands before him. "To think I owe everything I am to you."

His sarcasm galled her. "Right," she snapped. "All my doing." Her hands landed on her hips. She didn't remember getting to her feet. "Don't you go dissing me, home boy!"

He blinked. "I wouldn't dream of it," he answered in his bland, twenty-first-century voice. It sounded very odd coming from a man dressed in chain mail.

"I'm not showing you disrespect, Jane," he went on. "I did come looking for you. It was the least I could do. I never thought I'd find you, but I didn't stop looking," he went on earnestly. "Then when I did find you, I didn't recognize you, I fell in love with you."

Love was the last word she wanted to hear out of David Wolfe's mouth. The word would have been sweet coming from Daffyd. From Wolfe it sounded like the worst kind of mockery. How could she believe anything the man said? Trust anything he did?

She had to armor herself against him.

"Such a noble quest," she mocked him. "Such a perfect knight. Such a champion devoted to my cause. Ha. People don't go on Crusade where we come from. Or go on quests for the Grail."

He looked stung, stunned. There was hurt deep in his eyes. His voice was rough, less self-satisfied when he spoke. "It's what I did, Jane. People can still have consciences in our time. Try to right wrongs. I came looking. With very little to go on," he continued. "Records were lost. Your town house in De Kalb was destroyed. All the photographs I was able to come up with were of a younger you. I didn't know what you looked like."

"You knew *me*!" she reminded him. Loudly.

"Vaguely. My memory wasn't precise or objective." He gave a dry, humorless laugh. "I was twenty, Jane. You seemed ancient to me, at least six or seven years older. A dry, dusty woman in glasses, with long brown hair, who never took important research or me seriously."

"Dry and dusty!" she flared indignantly. "I was never dry and dusty. Even when I wore glasses!" She tossed her veiled head. "Hmmph."

He tried not to smirk but didn't succeed. "Yes, well. I was a bit immature for my age. My mind on my work. I'm afraid in my youth I was a bit of a—"

"Geek," she supplied with a nasty smile.

"Yes. Afraid so."

"You've changed." She eyed him closely. "How? What happened to you?"

He looked as if he didn't think she'd believe him. She probably wouldn't. He went on. "Fifteen years happened to me. Months for you, years for me. Time travel is a bit complicated, as I've said." His laugh was soft and hollow. "How does the line from the old movie go? 'It's not the years, it's the mileage'?"

He was being charming. She hated it when he was charming. And contrite. She didn't want to believe a word of it, even though the changes in him were so obvious. It was hard to believe a man like Wolfe—the Wolfe she remembered—could have such a guilty conscience. She might actually believe it of Daffyd. Daffyd her protector. Daffyd her savior. Her lover. Daffyd was strong and responsible. He had humor and wit; he understood duty. How could she reconcile Daffyd with David?

But maybe it was all a line. An excuse. Maybe he'd been arrogant enough to think his machine was perfect, and he'd stepped through for a little look himself. Stepped through and been unable to return. Maybe he'd been looking for her because he thought she held some kind of key for his own return to their time. Or he didn't have anything better to do.

"I arrived here three months ago," she said slowly, trying to piece together the differences in their arrivals and experiences. "But you arrived at—"

"Fontrevault Abbey in Anjou. In the west of France. I vaguely remember saying something in my drunken ramblings about Fontrevault being in the south. If I'd been a bit more precise in my geography, perhaps . . ." He trailed off with a shrug. "I've traveled a long way, in heart and mind as well as miles, my dear."

A shrug. He shrugged all the time. She should have noticed it about him. But it seemed such a natural gesture to her. It was so uncommon for this more formal era. She'd tried to be careful of her own body language. Of her speech. Of her behavior. Why hadn't she noticed the anomalies in him? His body language was wrong. And he didn't have any scars. He was a warrior. He posed as a warrior. Why hadn't she noticed something so obvious as his perfectly smooth, unmarked, gorgeous skin? And he didn't speak the language of the land he said he was from. "Why Wales?"

"What? Why did I choose to say I'm Welsh? My mother's family was from Cardiff. Will be. Tenses get to be a problem."

"Tell me about it. How old are you?"

"I told you, it's been fifteen years. I'm thirty-five."

Fifteen years. He'd been back here that long? How had he survived? "How'd you end up working for King John?"

"I've worked for King Richard as well. Interesting man, Richard. He asked me for a date, once. Wasn't particularly upset when I politely declined." He gave her a casual shrug. "Being in the king's service gave me the mobility and authority I needed to conduct my search. Being a fighter was the quickest route to the information I needed to access."

"Not to mention fortune and glory," she added.

"It's better to be a noble than a peasant, yes," he agreed. "As you seem to understand."

"I was lucky." She crossed her arms as goose bumps prickled up her skin. Some of the possibilities of what could have befallen her flashed across her mind. "If Stephan hadn't found me, I don't know what would have become of me. I ended up chatelaine of a castle by accident. You chose your career."

As she spoke the words, the dreadful implications of what the man had done hit her. "Oh, my God! Wolfe, how could you? You flung me back here to stop me from changing the future. Of all the stupid—"

"Rather a stupid idea, wasn't it?" he concurred.

"But what you've done is worse. Much worse."

"What are you talking about?"

"You deliberately took service with the kings of England. You move in the circles of power. You come into contact with the men who shape policy," she lectured him. She stalked the length of the room to look the man deeply in the eye. "You were so afraid I was going to change the future. You think nothing of using the very means that could change everything we know for your own purposes." Yes, this was the Wolfe she knew all right. "You hypocrite. What have you done that could change history? What inadvertent words or actions of yours have affected the course of history?"

He put his hands on her shoulders, holding her eyes with his. He said with conviction and sincerity, "I've been careful. Very, very careful. I haven't changed a thing. I assure you, sweet Jehane. I've done nothing to affect the energy flow we call history. And now that I've found you, I no longer need the use of kings and soldiers or any of the other tools I used to find you." He gave a deep, regretful sigh, his fingers tightening almost imperceptibly. "Perhaps now I can start to live my own life. If time allows."

For a moment the familiarity of his touch comforted her, the look in his eyes soothed her. Then he was looking inward, away from her. She didn't know what he was thinking, but it didn't appear to be a pleasant prospect. If time allowed . . . what did he mean? she wondered. Couldn't they leave? Were they trapped?

She took a deep breath and made herself ask, "Do you mean you can't go back? Can't be David Wolfe instead of Daffyd ap Bleddyn? There's no going home?"

His greenish eyes suddenly sparkled with angry fire. "Go back? Go home?" The words were laced with bitterness and pain. She wanted to hold him. "There's no way to change anything that's happened."

She stepped back and he released her. She turned her back to him. She didn't want him to see how much the knowledge of the finality of their situation affected her. She didn't cry. She didn't think there were any tears left. She hadn't had any hope. She'd coped with the world as it was. She was resigned. Until she'd fallen in love. But she'd even thought she could cope with that. Then she'd found out who Wolfe was, and for a few hours, if only in the back of her mind, hope of return to the twenty-first century sparked in her. The spark was dead now. Ashes. Nothing left. She'd have to go on. Survive as she'd been surviving. Alone. Without the man she loved. He didn't exist.

She would be all right, she told herself, refusing to give in to the weary despondency threatening to overwhelm her. This was her world now. After tonight she would never speak or think in English again. She would concentrate on what she had, be content with the world as it was. Her world was Passfair and Stephan and Sibelle and Jonathan and . . . and filth and disease and *routiers* and murder and rape and John and assassins.

Assassins.

John.

"Oh, my God!"

Her head came up sharply. Her hands flew to her mouth. She spun back to Daffyd. "King John! They're going to kill King John!"

28

Daffyd grabbed her shoulders with his hands as hard as steel. He shook her. "What are you screaming about, woman? Who's going to kill the king?"

"I was looking for you," she explained breathlessly. "I was going to tell you, but then you weren't you and I forgot all about it and now it may be too late, but I stabbed one of them and—"

He shook her hard. "Jehane! Stop babbling. Calm down. Talk to me. Tell me." Another hard shake. "Talk."

His face had turned to stone, hard, carved planes of cheekbone and aquiline nose and sensual lips thinned to a hard line. His eyes burned purposefully at her out of this carved stone mask. They caught her, calmed her.

"The two men who attacked me in the courtyard," she said more coherently.

"DeBourne and FitzWilliam. Two of John's favorites. Scum. They plan to kill John?"

She nodded. "Yes. I saw them earlier today. It's a long story."

"That's all right. Go on."

She drew a deep breath and tried to put her thoughts in order. Never mind Wolfe. Daffyd would take care of this! "I overheard them plotting to assassinate the king. They aren't going to do it themselves. Hugh of Lilydrake's in on the plot. He's to be the actual killer. They plan to blame Stephan, or Sibelle's father, I think."

"Lilydrake." He gave a sharp nod. "When?"

"Tomorrow."

His eyes looked past her, toward the alcove doorway. She turned her head to follow. The curtain was pushed back. Night sky showed through the window. "How long until dawn?" she wondered.

"Not long."

They stood together silently for a few heartbeats, antagonism put aside, thoughts of the future distilled to concentrating on the day ahead. Jane felt curiously at peace. This is the way it must be, she thought. One day at a time.

As the silence drew out between them she became aware of something different in the environment, something unusual and wrong. Silence. Where was the usual silence? She was so used to silence in the dark of her room. But she could hear noise. It was distant and faint, but still there when it shouldn't be. It puzzled and disturbed her. What was it? Where was it coming from? She concentrated, listening intently.

"The hall," she said, breaking the silence between herself and Daffyd. "There are people in the hall. Everyone was asleep when you dragged me up here."

"The party's been going on for some time," he said. "You just noticed?"

Jane nodded.

"I think your adventure in the courtyard must have gotten things stirred up," he told her. He ran his thumb along the line of his jaw, and she heard the scratch of beard stubble. "Perhaps we should join them," he suggested.

She stiffened, pulling away from the circle of his arms. Rounding on him, she proclaimed, "It's the *routiers* down there. Can't you hear their drunken shouting? I don't know what they're doing, but I don't want any part of it. What about the king?" she reminded him. "I thought you didn't want to change history."

"I don't intend to change history." His insufferable smirk appeared. "Where do you think the king is right now?"

From the look on his face, there could be only one answer to the question. "Partying hard with Louvre-caire's men?" she ventured.

"It seems a logical guess," he affirmed. "Otherwise Stephan would have driven the revelers out of doors by now. A young lord needs his rest, after all."

"You're clever," she complained. "And smug, and I hate you very, very much."

"Yes, love, I know. Come along." He urged her toward the door.

She resisted. She did not want to face the king. "What do you need me for?"

"You're the witness."

"Maybe the king won't believe me."

"You don't know John. Bring the accusation, he'll find the proof," Daffyd assured her. "The man's a complete paranoid. He's got informers planted in every noble's household. The weasel's an expert at staying alive." His fingers slipped around her wrist like a handcuff. "Come along."

She followed him with dragging steps, but with no choice. She reminded herself all the way down the stairs that Wolfe was an expert in not giving her any choice.

There were two guards posted at the bottom of the stairs. She looked across the hall and saw two more standing in the screen entrance. Paranoid, she repeated. Made sure his back was covered even when he was relaxing with the boys. Made sense to her.

Men were spread out around the hall. There was a great deal of laughing and drinking. There was a brawl going on over near the doorway. At least four men were punching, kicking, and gouging at each other. Onlookers were shouting encouragement. The king, still in his surcoat of multiple shades of green, was at the high table. He was involved in some sort of dice game with Louvrecaire and several richly dressed courtiers. Someone must have spilled wine into the hearthfire, because the hall was filled with an acrid, alcohol-laden smoke.

Daffyd put his lips to her ear and whispered confidingly, "Male bonding in its most raw, untamed form."

She almost laughed as he started to tug her forward again. The guards stopped them on the bottom stair.

"None of the household's to be allowed downstairs," one of the soldiers told them. "Go back to bed."

"I'm Captain ap Bleddyn. Let me through."

"Go back to bed."

"Bloody hell!" Daffyd grabbed Jane by the shoulders and thrust her in front of him. "This is the woman the king's been wanting. Do you want to deny him his pleasure?"

Jane glared back at Daffyd venomously. He gave her his best smirk. She kicked backward, but he quickly moved his leg before she could hit his shin. He shook her a little.

"Let go of me!" she said.

Her protest seemed to convince the guard. "Right. I remember hunting for the wench." He chucked her under the chin. "Too skinny for my tastes."

"You're not the king," Daffyd snapped impatiently. "Out of my way!"

The men stepped aside.

As they neared the high table, Jane was able to make out the faces of the men hovering around the dice game. Most were total strangers to her, though if she heard some of their names, she knew she'd be able to reel off facts about them. Perhaps she should go into business as a fortune-teller, she thought.

Her sarcastic speculations were cut short when one of the men in the crowd standing around the king's chair moved, revealing the man standing behind him. It was one of the conspirators. The one in chain mail with the boar's-head device. Daffyd said his name was DeBourne. Hugh of Lilydrake was standing on the other side of the king's chair. Both of them had eyes only for the king.

"Daffyd . . ."

He gave her a reassuring look, then pulled her up to the table. They stopped before the center chair, where the king sat with his men crowded around him.

"Sire," Daffyd said, bending the knee, then rising quickly as the king turned his small-eyed glare on them. "Lady Jehane must speak with you."

"That's her!" DeBourne shouted, pushing to the king's side. "The one who attacked FitzWilliam!"

The king gave DeBourne a look of lazy menace. "Lady Jehane is known for her impulsiveness," he replied.

The man's lividly angry face stayed bright red. It almost glowed above the white of his tabard. He looked at her with contempt and hatred. Jane looked back with a contemptuous sneer. "My liege," the man began.

John waved him off. "Let be, DeBourne. I've seen FitzWilliam. It's an amusing scratch. So the kitten has claws. She'll sheathe them for me." He turned a lascivious smile on her. "Welcome, lady."

What was this? Chivalry from the king? Well, he was a Plantagenet, she reminded herself. Perhaps he had a drop of the family charm.

The king stood. "Come to me, Lady Jehane."

She jumped and backed up, into the solid wall of Daffyd's chest. "S-sire," she stammered. Daffyd prodded her in the spine with a finger. It loosened her tongue. "There are men here who plot to kill you. Please believe me," she pleaded with the king. His expression had gone cold as she spoke.

"Assassins?" he asked, voice deadly soft. He pointed to his breast. "People trying to kill me? Where did you hear this rumor, woman?"

"I heard it from the men trying to kill you," she told him. "When the conspirators met at the tower in the woods near here. I was in the tower." She heard

DeBourne's gasp. She hoped the king did also. "The men are plotting with a pretender, a man claiming to be Arthur of Brittany."

The king looked her over slowly, carefully. The room was dead silent. Even the boisterous fighters in the lower hall had stilled. The silence had spread out from the high table like a shock wave. She could feel Daffyd's heartbeat, the rise and fall of his breathing, from where she was pressed against him. The warmth and size of him at her back was comforting. She wanted to look up at him, but her eyes were caught by the king's harsh scrutiny.

Please, she prayed, let him believe her. Don't let Daffyd be wrong.

"Who?" the king asked. There was death in his voice.

She swallowed hard. Words seemed to be stuck in her throat. She caught sight of Hugh of Lilydrake. The man was fingering the hilt of a dagger. Two large men were flanking DeBourne, one of them between him and the king.

"FitzWilliam, DeBourne, and Hugh of Lilydrake," she said as loudly and as clearly as she could. The silence thickened dangerously. Eyes flashed to the men she'd accused.

The king threw back his head and laughed.

Oh, God, he doesn't believe me!

"Sire—" Daffyd began.

The king wiped a tear off his cheek. He spoke as though lecturing a class. "DeBourne I knew about. And FitzWilliam. But it was the local lord in it with them I couldn't decide on." He laughed again, a little, wheezing sound. Jane gaped in astonishment.

"DuVrai seemed to have the most to gain," the

king went on as the people around him began to shuffle and look at each other questioningly. "Osbeorn's more Saxon than Norman. Sturry's claim to the throne might be popular with the English." He spread his hands out before him, tilting his head with the air of a much puzzled man. "Which one, I thought? So many choices. So hard to decide. Perhaps it was all of them, I thought. But no. There were no meetings where all of them were present. Not before the lad's wedding. And I knew about the conspiracy long before then."

DeBourne lunged forward, but the men flanking him already had him in their grasp. He shouted profanely, at her and at King John. Someone knocked him over the head. He sagged forward, blood streaming onto his white tabard.

"Lilydrake, of course," John continued, "is the worst fool of the lot. Of course it had to be Lilydrake."

No guards were next to Hugh yet. His response was with his dagger. It was out of its sheath and speeding through the air as quick as light. A deadly missile aimed straight at Jane's heart.

Daffyd moved as swiftly as the dagger, throwing her to the floor, covering her with his own body. She heard the swish of air as the blade passed over their heads. Then Daffyd was up, his arm thrown back.

Jane saw it clearly from where she crouched in the rushes just below the dais. It was framed in her vision with crystal clarity, even through the thin film of smoke that obscured the air with a dreamlike haze. It happened swiftly, but she saw it slowly. She saw Daffyd's blade poised on his fingertips. She saw the graceful play of muscle as the dagger left his hand. She saw it sail, a spinning mote of silver, the aim true and deadly. She saw Hugh of Lilydrake's head thrown back by the force of entry. She saw the hilt buried deep in the base of the man's exposed throat. She heard the gurgle of blood as he died. She saw the slow, crumpling fall.

She recognized the dagger as her own. She remembered David Wolfe taking it from her.

There was a great deal of shouting. A sea of feet and legs surrounded her. Hands hauled her upright. She was cold. So very cold. A mantle was placed around her shoulders. The hands straightening it were David's. How had he known she was cold? How could he know her so well when she didn't know him at all?

She pulled it tight around her as David Wolfe led her to the stairs, helped her to sit. She looked up at him, this stranger who had just killed, acting so quickly his motions had to be reaction driven by instinct. Where had he learned to do it? He was David Wolfe. David Wolfe was a physicist. A researcher. A soft-handed man of the twenty-first century. When had he become a savage?

She remembered him smiling as Pwyll died. How many more men had he killed? What else had he done?

She didn't want him near her.

"You're not hurt, are you?" he asked. He cupped her face in his hands. "Please say you're all right."

"I'm not hurt," she answered. She wanted him to go away. She didn't know him and she didn't like him and she didn't want to deal with him.

His smile was as bright as a nova. "Good. Don't worry," he soothed. "I swear nothing like that will happen to you again. I'll take care of you," he swore. "Forever and ever. I'll protect you, Jehane. Hugh was a mean, spiteful fool. He knew he was dead. He wanted to take someone he hated with him. It's over now."

She stood abruptly and backed up two steps. They now stood eye to eye. "Over. It won't happen again. No more violence," she concurred. She'd made up her mind. It had been the plan all along, hadn't it? "I'm not staying here," she told him. "I'm not going to be part of this world."

"It's all right. You don't have to stay here. I'll take you—"

"I'm leaving with Jonathan," she said. The words were adamant, etched in stone. "I'm going to Fontre-vault and taking my vows."

"The devil you are!" he shouted.

He opened his mouth to yell again, but the king's voice cut through the air. "Wolf! To me!"

"Damn!" David grabbed her wrist and pulled her after him to the king. "Sire!" he acknowledged tightly.

The king was grinning happily. Jane noticed he was missing at least three bottom teeth. The room was full of people, but none was DeBourne. Hugh's body was nowhere in sight.

King John clapped David on the shoulder. "That was the best sport I've had since we came here. Magnificent throw."

David bent his head in a humble nod. "Thank you, my lord."

How could the man be such a good actor? Jane wondered. How could he live the role so easily?

"Lilydrake's yours," the king told David. David looked up, face clouded with puzzlement. "Hugh's lands go to you," John clarified. "Been meaning to give you something for your service. An estate . . ." John peered at Jane. "And a rich widow. Not bad pickings for a landless Welsh mercenary."

A look of sly triumph lit David's face. It was the look of a man with a cunning plan. "No, my lord, not bad at all. You have all my thanks." Still holding Jane's wrist hard, David dropped to one knee. She was dragged down with him. "One more boon, my lord?" he requested, kneeling before the king.

The king's eyes narrowed with suspicious caution. "Yes?"

"Stand witness to my marriage. Right now. At dawn's first light."

Laughter broke out around them. Laughter and shouts of ribald humor. The king looked confused for a moment, his fat chin resting thoughtfully on his upraised hand. "If that's all you wish," he said as the noise once more turned into a riotous din. "All right." He raised his voice above the *routiers'* noise. "Somebody fetch that priest!"

Jane turned a poisoned look on David. She planned to open her mouth in protest, but David just shook his head. Light danced in his greenish eyes. His smirk was one of pure triumph.

Jane could find no words. There was nothing she could do. Once again David Wolfe was in control of her life. Once again he was giving her no choice.

29

Jane was so tired she could barely stand. Her eyes were burning from exhaustion. She thought she'd lost what was left of her wits some time ago, probably around the time Sibelle appeared, pushing her way through the crowd of *routiers*, Stephan a tall shadow in her wake. She was staring her hatred into David Wolfe's eyes when Sibelle arrived. It seemed a perfectly logical thing to be doing: kneeling in front of a fat, smelly man and trying to burn holes in the back of David's head with the strength of her will.

She didn't have any will at all when Sibelle hustled her off. A great deal of talking went on around her, to her, at and about her. Things happened. She was bathed by hands not her own, dressed and veiled in royal-blue silk and white linen, and led back down stairs she didn't remember climbing.

Stephan took charge of her hand and led her out here, to the castle steps. The world was lit by the first pale rays of dawn. The sky was pinky blue with clouds like puffs of artillery smoke high overhead. She looked around. Where'd all those people in the courtyard come from? Where was Daffyd?

"Where's Daffyd?" she heard her own voice ask petulantly.

"Here," the chocolate voice said. She looked to her left. He was standing right beside her.

"Not you," she said, awake enough to know she was too tired to make any sense. "I want Daffyd."

"I know," he soothed. "I'm here."

It wasn't worth arguing about. She yawned. When had she last slept? After she'd made love to Daffyd. But Daffyd wasn't here anymore. She wanted a cup of coffee.

Stephan was on her other side. Sibelle stood next to him. The king was next to David. David was back in Daffyd's red-and-black finery, his hair brushed to burnished gold. He was gorgeous. Why wasn't he Daffyd? Jonathan came out the castle door and approached them, smiling triumphantly.

You had better wake up, girl, a shrill voice in her head warned. *Something very bad is about to happen.*

Let it, she answered. *There's nothing I can do.*

Still, she'd shaken off some of the exhausted lethargy by the time Jonathan arrived before them. He unfolded a piece of parchment.

"What's that?" she asked.

"Your marriage contract," he answered. "Stephan, Daffyd, and I worked it out while you prepared for the ceremony."

An annoyance-fed shot of adrenaline brought her fully alert. "What?"

The crowd around them were staring. The king

looked impatient. She kept quiet as Jonathan read, his Latin flowing and beautifully accented. The gist of the agreement was that Daffyd got all she had; she was offered an allowance; Stephan threw in the dogs as her liege's portion.

"I knew you'd hate giving them up," he answered her curious look. As he spoke Nikki was patiently licking her toes and Vince had wandered off somewhere.

"I will hear your vows," Jonathan said after he'd finished with the contract. "Before God, the king, and those assembled."

Stephan placed her hand in David's. David was smiling tenderly at her. "Be careful," he warned in English. "Will you marry me?"

"I don't want to."

"I know."

"Do I have a choice?"

"No. Do you want to?"

"No."

"Fine. Neither do I."

"Good."

"I do!"

"So do I!"

David looked at Jonathan and lied easily, once more speaking French: "It's the Welsh rite."

"I see. The ring?"

David brought a wide gold band out of a belt pouch. She recognized it as the gold hoop earring he always wore. "The blacksmith did some work for me while we waited," he told her as he started to place the newly made ring on her left hand, following the custom of their own time.

"Right," she corrected. He switched direction

smoothly. It fit perfectly. She thought she could feel the warmth from where the ends had been closed to form a solid ring.

David took a step back. Everyone was looking at her expectantly. She didn't understand what they were waiting for.

Sibelle finally came to her rescue, stage-whispering, "You have to kneel now."

Jane's spine straightened with stubborn anger. Oh, no. No way did she show one bit of submission to any man. Especially not David Wolfe. She gave him the most pleasant, loving smile she could fake for the crowd. To David she said in their own language, "When hell freezes over."

She heard Sibelle whispering confusedly to her husband, "It must be a dialect of Welsh Granny Rosamunde didn't know."

David took her hands, drawing her close to his side. "It's not necessary," he told the priest.

"Not part of the Welsh rite?" Jonathan suggested helpfully. David shook his head. "I approve. Prostrations should be saved for God." At King John's thunderous frown, he amended diplomatically, "And kings. I pronounce you man and wife," he ended quickly.

David grabbed her in a tight embrace and kissed her, lips slanting sensuously across hers, parting them with his tongue, their breath mingling. Much to her surprise, heat raced from her lips down to her toes and back up again. It felt wonderful. She supposed the roaring in her ears was from the crowd, but she wasn't completely positive.

When David drew his lips away from hers, he smiled knowingly into her eyes. "Smug bastard" were the first words she spoke to her husband. He winked.

He released his hold on her and turned to kneel to the king. "My thanks, my lord."

John was pulling on a pair of gloves. A groom was bringing up his horse. The soldiers were forming into ragged ranks. From the pasture beyond the castle walls came the sounds of camp being broken and sumptuary wagons being loaded.

"I wish you joy of the wench. She looks like a hot bitch" was the royal blessing for their union. "I'm off to Calais." He gave Jonathan a hard look. "Come, priest. We'll talk about your order's contribution to my treasury as we ride."

Jane looked at Jonathan unhappily. "I must go," he said, taking her hand for a moment. "May God bless you." He turned and made equally quick farewells to Sibelle and Stephan. He had to run for the horse his servant held by the reins for him. The priest and his retainer hurried after the departing king.

The people on the steps were left standing, stunned by this quick exit of so many people.

"People come and go so quickly here?" Jane suggested after a time. David gave her a sour look. She shrugged. "I always wanted to say it."

"I think," Sibelle said, waving everyone to the door, "we should break our fast and celebrate."

"A wedding and our lord John's departure," Stephan agreed.

"I'm not sure there's enough left to break our fast with," Jane contributed, thinking as the chatelaine of Passfair once more.

"Oh, we'll contrive something," Sibelle said with firm assurance. She waved them all on into the hall.

Jane's steps were dragging by the time she reached

the hearth, every bit of energy she'd mustered for the ceremony dissipated. She found herself leaning on David's strong arm. She felt like a wimp. "I think I'm going to faint."

"Nonsense," he said cheerfully. "Sir Stephan," he said over her head. "My lady doesn't need food, but rest. I think we will retire."

"Now?" Stephan asked. "I wanted to hear about Lilydrake and the king. Couldn't you wa—"

"Stephan!" Sibelle hissed. "Not now!" She tugged him toward the table. "They just got married. Let them go to bed."

"Oh. Of course. Sorry," he called over his shoulder.

David urged Jane forward. She remembered setting her foot on the stair, then his lifting her onto the straw mattress in her alcove. The points in between were all covered in fuzz. The pillow felt wonderful against her cheek. She didn't have the energy to protest when he climbed in beside her.

She woke once in the middle of the day and found herself wrapped in a warm embrace. The man holding her was sleeping deeply, lids fluttering a little as he dreamed. She lay stiffly beside him for a moment, sleep trying to drag her back down.

She didn't know what was going to happen next. She knew it was better than sharing the bed with the dogs. She let sleep have its way.

30

Jane woke next when David got back into bed. She'd been vaguely aware of his moving around the alcove—heard him using the pot in the corner, the splash of water in the basin—but the sounds seemed so much a part of the routine of life that they didn't disturb her. It was the knowledge this was most certainly *not* part of the routine of her life that brought her fully awake.

She lay still, back against the wall. How long had they been asleep? The covering, if there'd been one, must have been kicked off while they slept. Yet she was anything but cool. She felt him lying close beside her, warm, unclothed flesh pressed intimately against hers. It was a small bed, and he was a big man. There was no way to scrunch over closer to the wall. She was practically inside the wall now. Any farther and the rats would be complaining of invasion of privacy.

There was no putting it off. She opened her eyes and looked at her husband in the dimness of what she thought was dusk. He was propped up on one elbow, head resting on his palm, one leg thrown over her hip. He'd shaved before the wedding, so there was no beard stubble yet to shadow his cheeks. In this light the man seemed to be all cheekbones and nose. There were still dark marks under his eyes. He looked tired despite the hours of rest. Tired and worried.

She found she wanted to stroke his shoulder reassuringly. And might have if she didn't remember just in time how much she hated him. This was Wolfe. He was her kidnapper. Was what he'd done technically kidnapping? Was there a formal charge for what he'd done? Illegal use of a time machine probably wasn't part of any legal code this side of "Star Trek."

Still, he was gazing at her with such an air of melancholy that it bothered her. Instead of feeling like a victim, she felt almost sorry for the man. Which was the wrong attitude. Everything was his fault. She tried to harden her heart against him. Unfortunately it refused to turn to stone. She had the feeling it was actually more the consistency of hard butter, just waiting to melt. Oh, no, not for him, she vowed. Still, there was no reason to act uncivilized. Uncivilized could wait for later, after the swords and daggers were put back on.

"You look terrible," she stated by way of a greeting. He reached out a finger and played with one of her sadly sagging curls.

She wished she could tell him she hated him and wanted him to go away. But after all they'd been through, such a childish action was impossible. Too easy.

"You owe me ninety-five dollars for this perm," she said inanely, glad to have someone who would at least understand what she was talking about. Even though the someone was Wolfe. "The thing's totally ruined. My hair's going to take months to grow long enough to trim off the curls. Makes me glad veils are in fashion."

"I don't remember this," he said, still playing with her hair. "There's so much I don't remember about you."

"We didn't know each other," she pointed out. They still didn't. Daffyd had warned her that she didn't know him.

"What am I going to do with you?"

She heard the bleakness in his tone and chose to ignore it. "The wedding was your idea, Wolfe." She didn't want to remember it had been her idea not long before.

He did not look happy at the reminder. "I know. I wasn't going to risk losing you," he continued. "It was all I could think of at the time." She felt a glow of pleasure. It was doused by his next words. "I'd been hunting too long to lose the thing I was looking for to a temper tantrum."

"Tantrum?" she asked, stiff and cold, trying to ignore the feeling she was just the prize he'd gained after a long quest. Was the quest more important than the prize? It often proved to be. She kept her tone cool and tried to hide her thoughts as she went on, "I don't recall any tantrum."

He conceded her a nod. "A fit of nerves, then. One of several. I don't blame you for any of them. The scene with Lilydrake was probably the most trying."

She almost laughed at this bit of understatement. She didn't laugh. She wasn't going to be entertained by him. Besides, the most "trying" thing had been finding out the man she loved didn't exist. Or existed in another dimension. Or something. She didn't understand anything.

She didn't want to talk to him. Why shouldn't she act childish if she wanted to? "Attempted murder can be trying," she answered, unable to keep from replying. She wished she could just turn her back to him and sulk. She wished she knew how to sulk. It came in handy in situations like this. A person shouldn't have an urge to communicate with someone they hated.

It was just because he was the only one here she could communicate with, she told herself. If she had a wider choice of acquaintances who knew about airplanes and computers and chocolate ice cream—oh, God, she missed chocolate ice cream—she wouldn't have to talk to Wolfe.

"You never quite get used to it," Wolfe said. "I never have, at least." He lapsed into silence.

The room was growing darker. There was a large, warm hand resting on her hip. She didn't know how long it had been there, or why she was noticing it now, but she wished it would go away. Or maybe move just a little bit farther down around the curve of her—

"Go away, Wolfe," she told him.

He edged closer, which wasn't really possible, but he managed somehow. She could feel all of him, from the chest hairs tickling her collarbone to the flat expanse of his stomach to his muscled legs. He was warm all over, especially around his groin.

He said, "You wouldn't tell Daffyd to go away."

"I might," she answered. It was ambiguous, but honest.

"I fell in love with Jehane, you know," he said. He sounded about as confused as she felt.

Go ahead, be honest, she thought, trying to deny her own conflicting emotions. See if she cared.

Then she kissed him. She didn't know why. Maybe to keep him from saying anything else. Maybe because she wanted to. What was there to talk about? He was a man and she was a woman and her body craved him like a drug.

He reacted first with surprise, then passion. She felt him whisper, "Jehane," against her mouth.

She thought, *Yes, I'm Jehane. You're Daffyd. I wouldn't tell Daffyd to go away. I couldn't. I so desperately love the man I thought you were.*

His sex was already straining against her as their lips parted. She opened her legs, rubbing against him, the hot ache inside her growing by the second. She felt the pulsing tip of his manhood between her thighs, and she thrust her hips forward, impaling herself. He shuddered at the entry, called out her name as he was buried deep inside her. She was hot with need, flesh quivering, out of control. She thrust forward, again and again, taking him into her. He growled something, heaved himself to his knees, and grabbed her hips with bruising strength, forcing the rhythm of her movements. She wrapped her thighs around his waist and gave up all control as a hot spasm of completion took her. She felt his shudder, and his seed filled her a moment later.

It wasn't over. She was too hungry to stop. She held him close, biting at his shoulder, his throat. His mouth took hers, tongue thrusting, then withdrawing. She craved his kiss, her response equally demanding.

They rolled over, off the narrow bed. Then their hands and mouths were all over each other, savoring heat and salty, sweat-moistened flesh. They were too frantic, too fast, too hungry, to be gentle. Within minutes they were coupling again.

The pleasure was incandescent. With her body splayed beneath Daffyd's on the storeroom floor, Jane begged for it never to end, cried out when the world exploded around her in ever-increasing intensity. Four or five times. She was breathless, with passion and a hint of laughter, by the time he collapsed on top of her. Laughter at herself, the situation, the sheer joy of being alive after the last day and a half.

She felt his silent laughter breathed into her ear. Knew it was for the same reasons. He lifted his head and kissed her nose. "The king was right about one thing," he informed her.

She barely had the strength to lift her eyebrows inquiringly.

"You are a hot bitch," he supplied.

"Kings can't be wrong all the time. Even John."

"I hope that's the last we'll ever see of him," he added. He shifted his weight until he was lying close by her side again, in much the same position as when the recent incident started. He felt a mark she'd left on his throat. "Bloodthirsty, aren't you? Or just hungry?"

She didn't answer. He was the one who shed blood. On a regular basis. Efficiently. Remorselessly. It was something she could understand of Daffyd, a man in his own time. But Wolfe . . .

He got up, padded toward the door. He seemed to be searching for something. Finally he said, "Ah."

He came back to her, sat down cross-legged beside her, and tugged her head in his lap. She didn't resist. All the confusion was still there. Sex didn't change anything. Complicated it, maybe. Wasn't sex supposed to bring a couple close? Enhance communication? What they'd just done had felt wonderful. It still felt wonderful, all over, even the bruised spots. It hadn't helped anything. It had just been sex. She sighed unhappily, her heart the most bruised spot of all.

"Open up." She opened her mouth because it saved having to say anything. Something sweet was dropped inside. She chewed. It was a blend of honey, nuts, and pastry. As she chewed happily he said, "It was the closest the cook could get to baklava. It turned into mush when you threw it against the wall."

She didn't remember throwing anything. "I'll take your word for it. This is good."

"Say, 'More, please.'"

This was all too comfortable, too cozy. He was too in control. She didn't like it. "I'm not hungry."

He stroked her hair. "You're never hungry."

He didn't know her at all. She was always hungry. Hungry and scared and lonely and uncomfortable. One bite of baklava after three months of garbage wasn't enough to change anything.

He'd tried. She had to acknowledge it. He'd tried to give her a present of something she'd really wanted. Daffyd had done it. For Jehane.

She sat up and rubbed aching temples.

He asked, "What's wrong?"

"Nothing."

"Or everything?" he asked softly. When she didn't answer, he repeated something he'd said what seemed like days before. "What am I going to do with you? With us," he added.

He didn't bother asking what she wanted to do.

She didn't know, but it might have helped if he'd asked. It might not. She didn't know.

"Why do you love Daffyd?" he asked.

"I don't!" she snapped back. It was a lie, but she had to protect herself somehow. She couldn't love Daffyd, because Wolfe came along as part of the package. All she loved was the shell. What it contained was full of poison.

He didn't pay any attention. "And why do I love Jehane? I miss Jehane, you know."

"Thanks."

He went on, still talking as if she weren't there. "I miss a great many things." He shrugged tiredly. "I don't know. . . ."

His words trailed off. A long silence stretched between them. Darkness settled comfortably into the room. Moonlight came sneaking hesitantly in the window.

The inhabitants of the room did not settle comfortably with each other. The room grew cold. Jane eventually got up and put on her undershift. Wolfe waited until she was done, then dressed by the moonlight.

He buckled on his sword as he told her, "You need some more rest."

She lay down on the bed. It seemed large without him in it. The door opened, then closed. She didn't call after him. Didn't ask where he was going.

After he was gone she rather wished she had.

31

After Wolfe left, she found the flint and lit a candle. She used the light to find the linen-wrapped pastry. She sat on the bed, gulping it down hungrily. It was slightly stale, but wonderful. She was glad she'd brought in a couple of barn cats to help cut down the rat population, otherwise there wouldn't have been any left for Wolfe to find.

Rats, she thought. Rats and wolves. Wolfe was a rat. But she already knew that, no reason to beat it to death. She rubbed an ache on her shoulder, the mark of his hand, she thought. She had to concede one thing about him: the man was great in bed.

A pang shot hotly through her. It might be nice if he was in love with her and not Jehane.

On that unhappy thought she blew out the candle and settled back on the bed, pulling the covering tightly around her. She couldn't deny she missed his presence in the bed beside her. His absence didn't prevent her from falling quickly back to sleep, though.

She woke up thinking, *I am Jehane*.

She sat bolt upright, repeating, "I am Jehane!"

She was also an idiot.

It was full daylight once more. Another breakfast missed. Work to do. Whatever would the peasants think? Not that she cared. She threw off the covers, muttering to herself as she dressed as quickly as possible. Once more garbed in linen and blue silk, her hair tucked decently under a wimple, she felt much better, much more herself. Much more capable of coping with the world at large and one of its inhabitants in particular.

She rubbed her hands together briskly as she said, "All right, where is that man?" Full of confidence, she marched down to the hall.

He wasn't in the hall, but she didn't really expect to find him there. The only people in the hall were a couple of servants sweeping up the old rushes in preparation for putting down fresh. She was glad to see the cleanup needed after the king's visit was proceeding without any direct orders from her. The whole thing had been a nightmare. Maybe only the least of it was the castle's depleted larder and ruined housekeeping.

There was nothing, she told herself, that couldn't be set to rights with a lot of hard work. Nothing.

She gave the workers a pleased nod as she passed them. One of them gave her a knowing wink and jerked a thumb in the general direction of the stables in reply. It was a firm reminder that everyone at Passfair was aware of everyone else's business. It was a community, she thought. A family of sorts. She hurried out.

It was raining, more of a gentle English mist than

real rain. The dampness felt good on her face. She could hear the ring of hammer on metal coming from the smithy. There was a smell of baking bread from the big outdoor ovens. The bakers weren't letting a little shower get in the way of needed work.

She supposed the geese must have gotten loose again, because the goosegirl's shrill young voice was floating up from near the gate. Why couldn't those birds hang out by the pond where they belonged? Jane wondered as she crossed the courtyard to the stables. Leave it to Stephan to have adventurous geese. That poor girl was going to have a nervous breakdown by the time she was nine if the birds had anything to say about it.

She looked around anxiously as she entered the stable. She didn't see David anywhere in the big building. She saw the well-kept stalls, noticing only two were occupied. She assumed the rest were either turned out to graze or being exercised in the paddock. Stephan kept more horses than a knight of his rank should be able to afford. The horsemaster had told her Stephan's father liked to breed the animals, selling them to his neighbors and at horse fairs. Stephan had inherited his father's love of horseflesh. She wished he could settle into horse breeding as a viable occupation instead of going through life as a head-bashing warrior.

She sighed and shook her head. It couldn't be. The world was the way it was. She was resolved to face the world as it was, not as she wished it to be. Stephan was who he was. So was David.

So was she.

She didn't find David anywhere in the stable. She did see Stephan, leaning casually against a post, watching carefully as Michael worked a curry comb gently over the hocks of his big black stallion.

Stephan turned his square-mouthed smile on her as she approached. "Up at last," he called. "You've had a merry time, I trust?"

"I slept through most of it," she replied honestly, then added with a slight, reminiscent smile, "but not all. Do you know where my lord husband might be?"

Stephan came away from the post and guided her outside. They paused beneath the overhang of the stable roof. "Gone to Reculver," he answered. "Then on to Lilydrake. He didn't tell you?"

There was only one word to describe the feeling settling in the pit of her stomach and suddenly weighing down her heart: bereft. He'd left her.

"No," she answered, her voice little more than a whisper of shock.

Stephan shook his head, the black silk of his hair swinging gently on his shoulders. "I can see Wolf's going to be a high-handed sort of husband."

He took her shoulders. With his black eyes looking deeply into her own, he advised, "Be patient with him. He'll be back in two days at the most. Greet him gently when he returns. Offer him a cup in welcome, and a wifely kiss." He shook a finger at her. "No man likes a nagging wife."

Two days. That wasn't so bad. The fist clenching her heart eased a little. She could almost smile at Stephan's solemn admonitions. Ah, the wisdom of the long married—it must be at least a week, now.

"Yes, my liege," she responded, lowering her eyes meekly to hide the amusement in them.

He gave a pleased sigh. "You two will deal very well together," he predicted. "Now, go on to the

bower and keep my lady company. If she isn't running around the fields grubbing for medicinal roots
in the rain, that is." He gently directed her footsteps
back toward the castle.

Sibelle, she thought. Yes, she would talk to Sibelle.
She didn't find her in the bower, sewing with the
women, but with Switha in the chapel. They were sitting on the floor beneath the altar in the full light of
the window, sorting some kind of dried berry from a
willow basket.

Melisande was lying close enough to have her head
on Sibelle's thigh. The girl was feeding her the occasional berry. The dog's tail thumped happily on the
stone floor as Jane approached the group.

Back from her poolside vacation, I see, Jane thought
of the wisewoman. She settled down with the pair.
"How's Melisande?" she asked.

"Mending," Switha answered. "The shoulder will
remain stiff. She'll never chase deer again."

"She never did that anyway," Jane answered.
Melisande was distinctly a house pet in a time when
such a privileged position was rare. Passfair, she
knew, was a rare and precious haven of peace and
kindness in the midst of a frighteningly brutal world.
She was a lucky woman to be a part of Stephan's
small domain.

"We've so much to talk about," Sibelle began
eagerly. "There's so much I must learn from you
before you leave."

Leave? She stared at the girl uncomprehendingly.
Leave? Were they sending her away. "Leave?"

Sibelle's gentle laugh echoed against the stones of
the little chapel. "I would love to have you with me
forever—perhaps someday we can be together at

Sturry when all our estates are secure and well managed. Meanwhile," she went on, "you can't be a proper chatelaine for Lilydrake if you remain here. Besides, I don't think Sir Daffyd would want you out of his sight."

"Bed," Swetha added succinctly. "Or protection," she added with a shrewd look at Jane. "I thought he might be the cure you needed when I led you to him," she added smugly.

Jane refrained from answering this statement, but she felt strangely happy. She and Swetha understood each other, somehow.

The berries went click, click, click into separate piles. Rain pattered in and ran in a slow stream down the wall. After a time, Jane let her historian's curiosity get the better of her. "Granny Rosamunde," she said. "Was she Rosamunde Clifford?"

Sibelle nodded. "Yes, that's who Granny was. I miss the dear old lady."

"'A sweeter creature in this world could never prince embrace,'" Jane quoted. No wonder Sibelle's father was proud to style himself LeGauche. Being half Plantagenet by Henry II's beloved mistress wasn't such a bad thing.

"What a pretty thing to say," Sibelle said.

"It's from a poem about her."

"There's lots of those. She didn't like hearing about them. She tried to forget such worldly things."

"I thought she died about thirty years ago?"

Sibelle smiled brightly. "So did the queen. Granny Rosamunde ran away from Woodstock after a nasty fall down the stairs. She was afraid Queen Eleanor was trying to kill her. She told me that later she supposed it was just an accident coupled with her own guilty conscience. She wasn't very good at being a mistress. Said she would have been much happier as a wife. She stayed in several priories before she settled at Davington and I met her." Sibelle gave a happy little domestic sigh. "Now I understand what she meant about being a wife."

Jane leaned back on her hands, feeling quite pleased at all this information. What a story. Too bad this footnote to history would never make it into anybody's monograph. Be a shame to wreck the romantic legends, anyway, she supposed. Not that it was possible to wreck legends, she thought. People believed what they wanted, despite what the thoroughly researched facts told them. Maybe you couldn't change history in some ways no matter what you did.

"About Passfair . . ." Sibelle drew her attention back to the original subject. "You must teach me as much as you can about running the household before Sir Daffyd returns."

When Sir Daffyd returns, Jane thought with a sigh.

"Of course," she answered. She didn't want to leave here, she thought. What was she going to do at Lilydrake? Alone. Alone with Daffyd.

She was going to make the best of it, she thought with adamant determination. She'd learned at Passfair that her one special quality was making the best out of a situation. She knew how to cope. She could cope with Daffyd. And David. And anything else the world threw her way.

She just wished he'd come home so she could tell him.

"About the rest of the demesne," Sibelle went on. "I think I can persuade my lord of the need to appoint a new steward to oversee everything else. What do you think of Bertram?"

Jane nodded, adding with a pleased smile, "Who else?"

"I know he can't keep accounts," Sibelle went on practically, "but I can get Yves to send a clerk from Sturry to help him. And eventually we'll have a priest back. I'll want one with some learning. My children will need a teacher."

Sibelle looked very determined, Jane noted. She also looked very happy. She and Switha exchanged a swift, knowing glance. "Are you pregnant?" Jane asked.

Sibelle lowered her gaze demurely. Her fingers played with the berries. "I believe so," she said. "My lord will be so pleased."

The kids worked fast. "Yes," Jane said slowly. "Yes, he will. Congratulations." She swallowed hard. She almost whimpered, an awful truth having just dawned on her.

Pregnant. She had never thought about getting pregnant. Why hadn't she thought about getting pregnant? Neither of them had taken any precautions. She wasn't on anything. And even if David had had a contraceptive implant, it would have stopped working years ago.

"There's nothing to worry about," Switha said as if she knew what Jane was thinking. She probably did.

Jane got to her feet. "I think I'll go wait for Daffyd."

She heard Sibelle calling, "But he won't be back for—" as she hurried out of the chapel.

She didn't care. She still went to linger by the gate.

She thought maybe wishing for him would bring him back to Passfair sooner.

She couldn't help but be frightened he wouldn't come back at all. The quest was over. The prize was won. Was there a new quest waiting for him beyond the horizon?

She prayed not.

She knew now he was all the prize she needed.

32

Two days crawled past before she saw David's horse approaching up the track leading to the castle. The day was harsh; a purplish-black mountain of storm cloud rode the sky at David's back. Lightning backlit the clouds. The wind whipped his pale hair; the light cape he wore around his shoulders stood out like black hawk wings. Jane watched anxiously from the spot by the gate where she'd spent much of the last two days. Villagers and castle folk were rushing indoors to escape the coming downpour, but she stood motionless as a statue, unafraid of the coming torrent. She had more pressing worries on her mind.

She hoped the things she wanted to tell him didn't come too late.

He gave her a disapproving look down his arrogant nose as he rode in the gate. He didn't pause but pointed at the hall without a word and rode quickly on. His actions didn't encourage her to think things were going to be settled between them. Her heart sank. She raced after him, skirts flying in the wind.

He dismounted and met her by the steps as a groom hurried the horse to the shelter of the stable.

"We have to talk!" she shouted, but a rising gust of wind blew her words away. He shook his head, grabbed her arm, and pulled her indoors.

He didn't stop until they reached the warmth of the hearthfire. Once there he threw back his cloak and shook raindrops out of his hair before turning to her. She held out her hands to the warmth and waited.

"Hello, Jane," he said in English.

"Greetings, my lord," she replied in French.

Puzzled brows lowered over his brooding eyes. "Jehane?"

She reached up to brush strands of damp hair off his forehead. She brushed his lips with her fingertips as well. The room was full of people. She didn't see anyone but David. "Call me anything you like."

He looked around. The presence of other people seemed to bother him. A sharp crack of thunder rolled overhead, loud enough to penetrate the stone walls of the fortress.

He took her arm. She was used to it by now. "We have to talk." She let him lead her up to the store-room.

"I'm packed," she said as he closed the door behind them. She went forward and struck flint to light the candles. It was early in the day, but the storm made the room dark as night. Rain hissed and beat at the outside stones. Water beat relentlessly on the thin-scraped oiled hide covering the window.

He took off his cape and the damp black surcoat underneath. She noticed he wasn't wearing mail, but the black undercoat, braccae, and hide boots. He unfastened his sword belt and set it aside as well. It seemed like a symbolic gesture to Jane.

"Packed?" he questioned suspiciously. "Where are you going?"

She swallowed an instant of panic. Perhaps she'd been wrong. Perhaps he was abandoning her. The quest was over and . . . Don't panic, she told herself firmly. Talk to the man.

"Sibelle and Stephan thought you would take me to Lilydrake."

"I see." He leaned against the door, crossing his arms. It was a very familiar gesture. She had never seen him more serious.

She wanted to go to him, take his hands and pull them around her. The unreadable expression on his face stopped her for now. "If you want to go to Lilydrake, I'll take you there," he told her. "I'll take you anywhere you like." He spread his hands before him. "It's your call, Jane."

She didn't understand what he meant. "Daffyd," she began, "I—"

"I've been doing a lot of thinking the last two days," he interrupted. He looked her over, his eyes raking her from head to foot. She felt as if she were standing in the middle of some bright, hot spotlight, every flaw and every good point being scrutinized and carefully judged. The feeling caused a shiver to run up her spine.

"Two days alone," he went on. "Trying to decide what I was going to do about you."

"Me too," she admitted.

His lips twitched, just a little. "Decide on anything?"

"Yes." She licked her lips nervously.

"Me too."

She put her hands behind her back and looked him squarely in the eye. "You first," she said, chickening out.

He came to her and put his hands on her shoulders. "I decided," he said after dropping a quick kiss on her forehead, "that if Daffyd is what you want, Daffyd is what you shall have. I offer you his heart, his holdings, his person without reservation. You mean too much to me, Jehane, for me to lose you now. Try to forget who I was and I'll make you happy. Here and now," he vowed. "I love you."

She was beginning to have a suspicion of understanding of what he was talking about. His words, his fervent intentions, warmed her. His words were all a medieval lady could hope for. She knew they could build a life together that would be as good and fulfilling as this time and place could offer. But she wasn't a medieval lady. She wished he'd get the notion she was out of his head.

He was looking at her expectantly. Hopefully. "My turn?" she asked. He gave a slow nod. "Maybe I don't want to forget who you are," she began.

"Uh-oh."

"Listen," she ordered, pointing an admonishing finger at him. "You seem to think I like you all butch and brawny."

"You do. Admit it."

"All right. I do." She kissed his cheek. "It was Daffyd I fell in love with. Daffyd is brave. He has a sense of justice. A sense of humor. He's strong—emotionally strong. He has charm. He's also the sexiest thing in or out of chain mail I've ever seen."

He inclined his head graciously. "Thank you, my lady."

"But David Wolfe's much more interesting. And just as difficult. Just as headstrong and sure he's always right."

"He is not!"

"Is too. Let me finish. It turns out this David Wolfe kid, whose guts I have every reason to hate, grew up into a pretty wonderful man. Seems he has a conscience. Seems he knows how to learn from his mistakes. Has the guts to try to fix things he's screwed up. He doesn't just live with his guilt like most people, he goes off and tries to make things right."

"Interesting assessment," his chocolatey voice rumbled. She noticed he didn't try to deny any of her praise.

"He has an ego, too. But all in all I think the kid turned out all right." She reached up to lightly slap one of the hands resting on her shoulders. "So get off the guilt trip, okay?"

"It's not so easy," he answered seriously. "I've been living with the guilt for a long time."

"You don't have to live with it anymore," she promised, and kissed him, her lips seeking his eagerly. He responded hungrily, but only briefly. It left her breathless and wanting.

"I love you," he told her, holding her close. "But Jehane—Jane—which one of you do I love? Is it love? Or just a guilty conscience trying to make an honest man of me? I've spent the last two days going crazy trying to decide who I am, who you think I am, who you want me to be, who I want me to be. I am *so* confused," he ended on a deep, breathy sigh.

"Ah," she answered, relief making the sound almost a giggle.

He lifted her chin in his fingers. "Don't sound so cheerful, woman," he complained. "I'm baring my soul to you."

"And about time," she commented. "I already told you I'm in love with all of you, you silly man. And you're in love with all of me."

"I am?" His eyebrows disappeared briefly into his bangs. "You have an explanation, I suppose?"

She gave an emphatic nod. "You think I spent the last couple of days doing nothing but tending my embroidery? Of course, I did, actually," she admitted. "Sibelle's taken to running the place. So I got a great deal of thinking done while ruining a lot of stitching."

"I see. No, I don't."

She hugged him, laughing into his shoulder. Everything was going to be all right. She knew it. Life was going to be hard. It was going to be terrible food and itchy clothes and cold rooms and no medicines and skirmishes to fight off and sieges to withstand and every other inconvenience she couldn't begin to think of. It was going to be short, brutish, and nasty. But she didn't care. She had David. What more could a woman ask for? Especially when she couldn't have it anyway. She'd make the best of what she had and be deliriously happy.

It would be all right. They'd be together. Forever. What a concept!

But first, to correct his little misapprehension. "It's been three or four months for me, David," she pointed out, speaking slowly and clearly. He was listening, studying her face carefully. "You never knew Jane Florian in 2002," she went on. "But you got a crash course in what she's like in the here and now. Time changed you, but it hasn't had a chance to get at me yet. And I know and love you. You. Not the twenty-year-old who's responsible for this mess."

The wind was setting up an unholy howling outside. Inside, in the romantic glow of the candles, David Wolfe pulled her into a tight embrace. "Three months. True. Hard for me to conceive, but true. You haven't had any time to change. You are just Jane. You are an amazing woman, Jane Florian."

"Yes," she agreed, and fluttered her eyelashes at him. "I have an ego, too."

"You're beautiful," he answered. "And absolutely right. Time." He sighed. "Time is a very confusing concept. For example," he went on, "the last forty-eight hours have taken at least ten years to creep by."

"For me, too."

"Happily ever after?" he suggested, tracing her lips slowly with the tip of a finger.

She considered very briefly, then shrugged. "Oh, why not?"

He swept her up in his arms and began to carry her toward the bed. She flung her arms around his neck. "Is sex all you ever think of?" she questioned with a delighted laugh.

"Yes," he answered. "Since I met you."

He set her on the floor next to the bed and they undressed each other slowly. It was a complicated process, and they made a long, sensually teasing game of it. They fell slowly onto the bed as they explored each other gently this time, trailing soft kisses and feather-light touches across naked flesh.

Jane knew she had all the time in the world. She savored every instant, every new discovery, as she learned the places where she could give him the most pleasure. He purred like a big cat when her tongue found just the right spot at the back of his neck, as it flicked across the palms of his hands, slid teasingly along the musculature between navel and thighs.

She worked her mouth along the hard length of him. He was smooth and hard and salty and sweet all at once. The smell of him excited her, as did every texture she encountered. The eroticism cleared every last doubt from her mind. She knew she'd never be able to give up the sensations making love to him brought her.

He groaned with pleasure, and she lifted her head to look at his face. Their eyes met. It was a transfer of heat, a jolt as powerful as the lightning dancing outside the window. He took her hand and drew her up the length of his body. She came, moving with slow sensuality, skin sliding over sweat-slick skin.

He turned her onto her back, taking his turn, his time, to explore her. She closed her eyes and gladly gave herself up to the heady sensations. He touched his fingers to her breast, stroking lightly. Excitement from his merest touch shook her. He suckled one nipple, then the other, turning them into hard points of fire. Then he moved down her body, moving slowly and thoroughly. Within a few minutes she was ready to scream with desire. She was so hot and throbbingly wet she didn't think she could stand any more.

When his head moved between her eagerly open thighs, she did scream. Scream, and arch hard against the tongue probing and lapping at the heated, swollen flesh. She screamed again, quivering body stiffening as a climax took her.

His mouth left her. She lifted herself to him, legs

wide and welcoming, needing him deep inside of her. He came into her, filling her as she strained upward to meet him. Their mouths met. She tasted herself on his tongue. His strokes were slow and steady, building the rising passion to a slow, devastating crescendo that took them together.

The world went away for a long, delicious moment. She soared. Coming down from the height of pleasure was a slow, sensuous glide.

Eventually she opened her eyes to look into his. He was a big, gold cat, looking smug and sated and thoroughly pleased with himself, the world, and her. She knew he was reflecting everything she felt. They shared one more gentle kiss. Then she curled up in his embrace, content just to be with him and drift in and out of light sleep while wind and rain continued to batter the castle walls.

33

Hours later, the rain was still pouring down, the wind howling just as strong. Lightning and thunder played across the sky. Jane lay on her side, tracing her finger down David's strongly beaked nose. He lay on his back, eyes half-closed, a contented smile tugging up his lips.

"You look like you need a dish of cream," she told him. "Big old tomcat."

"That's me," he agreed, and propped his hands behind his head. "What are you doing with my nose?"

She rested her finger on the slight kink just below the bridge. "I've been trying to remember what you looked like."

"It was only three months ago," he reminded her. "I was young, but hardly dashing."

"Promise me you won't shave your head again."

"It's hardly the current fashion."

"Thank goodness," she agreed. "If we'd been stranded earlier, you might have been stuck with the silly Norman soup-bowl cut. Of course, I would have looked great in the tighter-fitting dresses of the period. The long line would suit my figure better than the drapery in style now. And it's only going to get worse."

"The woman's a clotheshorse," he complained to the ceiling. He held her face cupped in his hands. "You're going to be expensive to keep, aren't you?"

"Yes." She turned her head to kiss his left palm. "Unless you prefer a dowdy wife locked up in the bower in rags." She sighed dramatically. "Whatever my lord chooses, of course." She lowered her eyes in mock humility. Then she went back to stroking his nose. "This bump," she went on. "I don't remember it at all. It looks like somebody broke your nose."

He lifted her chin so they were looking eye to eye. "Someone did," he told her. "And I deserved it."

"Hmm." From his tone and serious expression, it sounded like quite a story. She ventured a guess. "King Richard when you turned him down?"

He shook his head. "Cold."

"Someone's boyfriend?"

"Not even close."

"Father?"

"Warmer."

"Who?"

"Your mother."

She stiffened in surprise. "What?"

"Your mother," he repeated. "Colonel Elizabeth Florian, U.S. Army, retired. Quite a woman." His arm came around her, keeping her half on top of him. "I think I had better explain a few things."

There were things he hadn't explained. She eyed him nervously. "All right." What more was there to tell? "Explain."

"It's a long story. How I found you is a long story. I think you're under some misapprehensions. Where do I start?" He caught his lower lip between his teeth for a moment, then cleared his throat. A crash of thunder punctuated his first words. "The explanation that was given for your disappearance was that you must have been lost in the earthquake. I kidnapped you on a Friday night. No one reported you missing on Monday. You and I were the only ones who knew you worked late the night of the storm."

She tried not to be angry. All this happened a long time ago. "What about my car?" she asked, trying to stay objective. Trying to get the facts. It was really very interesting, in an uncanny, macabre kind of way.

"I drove it into Chicago and left it in the Grant Street parking garage. This was after I sobered up enough to realize the equipment hadn't functioned properly and that I only had a general idea of your location. The garage was under Lake Michigan a few days later. If there hadn't been an earthquake, I doubt I would have managed to get away with what I did. If I hadn't known you were alive and that I was the only one who could get you back, I would probably have admitted what I did to the authorities. Eventually."

"Eventually." She was very tempted to hit him. For the boy he'd been. She decided to forgive him and pretend they were talking about a mystery plot. "How did you know I was even alive?"

"The tracer sewn into your headdress was still registering body temperature. It was the only thing working correctly. Unfortunately, I lost contact with it. Also due to earthquake damage. It was two years before we had the apparatus up and running again. By that time, Time Search was a major gov-

ernment project, with me in charge. I was the only
one with the expertise to run the project. Nobody
knew my ulterior motives for the intense experi-
mentation."

"You didn't jump in right behind me, then?"

"No." He stroked her temples lovingly. "No. It was
two years before the bloody thing was working well
enough to use test animals. It was around then I met
your mother."

"Oh, yeah?"

He nodded. "I went to her. I wanted information
about you. Photographs. Anything. She asked me
quite a few insightful questions. She guessed something was wrong. She thought I killed you. I told her
what really happened."

"She broke your nose."

"She broke my nose."

"You have to watch out for her right."

"It was a left. But, yes, she's very good at unarmed
combat. And armed. And ancient combat tech-
niques."

"Better be." Jane laughed. "She was one of the
founders of the Medievalist Society. She thought I
was weird when I took her hobby as my profession."
It occurred to her that it was her mother who'd
turned him into such an efficient killer. Her mother.
The efficient soldier. The one who sent people into
battle and had taken life herself. David had had a job
to perform. She'd given him the tools to perform the
job. Jane discovered her throat was tight with emotion. She almost started crying. She was so proud of
both of them.

He ran his fingers lightly down her cheeks to her
throat. She didn't think he noticed what he was

doing. His eyes were looking inward. Somewhere far away. "The colonel was not pleased with me. She took a lot of convincing. But when I told her my plan she helped me all she could. Making my life hell in the process."

"So the colonel taught you to fight?"

He nodded. "Eventually. There was a great deal more to learn before we got around to even basic training. Language, customs, history. History for me was just energy readings. Time an elegant concept to manipulate. I had to learn about people, what I could and couldn't do to keep time flowing the way it ought. It was quite an education. In the meantime," he went on, "the Time Search Project became more and more refined. Five years ago a volunteer made his first trip back to the target area. To Anjou. Fontrevault."

"You?"

He nodded, his eyes full of old pain. "You weren't there. I returned again and again. I finally took on the Daffyd persona and spent most of my time back here. While I conducted my private search, carefully keeping the project in my control, we began the other work we'd been funded for."

"Weapons research?" she guessed. "Spying?"

He gave a sarcastic bark of laughter. "Nonsense. We can't expand the field beyond the late twelfth and early thirteenth centuries. Not yet. But it doesn't matter. We can get everything we need from this time period."

"And just what do you need?" she asked, almost frightened of the answer. What kind of exploitation was her time—

"The world's barely inhabited back here. We've

been able to find samples and bring them back without disturbing anything."

"Samples of what?" she demanded.

"Plants. Animals. Extinct and endangered species. Not the animals themselves, either," he hastened to add. "We just stun them with anesthetic darts and take cell samples. We're repopulating rain forests at present."

"Cloning?" she asked.

"Yes. Quite a big business these days. I'm considered quite the environmentalist." His lips curled in a sneer. "They've given me medals for it. I'm a hero. If only the world knew. You aren't going to tell them, are you?"

"Them? Them who?"

"The media, the world, whoever. Take your pick. If going back's what you want," he added.

She looked at him in confused shock. "What?"

"Though you might prefer Lilydrake and Daffyd." He kissed her. She was suddenly cold all over. His lips warmed her a little. "Your call, Jane," he whispered into her ear.

She stared at him. She saw the earnestness, the honesty. The willingness to give her whatever she wanted. "Are you crazy?" she demanded angrily.

"Just an average mad scientist," he responded.

"You'll make me chatelaine of Lilydrake?"

"If you like."

"Keep me as your lady fair? Be my champion? Wear my colors at tourney? Sing me troubadour poems?"

"All that. Promise." He was looking at her as if he thought she were about to break into mad hysterics.

Was he crazy for real? What kind of romantic, idiotic notion did he have in his head? This wasn't the Medievalist Society . . . this was the bloody thirteenth century!

Jane grabbed the wavy gold lock lying on either side of his face and hauled his head up until they were nose to nose. "Get me out of here!"

He flinched from her angry shout. "Yes, ma'am."

"Right now!" she demanded, shaking him.

He eased her fingers out of his hair. He got hold of her hands. "Not just yet," he said soothingly.

"I want a hamburger. Without onions. And chocolate. And coffee. Lots of coffee."

"That's not good for you."

"I don't care. And a shower. A lovely, long hot shower. A dozen. Books. My stereo. Every Mel Gibson movie ever made. Central heating. Bug repellent. My mommy."

He stroked her hair, gentling her. "Soon. Soon," he promised.

She collapsed against him, burying her head in his abundant chest fuzz. This was so frustrating! She wanted it so bad. And he was amused at her. She could tell. His chest was quivering with suppressed laughter. She looked up again, meeting his eyes. "How soon?"

He looked up at the storm-darkened window. "Soon as the weather clears," he said. "Storms still play havoc with the apparatus. On either end of the search."

34

"*Interested in what became of Sibelle* and Stephan?" he questioned as they crossed the hall hand in hand to join the couple seated at the high table. The lord and lady of Passfair were sharing a breakfast trencher, talking to each other in low, intimate whispers. The screen had been moved to one side and the doors flung open. A fresh, rain-washed breeze was blowing into the hall. The sky outside was a bright, clean, cloudless blue.

She stopped David just a few feet from the stairs. "How do you know what happened to them?" she asked very quietly.

"We've started picking up some extensive data from this area," he replied. "I looked them up when I was in the office catching up on paperwork."

Stunned shock covered Jane from head to foot. The look she turned on him was not friendly. She said very slowly, "When you were in the office . . . when?"

His Adam's apple bobbed hard as he gulped.

"Uh . . . yesterday morning?"

Sibelle was looking their way. Jane plastered a false smile on her lips, saying, "I'm going to kill you, you know."

"They lived happily ever after," he rushed on, trying to divert her. "Ten children. Most of them lived. Their family still lives in Kent. The Devrays are some of the most famous dog and horse breeders in England. Famous for it for centuries."

"Probably also the rightful heirs to the throne," she muttered to herself. Did King Charles know about the Plantagenets hiding out in Kent? "In the office yesterday?" She wasn't going to be diverted so easily.

He gave her an abashed look. "And talking to my counselor," he added. "There's one on staff who does nothing but remind me I'm not Daffyd ap Bleddyn, world-class savage, when I'm back in my own period. You'll get debriefed, too, love," he added. "Believe me, you'll need it. Even after only three months."

She believed him. And she was relieved to know he was smart enough to make sure he didn't let himself become totally lost in the role he played in the thirteenth century.

"Just how do we get back, anyway?" she asked him. She'd take up the discussion of his walking off into the future without her once they were safely returned to an environment where she could throw lamps, cups, crystal sculptures, or any other hard, breakable object she could lay hands on at him. Preferably expensive objects belonging to him. "Dear."

"First rule is we don't disappear where anyone can

see us. Or where we might accidentally take something with us. You sure there's nothing you want to bring along?"

"Not a thing. Stephan and Sibelle are welcome to all my treasure. I owe them a lot. I'm going to miss them," she added. She looked around the hall. "You see Nikki and Vince anywhere?"

"Who?"

"My dogs."

"No. I don't see those mongrels."

"Probably ran off and hid somewhere. Poor things are scared of storms. I think we better join our hosts."

He kissed the back of her hand. "I love you."

"I love you, too. Let's not stay for breakfast," she suggested strongly. He was sniffing hungrily as they approached the table. Well, to each his own, she reminded herself.

He looked disappointed but said as they reached the table, "My lady and I start for Lilydrake this morning. We wish to bid you good-bye."

"We'll miss you," Sibelle said, hurrying around the table. Stephan was right behind her. Sibelle hugged them both, planting kisses on both their mouths. "Go in peace," she told them. Tears brimmed in her large blue eyes.

The look Stephan turned on Jane held equal parts joy and regret. "It was merry while you were with us," he said, taking both her hands in his big, square one. "We will miss you."

"But we will see each other soon," Sibelle said. "Lilydrake's not so far."

David and Jane exchanged a quick glance. David turned back to the young couple. "It might be a while," he told them. "After we visit Lilydrake, I plan to take Jehane to my family in Wales. We may be there for quite some time."

"I'm with child," Jane said quickly. "Daffyd wishes his children to know their homeland." She gave David a quick, questioning look. It was possible. He shook his head and touched the spot on his inner elbow where a contraceptive implant would be. Oh. Well, they'd work on kids after they got home and had a nice, screaming fight.

Sibelle clapped her hands for joy. "A double blessing, then." A sad sigh followed. "Then you won't be here to stand godparents to our first child?"

"Maybe we'll be back for the second," Jane said. She gave David another look.

Well, why not? If he could just pop in and out, why couldn't they visit sometimes? She could go on with her research that way. A detailed biography of Rosamunde Clifford, perhaps?

She bet he wouldn't mind playing Daffyd ap Bleddyn now and then, either. It was a cunning plan. They'd talk.

"We must go," she said. "Get as many miles in as we can while the light is good and the weather holds."

There were more farewells. To the serving women and Bertram and Raoul DeCorte. The time went by both too fast and far too slowly before they were able to get on David's ungainly gray gelding and ride out the gate. They even made a stop in one of the fields where Cerdic was working to say good-bye. And Switha met them just before they reached the track leading into the forest. She smiled and handed up a pair of tiny cloth bags on leather thongs. The bags were full of some fragrant blend of herbs.

"A charm for fertility," she told them, adding, "I haven't any children of my own." She looked at them with a cryptic smile. "Not exactly." She shrugged, then headed down the road toward the village.

They looked at each other. And shrugged.

Jane directed him toward the tower where she'd first arrived. It seemed fitting, somehow.

It was cool under the trees. Branches shed rainwater on them as they passed. She held on to David's waist, riding pillion for the last time. Enjoying it far more than she had the first.

She leaned her head on his shoulder. "I'm very happy," she told him.

"Try not to fall off" was his loving reply.

They reached the edge of the clearing, and David stopped and got off the horse. They were taking it with them. Apparently it normally grazed on the grass over the acceleration ring at Feynman.

Jane was sliding down also when she heard the sound of running bodies coming up the trail toward them. She froze. This was still the thirteenth century. Just because Hugh of Lilydrake was dead didn't mean all danger was over. What if the outlaws were coming again? Her mouth went dry. She saw David had drawn his sword.

All she wanted was to go home, she thought, trembling more from frustration than fear as two long, sleek forms broke from the cover of the trees. The beasts moved with lightning speed. Speed bred for chasing down swiftly fleeing deer. David raised his sword.

"No!" she yelled, bumping his arm.

"What? Oh!"

"Nikki! Vince! What are you doing here?" she

demanded as the deerhounds screeched to a halt in front of her.

Nikki barked, while Vince jumped, trying to put his paws on David's shoulders so he could lick his face. David pushed him down.

He gave Jane an annoyed look. "Apparently they followed you."

"Well, they are my dogs." She smiled at him.

He backed a step. "Oh, no." He pointed a stern finger at her. "We are not taking these monsters with us." She kept smiling. "I couldn't afford to feed them even on my salary." Her smile turned toothy. "I'm not sharing a bed with them."

"*National Enquirer* still publishing?" she asked conversationally. She polished her nails on her kirtle. "Wonder what the media will think of my little adventures in Never-Never Land. Besides," she added reasonably, "you've got the horse."

"Yes, I've got the horse. All right," he capitulated. "We'll take the dogs."

She kissed him, even though Nikki growled a little as she did so. She could deal with Nikki and Vince. Get them a nice big doghouse and a couple of fenced-in acres to run in. Everything would be lovely. Just lovely.

"Let's go home, David," she entreated, her arms still around his neck. He nodded. His hand dropped to his sword hilt. He twisted the pommel to the right. "What do you do, just say 'Energize,' or something?"

The world went very weird. She was sucked upward through a sea of what felt and looked and, yes, tasted like blue paint.

"Or something," he agreed as the blue paint disappeared.

She, David, the dogs, and the horse they rode in on were now standing in a blue-walled room.

She stepped away from him. The recessed lighting was fluorescent. She touched the wall. It felt like cool steel. There was a thrum of air-conditioning in the background. It sounded loud in her ears. Air conditioning and other things. Her perceptions had definitely changed over the last few months. There wasn't much to see, but it all looked so . . . odd. She shuddered, suddenly afraid of this alien environment.

David's arms came back around her. "It'll be fine," he soothed. "We'll get you debriefed and you'll be fine. Then hot showers and chocolate and all the coffee you can drink."

"Promise?"

"Promise."

A door opened and several people dressed in beige coveralls came into the room. Some of them carried boxes with lights and dials. She didn't pay any attention to them. Neither did David. The dogs immediately tried to find someone to pet them. The horse lifted its tail and casually did what horses tended to do.

Jane hugged David tightly. "Get me to your shrink, then. As fast as you can."

He held her close to his side as they walked into a long corridor. "David?" she asked as they approached an elevator. She was a little uncertain about doors that opened and closed by themselves and little boxes that went up and down. She supposed she'd just have to cope.

"Yes?" he asked.

She rested her head on his shoulder. "How

should we celebrate our eight hundredth wedding anniversary?"

"Hmm? How about with a good night's sleep?"

"Suits me."

Together they walked into the little moving box.

COMING NEXT MONTH

A FOREVER KIND OF LOVE by Patricia Hagan

A sweeping novel of romance, suspense, mystery, and revenge, set in the turbulent reconstruction period following the Civil War. This bestselling author tells a story of two lovers drawn together in the blaze of passion amidst a world aflame with prejudice and deceit.

THE SEASON OF LOVING by Helen Archery

A delightful Christmas romance set in Regency England. On her way to visit a family friend, Merrie Lawrence's gig runs into the Earl of Warwick's curricle. Discovering Merrie is his mother's houseguest, the earl takes an immediate dislike to her, only to discover later his overwhelming interest.

THE BASKET BRIDE by Phyllis Coe

An enthralling historical romance spun from the historic event of the "Basket Brides" who came from France in the 18th century to help settle Louisiana.

ONE MAN'S TREASURE by Catriona Flynt

Adventure, intrigue, and humor are hallmarks of this delightful historical romance. Ruth McKenna travels to Flagstaff, Arizona, to make peace with her brother, but she's too late—someone has killed him. The only person to help her is big, redheaded Gladius Blade. A nosy, hard-headed woman only adds to Blade's problems. But when he falls in love with her, he knows he is in for real trouble.

Harper Monogram **The Mark of Distinctive Women's Fiction**